BECAUSE OF

Savannah

BECAUSE OF

Savannah

BY SARAH PATT

ARCHWAY
PUBLISHING

Archway Publishing books may be ordered through booksellers or by contacting:

Archway Publishing
1663 Liberty Drive
Bloomington, IN 47403
www.archwaypublishing.com
1 (888) 242-5904

Because of the dynamic nature of the Internet, any web addresses or links contained in this book may have changed since publication and may no longer be valid. The views expressed in this work are solely those of the author and do not necessarily reflect the views of the publisher, and the publisher hereby disclaims any responsibility for them.

Any people depicted in stock imagery provided by Thinkstock are models, and such images are being used for illustrative purposes only.
Certain stock imagery © Thinkstock.

ISBN: 978-1-4808-1990-0 (sc)
ISBN: 978-1-4808-1991-7 (e)

Library of Congress Control Number: 2015909985

Print information available on the last page.

Archway Publishing rev. date: 11/03/2017

This book is dedicated to the memory of Nathan Patt, whose love for my children was as big as the sea; my sister, Melissa Gervais, who will always be my one and only Missy Mouse; Matthew Rutter, one of the most humble mentors I have had the good fortune to work with; and to my father, Alan Rice, who instilled the idea, "You can accomplish anything if you put your mind to it!"

I am grateful to my friends and colleagues who read and critiqued my manuscript, and laughed at just the right parts. For my husband and children, who believed that I could, that I can, and that I will—always replacing my "ifs" with "whens!" And, lastly, I am thankful for my fur baby, who always keeps me company during the nights I write and write.

Contents

CHAPTER I

The Funeral

I was distraught, naturally. Perhaps that was too light a word. I was more like devastated—no, beyond belief. Yes, that was it. It was unbelievable. I was sixteen years old and attending my dad's funeral. I am an only child, and according to my dad, I was the best girl in the whole wide world. I was his sunshine.

I wanted to shout in hopes he'd hear me, "You're *my* world, Dad. You're what makes me shine!"

Sometimes I shushed him. He seemed always to walk in on the most intense part of the movie—right at the kill! I knew how it ended, but I just couldn't find it in myself to put it on pause. And now I wish I had. I never really put much thought into the adage *if you could turn back time*—until now.

Oh God, I thought; people were walking up to me. These strangers and acquaintances were asking me if I needed anything and telling me that they were here for me. Some lady was standing beside me. A tiny smile formed on her heavily made-up face—I could see the outline of her foundation. She smoothed down my hair. Her long, painted nails gently combed the back of my head as if I were a cat. I felt I should purr for her. I would have done anything to make her stop. Then she reminded me how strong and beautiful I was and how I looked just like my mom. I heard that a lot. I gave a closed-mouth smile, nodded, and silently prayed this crazy lady would leave. Oddly enough, she examined a strand of my hair, which remained fixed in midair, trickling down her fingers; she finally moseyed on. I gave myself a quick shake as if I were shooing a spider and thought, *Dear Lord, let this day end!*

Just the other morning I was flipping flapjacks—banana ones, Dad's favorite. The radio blared, and I was singing along, when he chimed in. We were dancing. We were having fun. I was on key. Dad wasn't. He was a goofball—my goofball—my adorably cute dad. He was always fun, making me giggle. Who's going to do that now?

I stood in a room full of people I hardly knew, feeling more anxious than usual, until I spied Uncle Travis, who gave me his familiar wink from across the room. That wink always seemed to reassure me that I'd be okay and that I should take three deep breaths.

Travis and my dad had been best friends since childhood. I could recite their story in my sleep. Wherever they were—local pub, church barbecue, or a friend's party—they'd tell their rendition of their first black eyes, and the more beers they put back the more uproarious the story became. In Mrs. Clark's third-grade class, they had fought over an empty seat, which happened to be next to Luanne. They were smitten with her looks: her long, auburn hair neatly falling to the middle of her back; her creamy, flawless face, with not one freckle; her perfect, little nose and soft, rosy lips; and eyes as blue as the sky.

Honestly, I wondered, *why can't boys look deeper?* I rolled my eyes every time, shaking my head, and asked facetiously, "How could you have let her go?" Then I demanded, "And what's wrong with freckles?"

Travis and my dad had duked it out at recess, and when the bell rang, they both were standing, looking straggly. Luanne took one look at their sweaty, tired figures with torn shirts and bloody faces and decided she didn't want either of them. She moved seats, and then she moved out of Texas within weeks when her military dad was reassigned. She was never seen or heard from again except as part of the black-eye story they recited habitually. They quickly got over her (out of sight, out of mind). And since neither one of them held a grudge, their friendship formed and became stronger with each passing year, like brothers. When I was born, Travis naturally became my uncle.

The black-eye story always finished with my dad telling me, "No guy is worth fighting over. Remember that, Dakota."

And Uncle Travis would chime in, "Any guy you date, Dakota, will have to get past me first!" I nervously laughed, picturing the two of them with shotguns in hand, sitting on the front porch rocking back and forth in their chairs (even though we didn't have a front porch or rocking chairs). I thought the prospect of a good-night kiss from the boy who dared to drive me home was highly unlikely. Eventually, I learned their bark was tougher than their bite.

Who's going to tell that story now, Dad? Uncle Travis can't do it alone. It takes two! It takes you!

I was twisting the handkerchief some stranger had handed to me at the start of the service, stopping any circulation I had in my right index finger. It was moist with my sweat—not my tears. For some insane reason, I could not cry. The embroidered, purple M disappeared. I hoped that dear old lady didn't want her hanky back. I spied her in the crowd and stared at her, wondering what the M stood for. *Was it her first name or her surname? She kinda looked like a Mabel, maybe a Mary Lou—definitely not a Margaret.*

"Darlin'. Dakota. Hello. You here, girl?" I heard Uncle Travis call, trying to get my attention. "You needn't worry about any living expenses. You'll be set for life, dear. I'll make sure of it." I nodded. Then he vanished. He had to work the room, graciously accepting the many condolences and trying to skirt the questions: *What's going to happen to Dakota? Will she be living with you?*

Good ol' Uncle Travis; my Uncle Travis. He was the top lawyer in Fort Worth—all of Texas, really. He was that good. He made headlines and talk shows—big ones, too. He was once on *The O'Reilly Factor* and actually befuddled Bill. That was amazing!

My dad was killed at his job on an oilrig. Some thingamajig went berserk—it wasn't properly maintained. It erupted on my dad's shift. It erupted in his hands and blew them off. It blew everything off. It blew him away to heaven, right that instant. I couldn't see him. There was nothing to see. It was a closed coffin—an empty coffin, a farce, really.

People were kneeling at his coffin. I wanted to shout at them, "Hello, he's not in there! He was burnt to death!"

Fried chicken was my dad's favorite. It was easy. I just followed Mom. I was her kitchen shadow. "Only the best girls know how to get the chicken just right!" he'd say with stuffed cheeks, grease glistening on his lips.

My mom would lightheartedly scold him, "Jethro, quit talkin' with your mouth full and use your napkin for God's sake. He invented them for a reason. Good Lord, sometimes I think you're like a child."

I had the urge to argue the inventions of God with her but didn't dare disrupt their moment. She planted a kiss on the top of his receding hairline as he sat devouring her chicken. She sat beside him, took a napkin, and wiped around his mouth like he was two years old. She scolded him again but affectionately questioned, "What am I going to do with you, Mr. Jethro Theodore Buchannan?"

He cutely puckered his greasy lips for her to dive in for a kiss. Gross! And even grosser, Mom did! I wanted to make the gag reflex sound but knew better. Instead, I took the, "aww, so cute" puppy stance as I skirted another lovey-dovey scene. They were so in love, and deep down I was really proud of that. Coming from a two-parent household was a rarity, and coming from a loving one was monumental! After she died, I followed her recipe—the index card was splotched with Crisco—but it wasn't as easy or as fun. Still, Dad always complimented me and told me, "You make it just like Mom." My mom and I were his best girls.

My mom has been in heaven for quite some time. I imagined her in heaven's kitchen—if there is such thing. I imagine her quickly taking out the hot biscuits, nudging the oven door shut with her hip, plopping the cookie sheet on the range, and easing each biscuit onto the cooling rack. Then my dad approached from behind, placing his hands on her derrière, and she lightheartedly scolded, "Quit your foolin', Jethro—this here's pipin' hot!" But really, she was smiling, relishing in his touch.

He was grinning, whispering in her ear, "I love you."

In spite of my dad passing through the pearly gates, I smiled knowing my parents were reunited. It was my first smile in three days. I stood smiling, picturing their embrace in heaven's kitchen.

Wait a minute! Stop! I was smiling at my dad's funeral! This didn't look good. Okay, now I was officially one very messed-up kid with this big-ass grin on my face.

"What's so amusing, Miss Dakota?" Uncle Travis asked with a curious grin, giving my back a quick rub.

"Just remembering good times," I answered, slowly letting go of my smile and stupidly studying my shoes. I was afraid I might cry if I looked into my uncle's soulful eyes and not be able to stop. I'd have one of those heaving cries, sounding like a wounded animal. I thought it best to be in denial about my dad's death. I could pretend this was some type of test to see how strong I was in the face of this practical joke gone way too far. But it wasn't a joke—I knew that. I'm not stupid. It was real. My dad was dead, and I hated it. My mother always said that "hate" is a strong word, but I often felt it was the most suitable. I knew she would make an exception just this once.

Uncle Travis put his hand under my chin and tilted it so that I had to look at him. He stared at me with a mixture of puzzlement and recognition and then spoke with slight urgency. "There's someone I want you to meet."

"Yeah? Is he cute? Would Dad approve?" I teased, looking up with a hint of a smile. Because my dad had died before I began dating, I would never experience or stress about his overprotectiveness or his awkwardness when trying to teach me about safe sex. I envisioned a boy clumsily trying to pin a corsage and lightly grazing my breast as my dad eyed him with dubious contempt. I would never have to worry about this, would never undergo that suspicious-father syndrome that asserts that all boys are after just one thing.

Uncle Travis chuckled once, but quickly his soft eyes grew serious, and his genteel smile vanished. He seemed nervous. Uncle Travis loved me as if I were his own daughter. He was always genuine and candid toward me. He said I was too smart to be fooled with. I'll admit when I was younger—way younger, like eight or nine—I sort of had a crush on my uncle Travis. Remember, he isn't blood-related, so this wasn't all that perverse. He is handsome, smart, and funny. And according to some magazine, he was once the most eligible bachelor in the Fort Worth area. That crush no longer exists. It's not because of his age—fifty-seven—I just outgrew it like any normal teenager would. Besides, I wasn't one to condone being a Lolita.

"Dakota, darlin', this here gentleman ..." I heard my uncle start to introduce us. Out of nowhere, a man who was the spitting image of my dad was standing beside my uncle. Oh my God. He looked just like the photo of my dad when he was in the service. I suddenly felt sick. I thought I was going to throw up.

"Your dress is pretty," said a small child sneaking out from behind this man's legs. Her little hand tugged on the hem of my dress. "What's your name?"

I was speechless. I felt dizzy.

"This here is Dakota," Uncle Travis answered for me in a friendly manner. He continued, speaking slowly and clearly as if *I* were little and it were my first day of kindergarten. "Dakota, this here's Luke and his daughter, Savannah. This pretty little girl is your niece. Luke's ... well, that makes Luke your brother."

Oh my God. I was going to puke on Savannah's shiny black patent-leather shoes.

CHAPTER 2

Who's Luke?

"Why thank you, ma'am. I can handle it from here." Uncle Travis politely dismissed someone. A cool sensation compressed my forehead. It felt good. "Why, Miss Dakota, you fainted. My dear Dakota, I can't imagine what you're going through." He took my hand while seated on a rickety-looking coffee table. I was surprised it could even take his weight. He continued, "You know I am here for you with all my heart and soul."

"Uncle Travis, who's Luke? Who's Georgia?"

He chuckled. "You mean Savannah?" His soft eyes and genteel smile returned. I smirked, still dazed from the fall but thankful I didn't puke. That would've been downright nasty to do at my dad's funeral.

Uncle Travis continued, "Luke arrived the day of the accident looking for your dad. He only just found out who his daddy was."

His words hung in the air as I tried to understand. My uncle's face showed empathy, as if he felt sorry for this Luke guy. Perhaps I should, too. "Dakota, I had no idea. Jethro neither. Your mama ..." His voice softened. "God rest her soul."

He released my hand and took off his Stetson. He held it against his heart and stared into the distance at the American flag. A collage of framed pictures—Jesus Christ, Mother Theresa, Martin Luther King Jr., and a signed photograph of forty-first US president George H. W. Bush hung on the wall surrounding the flag, behind the reverend's desk. For a moment I thought my uncle was going to stand and recite the Pledge of Allegiance. I waited, noticed the peeling paint curling up like corn flakes, and thought, *If Mom were alive—and Dad—she'd volunteer his service.* Mom had a knack for making my dad feel indispensable with her honey-do list, which was not limited to our own household but included odd jobs the community needed completed, such as building wooden herb boxes for the food pantry. I remembered fondly planting the herbs and loving the aroma rosemary exuded. My mom had said, as she and I were digging in the dirt, *Just cause you need a little help putting food on the table don't mean you lost your taste buds.* I hummed in agreement and tried picturing someone sprinkling fresh oregano in his pot of canned SpaghettiOs. Maybe a minute lingered before Uncle Travis beamed, recapturing my eyes and hand. "I smell wood burning," he joked. "What's going through that pretty little head of yours?"

"Nothing," I said.

He didn't push. Instead he professed, "Your mama, sweet Loretta … she won your daddy's heart and never let go." Then his grin quickly squashed as if he just bit into something vile. His handhold grew tighter, as if he were about to get a shot! The suspense, let alone his theatrical ways, was killing me. "But Luke's mama—she left town like there was a tornado comin'. She never let on she was carrying his baby. She left him a note sayin' she *outgrew* him, like he was some pair of old shoes! I never cared for her. Geraldine … Geraldine Lockwood. She liked to be called Gerry—a man's name, if you ask me. She stepped all over your daddy. She knew his weaknesses and played him like a fiddle. He was heartbroken, but he was one stubborn son-of-a-bitch. He was determined to win her back."

Uncle Travis took a breather and sighed, loosening his grip—thank goodness. "He found her in Houston, near Rice University, at some professor's home. She traded free room and board for some light housekeeping and taking care of their three-month-old baby."

He paused again as if trying to remember it all. "She wasn't showing yet. She told Jethro to leave immediately because there was someone else and that someone was going to be back real soon. Dakota, dear, you remember the Luanne story, right?"

I nodded. How could I forget?

"Throwing punches wasn't his way of winning a girl's heart no more. He left. He left Houston, left Geraldine, and left his unknown, unborn son behind."

I took the face cloth off my forehead as I slowly got up from the surprisingly plush velour sofa the reverend had in his office—probably a donation from the Peterson family. Mrs. Peterson was always redecorating and spared no expense. Even though her husband faulted her spendthrift sprees, she was very generous. I gave a quick guffaw, thinking, *why hadn't she had the room painted?* My uncle shot me that inquisitive look again, but I waved him off.

We stood for a moment motionless and quiet. I didn't know what to do. I didn't know whether to embrace this new situation or to throw my hands up and say ... *whatever!* Luke was way older than me. He had a kid, for God's sake. It wasn't like he and I could watch scary movies together curled up on the couch, sharing a big bowl of buttery popcorn. But I was parentless. That sounded worse than being homeless. How could anything sound worse than that? I finally asked, "Is he married, Uncle Travis?"

He nodded but that was it. He said nothing.

"Have you met her?" I asked quizzically. He nodded again. She had to have been a loser, then. My uncle was a good reader of people, and whenever he met someone he liked, he boasted about them. "What's she like?" For goodness's sake, spill it!

He fiddled with his Stetson before putting it back on and said coldly, "She's a New Yorker." He made it sound like she had cancer.

Cancer. That was what my mom died from. Ovarian. I didn't know what cancer was or even if it was contagious. I remembered ferociously looking it up at the library. And when I checked out some big book on it, the stupid, dumb, nosey librarian pouted her lips like I lost my puppy and asked in her stupid, dumb, sticky-sweet, overly exaggerated Texan accent, *You know someone dying of cancer?*

What? She was going to die? I ran for the door. The stupid, dumb librarian's voice got an octave higher. "*Dear, your book. You're forgetting your book.*" I wanted to get out of there as fast as I could. I didn't even hold the door open for some old guy coming in—he even had a cane! I'm sorry, old man. My mom would have been very disappointed in me. Respecting my elders and following etiquette were sacred to her.

CHAPTER 3

Janet Powers-Trenton

"Hi. You want to see my room?" Savannah said. She took my hand before I could answer and led me to her very pink bedroom.

Etiquette took over. "Why, I think this is the prettiest room I have ever seen. And this here is the biggest and cutest bear!" I said as I picked up one of Savannah's incredibly soft, enormously large stuffed animals. Her room was home to at least fifty. I asked, "How old are you?"

Savannah held up four fingers.

"Four! I loved being four!" I said in a big, jovial voice. I actually didn't remember, but it sounded like a nice thing to say. I'm sure I was happy. My mom was alive then. It was a month before my tenth birthday when she began looking like the grim reaper already had his claws in her, ready to take her at any moment. He did. She died six days before I reached double digits. A few weeks after her funeral, Dad insisted I have a proper birthday party. He said it would be good for me. It drove me crazy when adults said that. I really didn't feel like celebrating. But I had the feeling Dad needed a day full of squealing kids to cheer him up, so I invited ten friends over. I got more joy watching my dad howl at our water balloon fight than opening my presents and getting everything I wished for.

"Dakota, will you be my friend?" Savannah asked with tenderness.

"I already am your friend—and his, too!" I said, hugging teddy and kissing him on his button nose. Savannah giggled and told me I was funny.

"Girls, what are you doing? We're out here on the porch. Come join us." A loud female voice called, sounding a bit like Sigourney Weaver—the renowned actress who also had narrated many of the documentaries on the Discovery Channel that I enjoyed. Horror movies weren't the only things in my repertoire.

"Pleased to meet you, Dakota. I am Janet Powers-Trenton." She spoke with great vigor, shaking my hand in a firm grip as if sealing a business deal.

Luke hugged me from behind while planting a light peck on the top of my head. He said excitedly, still holding me, "I see you've met the missus, and you already know our sweet Savannah." He let go of me to pick up his daughter. He Eskimo-kissed her cute, teeny nose. She giggled, held his face in her little hands, and kissed his nose back. They giggled in unison. My dad and I were a lot like them. I smiled. Then the sweet moment was interrupted when Janet asked if I wanted a cold beverage. She handed one to me before I could answer. She had decided for me. It was grape juice.

"My favorite! Thank you," I lied. What did she take me for—a child?

The grape juice was putrid. Her coiffed hair was stiff, like her. At that moment I understood why Uncle Travis had kept quiet about her. Suddenly out of nowhere a dog came barreling up the porch steps and jumped up on *me!* My juice went flying, right onto the front of Janet's baby-blue linen dress. Her nipples were showing through the wet purple stain—she wasn't wearing a bra. I kept back my shocked expression, but I had to bite the inside of my cheeks to keep from laughing. I apologized even though I knew it wasn't my fault but this great, big, wonderful dog's. Well, it was quite smelly, but what it had just done was priceless! Janet shouted, "Bad dog! Bad dog!" while holding her breasts as if she were topless. Served her right for giving me grape juice. I really just wanted water. The dog seemed unfazed by her yelling and was happily wagging its tail and licking up the spilt juice.

"Belle, get over here, girl," Luke commanded while grabbing her collar with one hand and petting her back with his other as if he were rewarding her. Luke then looked my way and asked, "Are you okay?"

But Janet assumed she was the center of attention and barked loudly, "No, I am not okay! Just look at my dress! Do you know what this cost? No, of course you don't! You only shop at Walmart!"

"I was asking Dakota," Luke calmly claimed, ignoring his wife's gibe.

"I hate your dog!" Janet retaliated while storming off the porch, letting the screen door slam behind her.

"I'm sorry about that, Dakota. She's been acting a little crazy lately," Luke confessed.

"Who, the dog or your wife?" I returned with sass.

He grinned at my sarcasm and playfully discharged Belle, telling her to go get her ball. "Hope you like burgers and dogs," Luke said with his back turned to me, tending to the grill.

"Yes. I'll have one of each and a slice of cheese on my burger, please—if you have it." I was famished and giddy.

"You got it, kiddo!" Luke cried.

I took a seat on the glider, and Savannah instantly plopped on my lap. It was a natural fit. I couldn't help but wrap my arms around her petite waist. Her golden hair brushed along my face, and I was taken in by its sweet scent—that heavenly clean baby aroma that really ought to be bottled and sold. I secretly sniffed again and then topped it with a kiss. She folded my hands into hers and fiddled with my ring—my mom's turquoise ring—twisting it so it rotated around my finger a million times.

Janet returned wearing a duplicate dress but in black, carrying a tray. She ignored everyone. She placed the condiments, rolls, and salad on the table and began tossing the salad with vinaigrette. I preferred ranch but didn't dare say anything.

"You look even more beautiful," Luke told her while caressing her shoulders—something my dad would have done to Mom. Janet cringed, showing no hint of a smile—entirely opposite of my mom. It seemed as though Luke understood his wife's negative body language. He released his hands but mumbled, "I try," before returning to the grill.

Shortly after, he carried a platter of meat to the table and announced,

"Time to eat!" We all sat. Unexpectedly, Janet took hold of my left hand, and Luke took hold of my right. Sitting across from me was Savannah, who was holding her parents' other hands. Their eyes were closed, and instinctively I closed mine. We listened to Savannah recite a prayer, "Thank you, God, for the food we eat. Thank you, God, for the people we meet. Thank you, God, for the birds that sing. Thank you, God, for everything."

We opened our eyes and smiled … even Janet. Her looks had potential. Then she dropped my hand. Potential to be a vampire! Luke squeezed my other hand before letting go and softly said while looking into my eyes, "I feel blessed to have you in my life, Dakota." Savannah mimicked her dad's low voice and added, "Me too," smiling from ear to ear. Of course, Janet didn't say anything and started piling salad on her plate.

"Honey, you want a burger?" Luke warmly asked his wife.

Her response was as quick as it was cold. "You know I don't eat those things."

"Oh, are you a vegetarian?" I asked, trying to make conversation. *Or is it not rare enough for your vampire liking?*

"No. I eat filet mignon," Janet stated in a terribly proud manner, as if confessing to a good deed.

I nodded to her as I took a big bite of my cheeseburger. The ketchup and relish gave me a mustache. I complimented Luke while still chewing, moaning like my dad used to over my mom's chicken, "Mm, this is delicious!" Forgive me, Mom, for talking with my mouth full, but Luke needed it. I quickly wiped around my mouth to make up for it and swallowed the food I purposely chewed loudly before I asked, "So how did you two meet?" *What does Luke see in you?*

"Luke fixed my parents' pool," Janet flatly stated.

Luke continued to play the perfect, loving husband and said so romantically, "It was love at first sight," ending it with a sexy wink.

"Oh, so you fix pools?" I asked, sounding very enthusiastic.

"My daddy builds pools!" Savannah said, sounding even more gung-ho than me, as if her dad were the US president rather than CEO of Lockwood Pools.

"Oh yeah, Uncle Travis and I saw your billboard. Lockwood Pools: You'll be swimming in no time! Duh, that's you," I said while giving my head a light slap, punishing myself for not making the connection earlier. I complimented him some more, since his wife remained unsupportive of his career. "Very cool!"

My mom always bragged about what my dad did—made it sound like he was a saint. One time she volunteered him to mend a leak in our church's roof. On rainy Sundays my mom had no qualms telling the parishioners, *We have the Lord to thank for being here today ... but we have Jethro to thank for keeping us dry!* And they all agreed and said in unison, *Amen!*

Vampire interrupted my fond recollection, and speaking harshly. I was beginning to feel very uncomfortable and couldn't help but feel sorry for my brother. "It wasn't built right to begin with, so my dad demanded to have the owner of Lockwood Pools come out to fix it himself, free of charge!" She uncrossed her arms and took a gulp of her Pinot while her other hand tousled her hair as she eyeballed Luke, shooting invisible daggers.

Geez, could she lighten up? Poor Savannah—all this negative energy bouncing off her mom. Thank heavens Savannah wasn't a "Mini Me" and had her dad's disposition. Finally Luke said with some authority in his voice, "The pool was twenty years old, and I didn't build it. I bought the company a year before I met you ... and your dad."

And Savannah chimed in with her version: "My mama was lying down in the sun looking very pretty, so my daddy asked her to marry him ... after he fixed Grandpa's pool!"

Savannah's rendition was sweet like the gherkins she offered me, which ignited me to tell a pickle joke. What had come over me? This was so not like me. It was more like my dad. I asked, smiling, "Why do gherkins giggle a lot?" I didn't wait for a response. "Because they're pickle-ish!"

Luke and Savannah laughed. Janet poured herself a second glass of wine and took a sip before prematurely asking, "When is your uncle coming to get you?"

"He's having dinner with clients. He said he'd come get me as soon as it's through," I answered, sounding apologetic. Vampire implied I had overstayed my welcome.

"She can't go yet, Mama! We haven't had the pie and ice cream!" Savannah professed loudly with a pout and furrowed eyebrows, disappointed her mom had forgotten about dessert.

But I had a strong suspicion she really didn't forget. A good host offers dessert before ever thinking to ask their guests if they have to go—at least, my mom always did, and she'd say it so sweetly. *I've got a fresh pot of decaf brewing and the best pecan pie in Fort Worth topped with homemade whipped cream, so don't you go traipsing off anytime soon!*

"That's right!" Luke concurred. "We've got Miss Crystal's pie."

"I know that. Just asking a simple question," Janet said, rolling her eyes and pouring her third glass of wine.

"Miss Crystal makes the best peach pie!" Luke declared as he cleaned the last morsel off his plate.

"Who's Miss Crystal?" I asked, also joining the clean plate club.

"She is one of my dad's servants," Janet answered with a voice, the epitome of snot.

I had to investigate this bizarre union between my loving brother and this vampire wife of his. "So your dad's a Texan and your mom's a New Yorker?" I enquired, looking straight at Janet.

Janet boasted, "Yes. When they divorced—" She was actually smiling!—"My mother, Constance Powers, ran back to New York to immerse herself into the society she had left behind. I was only four—Savannah's age. I was cared for by multiple nannies. I was given the best education. My debutant ball made the *New York Times*. Even the mayor made an appearance. I adore everything about New York."

Luke looked forlorn. Janet was pathetic. And I wondered, was she a bad kid? Or was her mom difficult? Why had they cycled nannies?

Precocious Savannah announced in a rambunctious voice, "Grandpa was the monkey today! He couldn't get the ball from Alexis or me. It was so funny!" And she giggled her infectious giggle. Only Janet was immunized—our laughter annoyed her.

"Who's Alexis?" I directed the question to Savannah, but Janet answered for her, "She's Crystal's granddaughter. My father, Drew Trenton—CEO of Trenton Construction, responsible for most of the skyscrapers adorning downtown Houston—allows his workers to bring their kids or grandkids over to his estate to use the pool, hot tub, tennis court, even ride the horses—all his expense."

"That's so nice!" I said, smiling.

"Nice? More like stupid. Do you realize the liability? Never mind. You probably don't know what that means," she shot back with ugliness.

Janet must be more like her mom because her dad sounded like a gem. Belle returned with a tennis ball in her mouth. Janet made an "Ugh" sound and matched it with a spiteful look. It seemed to come natural to her. She cried, "You get her out of here!"

I knew she was referring to the dog, but I got the feeling she was inwardly screaming those six words for me as well. She stood and announced, "I'll get this" as she began to clear the table. Being polite, I started to help her, but she made a shooing motion to all of us. We obeyed and were exiting the porch when the theme song from *Halloween* sounded—my cell phone was going off. Janet looked mortified and gave me a look like I was a freak. Luke and Savannah ignored the ring tone, stepping off the porch onto the yard. They started playing catch with Belle. The dog was in her glory.

I answered my phone, "Hello."

"These sons of bitches just ordered another bottle of wine while I was taking a leak. I won't get out of here till late, Dakota, and you know how I hate wine! I'm sorry, honey. How's it going? How's Big Apple?"

I knew he was referring to Janet, and for a second I wondered how New York City had earned its nickname. I made a mental note to Google it later. I chuckled at the code name and answered, "Very sour."

He chuckled back and said, "I couldn't agree with you more. Do you think you could ask Luke to drive you back to the hotel?"

"Let me see—wait a minute." I walked toward the three of them. Belle didn't jump up on me but dropped her tennis ball at my feet, which told me she was a very smart dog and it was her ploy to have Janet bathe in grape juice!

"Uncle Travis can't come and get me. Can you drive me back?" I asked as I picked up the slimy tennis ball and threw it as far as I could. Belle charged.

"Of course!" Luke answered without any hesitation whatsoever. He truly was a gentleman, a loving dad, a subservient husband, and so far a very cool brother. Even though he had never met my dad, it was uncanny the mannerisms they shared.

I returned to my cell phone. "Yes, Luke will drive me back. Yes, I'll tell him. I love you too."

I clicked END and slid my cell back into the front pocket of my faded jeans while telling Luke my uncle sent his regards and was looking forward to skeet shooting on Sunday.

CHAPTER 4

The Drive With Luke

As we pulled out of the driveway, Luke immediately apologized and said he hoped I had a nice time in spite of his wife's behavior. I had the feeling this wasn't the first time he had apologized for her rudeness. Then the words just blurted out.

"Why'd you marry her?" I brazenly asked.

He concentrated on the road with both hands on the steering wheel and momentarily answered, "She was five months pregnant and didn't know it."

Another unequivocal question escaped my mouth, "So it was too late for her to abort?"

"Geez, Dakota, how do you know so much? You're too young to know stuff like that."

"First of all, I'm sixteen—not far from turning seventeen. With my mom dead and my dad working long hours, drowning myself in books and horror movies relieved a void. The genre of books ranged from the human anatomy to medical science and procedures. One of them illustrated an abortion. I know—gross, but it caught my attention."

"Maybe you'll become a doctor," he said.

"Hate blood. No can do," I shot back and rephrased, "So what'd you even see in Janet to go out with her in the first place, besides her slim figure and somewhat okay face?"

"She's pretty!" Luke countered.

"Maybe a little, but so was Snow White's evil stepmother."

"You're something else, Dakota." He chuckled. "Honestly, when I first met Janet she was a lot ... a lot nicer than she is now."

"So what changed?"

"I wish I knew. Janet's an independent woman, but raising a child alone terrified her. She demanded I marry her, even though I naturally would propose to her or any woman carrying my child."

I nodded and made a "hmmm" sound. How uncanny—it was just the opposite with his mom. She wanted to raise Luke alone.

Luke continued, "She didn't even give me the courtesy to do the old-fashioned thing—you know, ask her father for her hand in marriage."

On top of his good looks and charm, he was also so respectful. He was truly a catch. What was Janet's problem?

"She arranged a small ceremony at her dad's ranch. She didn't even ask her dad's pastor to do the blessing—some justice of the peace dictated the words for me to recite. When it was her turn there was no tenderness in her voice. Casually she said, *I take thee, Luke Theodore Lockwood, as my husband from this day forward.* But she didn't take my name. She kept her maiden name, like somethin' was wrong with Lockwood."

"Did you say Theodore?" I asked, tickled pink. He nodded, still concentrating on the road. It had started to rain.

"That was my dad's middle name!" I joyfully exclaimed.

Luke beamed, but then tears started to form in his beautiful eyes. He softly said, "I really wanted to meet your dad—my dad—our dad. I couldn't believe it when I read the headline: Long-Time Resident of Fort Worth and Dedicated Employee of Jennings Petroleum Dies in Accidental Explosion."

Shivers just ran through my body. Goose bumps formed, and tears began streaming down my cheeks like water from a faucet. What the heck—I was crying. I was finally crying. It had been nine days since Uncle Travis had pulled into the driveway with the CEO of Jennings Petroleum following in his phantom black Cadillac Escalade. I knew something was wrong. Jake Jennings never visited employees' homes.

He rarely attended the lavish corporate Christmas parties he threw. He was always generous, though—spared no expense. He even had lobster flown in a few times. And kids, spouses, boyfriends, and girlfriends were included in the invites. But Mr. Jennings gave off the impression he was too cool for the room. Even though he tried to be PC, I once saw him give a nasty look like he stepped in dog crap when his assistant, Derek, introduced his male friend, Jason, as his soul mate. A few days later Mr. Jennings had a new assistant. I was only thirteen at the time, but I could tell from a mile away Derek was gay. So why Mr. Jennings was so oblivious was beyond me. And why did he care what sexual orientation his assistant had, just as long as he did his job?

More importantly, why did Mr. Jennings let the machines that dug him oil and made him millions of dollars go askew? Hinges on kitchen cabinets could get off-center and still work for months, and nobody would get killed! But a machine that weighs tons gets wiggly and rattles, and it goes unnoticed? It didn't make any sense. He gave off the "I am so perfect" air, but his business wasn't so perfect—at least not since the accident. And it would be worse after Uncle Travis garnered a settlement for me. I wondered if Mr. Jennings would have to cut back on the employee Christmas bonuses.

I remembered Dad's Christmas bonuses. My very generous dad proudly declared, holding up the envelope, *Dakota darling, this here check I got is all to be spent on you!* I was not your typical teenage girl ready to go on a shopping spree with Daddy's money. I preferred a movie marathon, a bucket of extra-spicy wings, and a liter of Pepsi. Maybe some onion rings if they were killer big and crispy—God forbid soggy. After watching me eat, Dad would always declare, shaking his head, *I don't know where you put it, Dakota. I swear, you must have a tapeworm.* It's true—I am rather skinny but can eat like there's no tomorrow!

Naturally, being the incredible dad he was, he obliged. We sat on the sofa all afternoon watching the *Omen* series. After movies one and two we broke for ribs at Red Hot and Blues about a mile from our house. Everyone there knew my dad, which delayed us from heading back on schedule to watch *Omen III*.

I thought it was awesome, though, how popular my dad was. I savored the flattery bestowed upon him. He never got a big head, either. He was always helpful and remained humble. The widows especially were very fond of his charming ways. He'd say persuasively, *Miss Clara, it was nothing, really—just a loose wire. Miss Su Ellen, I told you already, I am not taking your money.* Old Miss Su Ellen wanted to pay for our dinner since my dad unclogged her kitchen sink one Easter. She tried taking the tab off our table, but my dad gently nabbed her hand, brought her leathery skin to his lips, kissed it ever so softly, and said, *Miss Su Ellen, you keep baking your delicious strawberry-rhubarb pies for the church's potlucks and I'll fix whatever needs fixin' in that grand house of yours. Okay?* I think Miss Su Ellen nearly fainted. That was a lot of romance for any eighty-six-year-old to endure. My dad was so winsome—and also respectful to have referred to her house only as grand. It was starting to look haunted.

CHAPTER 5

Skeet Shooting

"Ready … aim … fire!" Luke shouted. I pulled back and shot. I missed, but it was still invigorating. Just FYI, skeet shooting is a lot harder than it looks. Naturally, my rugged Texan uncle and brother were incredible. The clay disks instantly smashed at their pulls. I was having so much fun. The only void was my dad's absence, but I didn't let my missing him put a damper on my day. I continued to smile because I felt Dad's presence. He was looking down at me, also smiling, happy that I had Luke in my life. It made me think about how my life might have been different if we had known about Luke from day one.

My mom would have embraced him. She always preached, *there's enough love in this world to go around, but some people close their doors and never know the power love holds. Dakota, you remember, we are all God's children. Never turn people away because of their differences, okay?* Those words were forever inscribed in my mind and soul. I promised Mom I wouldn't. *Mom* —the very word ignited my curiosity. Where was Luke's mom?

"I'm starvin'," Uncle Travis declared after our clay disks were all used up.

We headed back to the lodge, where a sumptuous luncheon awaited—a roasted pig with an apple in its mouth adorned the twenty-foot table. The cute chef sliced me a juicy piece of pork. I thanked him, and he winked in return. I thought, *He's too old for me.* I piled on the mouthwatering sides—garlic-infused mashed potatoes, pan-fried okra, and string beans with sliced almonds. I noticed cutie watching me. He smiled. "Come back for seconds."

I moseyed to our table. The sight of Luke and Uncle Travis' plates was deplorable—piled too high, higher than mine, as if the lodge might run out of food. "You both know you can go back for seconds," I reminded them, sounding like Mom. They ignored me and dove in. The empty fourth chair at our table made me think of Savannah, not Dad. Savannah would absolutely go bananas at the dessert table. I now wished she had come but understood why Luke didn't want her to— guns and kids don't mix.

"Luke, I am so sorry I couldn't join you and your family for dinner the other night. I really didn't think my clients, after spending most of the day in a stuffy conference room with me, would insist on dinner with me. But they're top-dollar clients, so unfortunately money deter-mines many outcomes." Uncle Travis took a bite of his chutney-smoth-ered pork and said with his mouth full, "Speaking of money, you had a good write-up in Houston's business journal. Lockwood Pools is doing well, yes?"

Luke hesitated. He smirked, took a gulp of his cold draft beer, and finally remarked, "Money isn't everything, Travis."

Uncle Travis became defensive. "I know that, boy. You're preaching to the wrong choir. I was very poor growing up. The five of us would trudge to school with holes in our shoes. We didn't care what the rich kids thought of us. We knew our minds were just as keen if not smarter. My mama always said I'd make a good lawyer or politician 'cause I was as sharp as a whip and could lure a bear away from honey."

"Travis, I didn't mean to offend you. I'm sorry. You're the last person I want to upset."

Travis nodded in acceptance to Luke's back-pedaling and also apolo-gized. "No, I'm sorry, Luke. Sometimes I get carried away. I persevered through so many goddamn injuries playing football so I could get college paid for. I played eight years, and I don't miss it one damn bit. Books are what mattered the most to me. The law was so important to me, and understanding all the bullshit and loopholes the poor are blindsided by. Ever since my grandpa lost his land because of a missed, added fee that he swore on the holy Bible he never received, but the bank claimed they sent …"

He shook his head and took a gulp of his beer. "I vowed to him on his deathbed I would never let that happen again to any law-abiding citizen of this great country."

While all this was going on between Uncle Travis and Luke, I couldn't help but visualize Luke's very modest home—without a custom pool, even though that was his business. I interjected, "Luke, why don't you have a pool?"

They broke away from their very intense conversation for Luke to answer my question point blank, "That was my bachelor pad before I bought the business, before I married, and before I became a daddy."

I was surprised vampire Janet hadn't pushed for a more palatial setting to live in. But deep down I had the feeling she was going to return to New York, and sadly I felt Luke had that same premonition. I was all for a two-parent household—but a happy one. However, the binds of their child … if only he could get custody of Savannah. Then it hit me. Uncle Travis being the brilliant lawyer he is, Luke had a chance! I then rudely asked, "Have you thought about divorcing Janet?"

I couldn't believe I just said that. They were surprised too. Uncle Travis gaped. Luke choked, but a quick chug of water relieved it. Then Uncle Travis demanded, "Dakota Summer Buchannan, what has gotten into you?"

I immediately apologized, "I'm sorry, Luke. Janet's lovely."

But Luke dismissed my apology and my superficial compliment, telling my uncle, "It's okay. Don't punish Dakota for being straightforward. She's an honest and curious kid."

"You're lucky," my uncle said, looking directly at me.

"I have thought about divorcing Janet, but I love Savannah too much to let her go. Janet would return to New York just like her mother did and take my little girl with her."

Now Uncle Travis asserted, "Luke, I can help you."

A sense of relief came over all of us. We were on the same page. Janet's a B-I- T-C-H. She's got to go—Savannah stays!

I wanted to ask Luke about his mom, but he seemed overwhelmed. I supposed there had been enough drama for one day, and it just wasn't the right time or place. What if it made him cry? Then I'd start to cry. Besides, my uncle might not let me off so easy a second round.

CHAPTER 6

Bible Camp

Uncle Travis and I took the four-hour road trip again to good ol' Houston. He had business, and I had my new and wonderful brother with his equally adorable daughter—my niece, sweet Savannah—to revisit. It was nice, being called "sister" and "aunt."

We rolled in about two in the afternoon. We had already stopped for lunch at a roadside diner that served the most scrumptious chicken-fried steak over a mound of mashed potatoes with gravy. I felt totally bloated. I was ready to be a couch potato in the suite Uncle Travis had booked. I anticipated slipping on my sweats—anything with an expandable waistband—and scouring the channels for a horror flick or reading … probably both, but TV first. I had stashed my mom's copy of *To Kill A Mockingbird* in my duffel bag. We were supposed to read it together when I reached ninth grade. I never asked my dad to. I knew he'd oblige, but I also knew books weren't his thing, and he would just be pretending to like it. When I entered high school, the English teacher's syllabus didn't include Harper Lee, so I had put it off until now.

I prevented any valet delays by taking the bags out of the trunk myself—being careful not to scratch my uncle's pristine Jag—and scurried to the front desk.

"Good Lord, child, hold your horses. Your Uncle Travis isn't getting any younger!" He cried, sounding out of breath, trying to catch up to me.

The front desk recognized him, greeted him, and gave him the royal treatment. Blah, blah, blah, just give him the damn room key— I've got to poop!

Since my Uncle Travis had work to do and Lockwood Pools had just been commissioned to build a community pool in some fancy gated neighborhood, Luke could not take the day off. So, I had two options. Option one: revisit the hotel's spa for more pampering, be a lounge lizard, and finish Harper Lee's book—I was enamored with the protagonist, Atticus Finch! Rascally Uncle Travis had hidden the remote so I wouldn't be tempted to channel surf! Or option two: attend Bible camp with my sweet Savannah. You'll never believe what I chose.

A pleasantly plump woman announced while giving her hands two loud claps. "God's children, please take a seat. The sooner you sit and close your mouths, the sooner we can listen to the wonderful stories of our good Lord."

Surprisingly, the small group of four- and five-year-olds adhered to this woman as if she were Mrs. Claus about to pass out presents. They each took a seat in the semicircular row of small plastic chairs and sat with their hands clasped on their lap. I was leaning against the back wall next to a colorful poster. The picture of flying doves forming from a rainbow and blazing in crimson script across the bottom read, "Do unto others … like you would want others to do unto you."

These were the best-behaved children I had ever seen. It was like they had been brainwashed. The robust woman continued, "Children, we have a very special visitor here with us today. Her daddy and mommy are with God, and all three are looking down at this brave and beautiful girl, so happy she chose to attend Bible camp."

She gave a heavy sigh, motioning her stout body toward me. The children followed, turning their little heads toward me, looking as intense as if they were searching for my halo! Oh my God, how in the world did she know? Perhaps it was thanks to Janet and her big mouth.

I wanted to tell Miss Humiliating Bible Thumper I was only attending Bible camp for this one day, and only for Savannah's sake, not Jesus's. And why did adults refer to me as brave? Because I no longer had a mom or dad, I was brave? Didn't make any sense to me whatsoever. And I was far from beautiful. I was very ordinary-looking. Why couldn't they ever refer to me as smart? I would be taking all AP classes in the fall. My junior year had been a joke, and I was hoping my senior year would be more challenging.

Savannah was beaming. She was absolutely thrilled I was her "Show 'n' Tell." She ran over to me, took my hand, and led me to the front of the semicircle of friends. Miss Tubby was unintentionally pushed away. I knew I shouldn't feel any animosity toward this well-endowed Bible school teacher—it had to be a double-D bra she harnessed her bosoms into every morning—but really I didn't think it was anybody's business that I was permanently parentless, especially a roomful of tots.

A little boy wearing a shirt that matched his bright blue eyes asked before Savannah had a chance to introduce me, "What's your name?"

Savannah proudly answered for me, "She's my Aunt Dakota!"

Now I was the one beaming. Suddenly I felt like the most popular girl in school. And just as suddenly I was bombarded with questions. "Where are you from? How old are you? What's your favorite color? Do you like broccoli? Do you have a hamster?"

None of them waited for a response, and everyone seemed to be talking at once—so much for my theory that they were the best-behaved children! I actually didn't answer any because Miss Zaftig called them over for lemonade and gingersnaps.

CHAPTER 7
Rhonda's Rodeo Roadhouse

Vampire's distinct quirk of wiping down her silverware the minute we were seated irked the shit out of me. Remembering the dog and grape juice fiasco, I wished one of the busy waitresses delivering mounds of ribs from kitchen to table as fast as their little feet could go would accidentally bump into Janet and topple one of them platters over onto Janet's too-perfect appearance. Then she would simply have to run home and change—and decide not to return! She just didn't fit in at this old-fashioned Texas-style restaurant. If my mom were here, she'd teach Miss New Yorker a few rules of conduct. I had a feeling Janet knew better. She wouldn't dare act that way in Manhattan. It was like she was saving herself—like we weren't good enough for her etiquette. She thought she was better than us. Bottom line, she wasn't. Unfortunately, as the night played out, my wish never came true!

A gorgeous, Dallas Cowboys cheerleader–type girl approached us with a "Howdy! How's everyone doin' tonight? Can I start you off with something cold to drink? It sure is hot in here."

Uncle Travis was in absolute heaven and devilishly declared, "It just got hotter!" The waitress smiled at his impish grin and sexy implication. My uncle wooed her with, "You are just the prettiest girl ..."

He quickly looked at me and winked, his way of telling me in an osmosis kind of way, *Except you, Dakota.* I picked up on it and nodded, letting him know, *go on and have your fun!*

"And you, sir, are very handsome! Now, what can I get you to cool you down?" she said with a seductive overtone while bending toward him so he could get a better look at her cleavage. I was inwardly laughing at this brazen flirting between this maybe twenty-three-year-old and my uncle. Uncle Travis had to be aware that this waitresses acted sugary to all her customers—especially male ones—for higher tips. But knowing my uncle, he'd never pass up a consensual flirting opportunity. And I loved it when he was this way. It always put him in a feeling-younger mood.

Janet rudely interrupted the love fest and demanded a cold glass of water with a lemon wedge. Luke ordered a Bud Lite. Uncle Travis said merrily, "Copy that with two shots of Wild Turkey, please," gesturing that the second shot of bourbon was for Luke.

Again and abruptly, Janet put the kibosh on. She said sternly, "*I wasn't expecting to be the designated driver*." And she motioned to Miss Cheerleader—with her index finger in the air—to make that *one* Wild Turkey! Uncle Travis was pissed—not because he didn't have a drinking buddy but because Big Apple had corrected him.

Savannah bellowed over the turned-up music, "Two Shirley Temples, Pease." Like Uncle Travis, she was ordering the second one for me. I was relieved her mom didn't correct her pronunciation of the word "Please."

Uncle Travis looked over at me again. He understood my take-it-easy-look and gave me a wink, agreeing that Big Apple wasn't going to ruin our night. The music was loud. He stood up and shouted over to Savannah and me, "Let's dance!"

We smiled and obliged but not without Luke. We walked over and grabbed him. I pulled one hand and Savannah the other. Janet quickly crossed her arms—again that negative body language—telling us to leave her alone. *Honestly, don't flatter yourself, Janet. You aren't worth any dance ... first or last!*

The four of us were working up a sweat and an appetite, having a blast dancing to the music of Brooks & Dunn. Then suddenly in between songs my uncle slowed down, stopped, and put his hand to his heart. He saw how alarmed I became and quickly repositioned it, pantomiming the act of drinking. I got it and was quickly relieved, but still I yelled at him as we left the dance floor, "Don't you ever do that again! I thought you were having a heart attack!"

We adjourned to the table. Vampire was on her cell talking to her mom, but because the music was so loud, Janet was shouting. Why she didn't go outside is beyond me. As smart as she thought she was, she was stupid!

Our drinks were on the table along with a variety of appetizers Janet took the liberty of ordering. She loved deciding what people should drink and eat. But inwardly I declared, *Bravo, Janet. I am one hungry girl who happens to have gotten her period today, and salty food is like heaven!*

Savannah was masked in barbecue sauce as she devoured her hundredth chicken wing. She was so darn cute. I took my own napkin, dabbed it in my glass of water, and started cleaning around her mouth before the sauce and spices of Rhonda's famous recipe irritated her delicate skin. Janet was oblivious—still staring down at her iPhone. What in the world was she researching? Divorce lawyers, I hoped.

After dinner, outside the restaurant, Savannah sweetly asked me, "Can I stay with you?"

I answered, "I would love it if we were snuggle bunnies tonight, but it's up to your daddy and mommy."

She looked at her parents angelically, clasping her hands in prayer form, and begged, "Pease, pease, pretty pease."

Luke got down on his knees so he was level with his daughter, took both her hands in his, and declared while smiling and looking into her eyes, "This will be your first sleepover, Savannah!"

Vampire nonchalantly conceded, "Sure." She finished her text, not looking at Uncle Travis, me, or her adorable daughter and husband. Their pose was like a Kodak moment. She shocked all four of us with her approval. Boy, did she have a conflicting personality.

Back at the hotel, Savannah was draped in one of my T-shirts as a nightie, naturally looking like a cutie pie. I was taking off my mascara, standing next to her as she brushed her teeth and paying attention to her counting through her foamy mouth. When she finished I curiously asked, "Why were you counting, Savannah?"

"My dentist told me to count to ten three times when I'm brushing so I won't get a cavity," Savannah answered with certainty. She opened her mouth wide for me to take a look inside. "See!"

I just couldn't believe how responsible this four-year-old was. I congratulated her, "Good for you!" as I checked her teeth. "Yup, you got 'em. No sugar bugs in there!"

She giggled.

We climbed into bed, and Uncle Travis approached us, looking debonair in his burgundy silk pajamas, "All right, girls, time to get some shut-eye. When I see you in the morning, you'll be even more beautiful." And he kissed us both on our foreheads. "Good night, my princesses." He is so affectionate, and it saddens me he doesn't have a woman to appreciate all he has to offer.

CHAPTER 8

The Property

L uke picked us up at ten in the morning. We piled into his Ford
truck. As I buckled Savannah into her car seat she innocently asked,
"Where's Mommy?"

Luke was hesitant. Savannah rephrased her question. "Daddy, is
Mommy shopping?"

Luke was apprehensive but finally answered his daughter, "Mama's
in New York."

"What?" I shouted.

Luke quickly blurted, "She wanted to be with her mom."

Uncle Travis remained speechless.

What a B-I-T-C-H. How could a mom not say good-bye to her kid,
especially when leaving town and getting on a plane! I saw the crushed
look on Savannah's face, and I wanted to cry.

Savannah made a pouty face for a split second but then announced
with a smile, "Grandma's lucky! I wonder what Mommy will bring me
back—this time."

This child is amazing. Her ability to see the glass as half full is re-
markable considering her young age.

We drove down a dirt road and approached a Private Property sign,
which Luke whisked by. He was acting proud. We soon came to a stop.
We got out and took in our surroundings. The variety of plush trees
indigenous to Texas spread throughout. Some of the cedar elms and

live oaks were massive—they had to be at least five decades old. Luke asked, "What do y'all think?"

Uncle Travis chimed in, "What's not to like?"

Luke beamed and happily declared, "I bought it! I've got forty-two acres to do what I want with!"

Luke was radiant, and Savannah started jumping in place as if her dad had just won a prize at the carnival. She anxiously asked, "Daddy, are there horses?"

Luke caught her, swung her around, and answered in the same jovial tone as his daughter, "No … but I'll get some!"

I smiled but stayed quiet. Uncle Travis exclaimed, "Looks like you got a nice piece of property here, and I wish you all the best." He sounded happy for Luke but seemed concerned, too. He knew as well as I did that Big Apple wasn't going to go for this. This place was over forty minutes from downtown Houston. Their house now was maybe a ten-minute drive from the city center. Uncle Travis then asked the inevitable. "Does Janet know?"

Luke, still holding Savannah, gave her an affectionate squeeze and told her he loved her as she rested her head on his shoulder. She seemed tired from the long drive and big hotel breakfast. She actually was closing her eyes and falling asleep. Luke whispered to us, "I thought a lot about what you two said the other night … leaving Janet."

Simultaneously Uncle Travis and I glanced at each other. We shared a look of panic. A tinge of guilt riddled us. We were home wreckers! Luke didn't take notice of this and continued, "I know we aren't a match made in heaven, but we have a slice of heaven right here." He was referring to Savannah as he slowly and gently rubbed her back. She was passed out on his chest with her legs dangling.

He found a three-foot tree stump to ease down onto. Uncle Travis leaned against the hood. I decided to sit cross-legged on the dry, hard earth. I started fidgeting with a short stick I found near me, poking the dirt with it, and candidly asked Luke, "When are you going to tell Janet?"

He briefly hesitated. I could see by the way his face reddened and his eyes blinked that he was trying hard to hold back his tears. He slowly breathed in and out as one would for a doctor and confessed, "Janet asked for a divorce when we headed home from the restaurant last night."

No wonder she had agreed to let Savannah spend the night with me. Uncle Travis and I were like deer caught in headlights. We didn't expect this so soon. Luke divulged, "At a red light, she just came out with it. She said, *Luke, you are a wonderful provider and loving dad, and you try to make me happy. Your attempts at romance and flattery are nice, but but I just can't do it any longer. I can't pretend anymore that I'm in love with you. I'm not—I'm sorry. I think it would be best—better for Savannah, and better for you—if we parted ways.* She actually sounded poetic! At our damn wedding she couldn't make our I-dos sound romantic, but when she asked for a divorce she made it sound like … like a scene from *The Way We Were!*"

The Way We Were? Luke knew *The Way We Were*, the best American romantic drama film ever made? I had watched it with Mom ten, fifteen, maybe twenty times! She loved the classics, and I loved curling up with her. I am not exaggerating when I tell you we went through a whole box of Kleenex each time. I was a bit surprised my rough and tough–looking brother had seen the chick flick. But then again, he did exude a romantic side.

Those who knew my parents referred to them as the couple from *Love Story*—another chick flick. I wondered if Luke had seen that one, too. My parents weren't Harvard grads by any means, but they were just as smart. They weren't rich with money but had class. And if love had a scent, you could smell theirs for miles. I think the author, Erich Segal, would have been impressed with my metaphor. It wasn't as good as his, though: *Love means never having to say you're sorry.*

Like Jenny in *Love Story,* my mom was dying. Dad would have done anything to save her, like Oliver tried to save Jenny. Some of my parents' friends even thought my mom looked like the actress who played Jenny, Ali MacGraw. Of course, I was biased. I teased, *She's prettier!* And even though none of those friends ever remarked that my dad looked like Oliver, I thought he was just as good-looking, if not better-looking, than the actor who played Jenny's husband, Ryan O'Neal.

Although no one died at the end of *The Way We Were,* I thought it was sadder than *Love Story.* Hubble never surrendered his love, and because of that, his life had regret. In my opinion, feeling regret about not being with your true love is far worse than losing someone you do surrender your love to.

My mom bought both soundtracks, and because of *Love Story* I have a great appreciation for classical music. It isn't boring or stuffy—just the opposite. In fact, it freed me. Barbara Streisand has one of the most beautiful singing voices I have ever heard. It was so powerful. It captured me and swallowed me, and I just wanted to sit still and listen. The lyrics spoke the truth. Mom played her so much that the three of us had the lyrics embedded in our memory. The theme song from the movie was played at her funeral. I silently mouthed the words as her coffin was being carried out of the church.

Unexpectedly, it was time to leave. I must have zoned out during the rest of Travis and Luke's conversation. As I got up I stared at the heart I made in the dirt.

CHAPTER 9

Pamela

Luke took an emergency call. Some pool fountain wasn't working, and it was the backdrop of someone's wedding photos. Understandably, that took precedence over joining us at his father-in-law's for the day.

Savannah was playing in the shallow end of the pool with Alexis. Crystal, of the famous peach pie, had set a tray of cold beverages and snacks on a table under one of the umbrellas.

Uncle Travis shouted, "Cannonball!" as he plummeted into Mr. Trenton's pool. Sometimes I was embarrassed by my uncle's childish actions. But as soon as I heard Savannah's howl of laughter, I couldn't help but smile and give in myself. Mr. Trenton, who preferred for me to call him Drew or Uncle Drew, challenged Travis, but his splash wasn't as big. He looked about thirty pounds lighter than my uncle. I wished my uncle were in better shape. I couldn't bear losing him, too. He needed to walk me down the aisle one of these days.

A gorgeous, Latin-looking, woman about Luke's age, wearing a swimsuit that accentuated her every feminine curve—no body fat in sight—tootled out. Alexis gleefully shouted, "Hi, Mommy!" Of course, my uncle's jaw dropped. Then Mr. Trenton, wearing a playful grin, called out, "Looking good, Miss Pamela!"

She blushed. I wanted to shout to my uncle, *Close that mouth of yours and stop staring. You're not a frat boy anymore!* He finally caught my scolding glance and plunged under.

Okay, so this here goddess was Alexis's mom and Crystal's daughter, Pamela. I silently prayed, *Dear Lord, please let her be as beautiful on the inside as she is on the outside.* I really couldn't deal with another Janet.

I decided to climb out of the pool and take the chaise lounge near Pamela, even though I was wet and preferred the sun to dry me. I reached for a towel and lay under the umbrella next to Pamela, who was sewing! She totally didn't strike me as the Suzie Homemaker type, so immediately I asked, "What are you doing?" in a somewhat cynical manner. I realized seconds later that my tone had been rude. Maybe I was on the defensive, preparing myself for a bitch.

Pamela looked up from her sewing, smiled, and greeted me with a bubbly, "Hi! You must be Dakota. I'm Pam."

"Hi," I returned with a smile, hoping she didn't think I was a brat.

"I'm almost done. This is Alexis's favorite cover-up. The button came flying off just before we got here. She was in tears, like it was her wedding dress and this here day was her wedding!"

I smiled at her sense of humor as she conveyed, "My daughter always gets so excited when she hears Savannah will be at her grandpa's. And then you and your uncle were going to be here too, which got her more excited. You're all Savannah talks about now. And I'm so glad I finally got the chance to meet you both."

Thank you, Lord—this woman is nothing like Janet. I beamed. "Really? She talks about me? I think Savannah's incredible! And so bright, too— that mind of hers. She's like a sponge. Just the other day I took her to a bird sanctuary, and she was pointing out all the different species, listing their names and traits. I couldn't believe it. Did you know there's a bird called the Savannah Sparrow?"

"Of course! That's how Savannah got her name. Luke's mom, Gerry, volunteered there—her favorite species was the Savannah Sparrow. Naturally, Janet had to like it. She said it had a nice ring, and lucky for them it had three syllables. She was only considering three-syllable names and would highlight them in the baby-naming book with a pink marker. She found out the gender as soon as she could, even though Luke suggested they wait and be surprised at birth. But she didn't care about what he wanted, nor did she keep from telling him when she found out—she was carrying a girl!"

"Oh, so you don't like her either?" I presumed.

Pamela shook her head and continued, "My mom said she went on a shopping rampage, buying all the nursery furniture and pink bedding. She charged it on her daddy's credit card, claiming Luke could never afford it. Naturally, Mr. Trenton paid it. He never said a word to Luke other than that he got a big discount and to consider it his baby gift. But you and I both know it didn't end there. Savannah gets anything she wants."

"Yeah, I suppose with a rich grandpa—why not? But she doesn't come across as spoiled or rotten."

"No. She rarely whines for anything. She's the type of child who's content playing with the box the toy came in!"

I laughed and reminisced, "My dad told me about a Christmas I was more intent on making a bed for my new doll with the box it came in than playing with any of my other presents."

Pamela smiled. I was dying to know why Gerry had waited so long to reveal my father's identity. "Were you close to Gerry?" I asked.

"Well, she was here a lot. Mr. Trenton is such a sweet, caring man and so generous," she said as she tidied the sewing tools away in a small fabric box. What did that have to do with Gerry? It was as if she wanted to set precedents. "My pregnancy was a difficult one, and if Mr. Trenton saw me looking ill at ease, he insisted I take it easy. He kept offering me money, insisting I take hundred-dollar bills from his hand. He told me he'd sneak it in my purse if I didn't take it then. And then he headed down the corridor to Gerry's suite."

"Gerry's suite? She didn't live here. Luke and Gerry didn't live here!" I said as if Pamela had made a terrible mistake.

"They didn't—I know. But Gerry had a room," she reiterated.

"Do you mean Mr. Trenton and Gerry were having an affair?" I asked, shocked.

"If you call a thirty-six-year relationship an affair," she answered with a sardonic tone.

"What?" I shouted in utter shock. This was like a soap opera—and I didn't even watch them! My mom banned me from watching those television dramas where infidelities and illegitimate children were considered the norm. Luke looked too much like Jethro, so there was no doubting he was my brother. Even though we had different moms and different last names, I wasn't putting "half" in his title, and I hoped he wasn't putting it in mine.

"I thought Luke met Janet five years ago when he came here to repair this pool?" I said, pointing to the pool as if that would clarify my confusion.

"They did. Gerry wasn't on the books as one of Mr. Trenton's employees. She never brought her son here for the family swims. Everyone who worked here knew which suite in the guest quarters was off-limits—it was Gerry's. There were certain times throughout the day when Mr. Trenton wasn't around, but his car was still in the garage. We knew where he was. It had to be a dire emergency before any of us would dare knock on the door. Constance, his wife, knew too. She was aware of this weird arrangement even before they wed, but she still married him—for his money, of course."

"I thought Constance was a New York socialite?" I asked, sounding more confused.

"Yes, but she was becoming a poor one. Her inheritance was dwindling. She never invested it—only spent it. Constance and Drew slept in separate quarters. Conceiving Janet was like the immaculate conception!"

I let out a chuckle, savoring her intense gossip with her added quips.

Pamela continued, "They made a handsome couple. She knew how to look radiant and act in all the right social situations … except for one dreadful night. That changed everything."

She gave a deep sigh with a pensive look, as if she were an oncologist about to reveal to her patient that the cancer had returned. "She took a painkiller right before she left—the pinched nerve in her back was throbbing. She hadn't eaten all day, but that didn't stop her from downing a glass of champagne right away at the party's entrance."

"So, she got drunk and what … fell?" I asked. That didn't seem like a big deal—majorly embarrassing, though.

"Worse! Mr. Trenton supported the governor's campaign. He was one of the highest-ranking contributors."

"I'm not surprised," I interrupted.

"Constance got sloppy at this big fund-raising gala and told Drew very loudly to go …" She looked around to see the kids weren't in earshot. They were splashing around, not paying any attention to us. "Well, you know, the F word—to go F his whore, Geraldine Lockwood!" Pamela finally divulged.

I let out a big laugh. I was really surprised, and pleased, that Pamela was so forthcoming.

Pamela laughed, too, and concluded, "Constance actually said the surname, Lockwood, which grabbed the attention of another bigwig contributor who was seriously seeing Gerry. Rumor had it this bigwig was literally carrying an engagement ring in his pocket, waiting for the perfect opportunity to propose to Gerry. Supposedly when the governor was re-elected, which was only in a matter of weeks—he was way ahead in votes—this bigwig—I forget his name—was going to pop the question. You know, when the balloons and streamers showered the ballroom."

Both of us looked up into the sky as if expecting confetti to fall on us. "I feel sorry for Bigwig," I said heartily.

Pamela nodded and stated solemnly, "Gerry wasn't at that fundraiser because she knew both her lovers were going to be there."

"I recall my Uncle Travis telling me, *Gerry played Jethro like a fiddle.* Is that what that means—another term for cheating?" I asked, looking at Pamela for guidance. I never did understand that terminology my uncle had used, and I didn't bother to ask him what it meant. I was in that mind-numbing period of adjustment at the time.

"No, not necessarily. You don't have to cheat to toy with someone's emotions. Although Gerry did both—manipulate the heart and cheat! She was definitely the expert at that."

I loved Pamela's honesty. I found it so refreshing for someone I hardly knew to tell me like it is. I summoned Pamela back to Uncle Travis's story. "Gerry told my dad there was another man and Jethro needed to leave immediately and never return. Was Gerry planning on pretending Luke was Mr. Trenton's baby? Did he do the math? Did he have a blood test done? Why would he continue seeing her when she was carrying another man's baby?"

"Hold that thought," Pamela gently said to me. Then she called, "All right, girls, get on out and get some lunch." She held up the cover-up. "Come here, Alexis—it's fixed."

"Wait, you can't leave me hanging! I can't talk about this in front of the girls," I said. I sounded frantic, as if it were a matter of life and death! But Pamela ignored me. She wrapped her daughter in her cover-up and then playfully swatted her bottom, edging her to go get some lunch. Savannah and Alexis tootled off like two peas in a pod. I was curious as to where Pamela's husband was. Did she even have one?

Mr. Trenton and Uncle Travis were way at the other end of the pool in the cabana. I could smell cigar smoke, probably coming from the best Cubans accompanied with single-malt scotch. The last time I saw my Uncle Travis relaxed like this was with my dad, just a week before he died. They ordered Chinese take-out and ate it while watching some crazy, stupid wrestling show. It was really outlandishly ludicrous, but hearing my dad howl made me happy. My uncle hinted that his moo shoo pork would taste much better accompanied with a Mai Tai. I was willing to try—I Googled how to make them with my smartphone, and lucky for him our pantry did house a can of pineapple juice, and our liquor cabinet had rum. It was the same bottle of Bacardi my mom had bought to make a punch when she hosted Bunco—a dice game twelve ladies played once a month, rotating houses. I didn't think liquor expired, so I concocted a pitcher and served it to the boys, which earned me great praise. My mom also liked her rum and Cokes on Saturday evenings, and when Sinatra's "Fly Me to the Moon" blared, I knew she had a few too many! But before the song even went into its second verse, I could rest assured, knowing my dad had her safe and sound in his arms as they danced the night away.

I was glad my uncle had found a friend in Mr. Trenton, but was this all going to change when he found out about his daughter's impending divorce, with Travis representing Luke? I hoped not.

We devoured the delicious lunch Crystal served in the veranda. She brought the boys theirs—a small platter of club sandwiches with chips. God forbid they get up! The preschoolers were back in the pool frolicking. The boy's roars sounded like cheers. What were they watching? It wasn't football season. It was no surprise that the cabana held a TV. And my newest best friend, Pamela, continued to divulge as we relaxed in the bubbling hot tub fit for ten. I really appreciated her candidness and that she didn't treat me like an orphan.

"Sex!" she blurted out.

"What?" I said discombobulated.

"You asked me why Mr. Trenton would continue to see Gerry, knowing she was carrying another man's baby. The answer is sex. And even after he wed Constance … sex. Their honeymoon was a complete disaster. It ended earlier than expected. Mr. Trenton returned to Texas—to Gerry—for her sex, but Constance stopped over in New York for a week."

"Who does that?" I said, dumbfounded. I divulged part of my upbringing. "My parents were so the opposite. Their honeymoon never ended—every night was like date night! And even though at times I acted nauseous, deep down I delighted in their adolescent way of showing how much they cared for and loved one another."

"Speaking of adolescence, do you have a boyfriend, Dakota?" Pamela asked, smiling. She added, "I bet all the boys salivate over you!"

"No … not exactly." I blushed. "Thanks anyway, though."

"Really? That's hard to believe."

The hot water, and tantalizing jets were really relaxing me, making me yearn for an equally tantalizing guy, preferably an older one. "I'd like one," I said. "Do you know of anyone?"

"I'll see what I can do," Pamela answered coyly as she stepped out of the whirlpool and added nonchalantly, "I'm making myself a drink … do you want one?"

Did she mean with alcohol? Should I just go with it? I answered, "Sure, whatever you're having."

CHAPTER 10

Hank

Suddenly I was being doused! Luke was standing over me with an empty bucket and laughing. I quickly jumped up with an exasperating, "Whaaat?"

"Geez, girl, I needed to do something. According to my daughter, you've been napping all day—and seeing these three empty martini glasses on this table, I think I know why!" Luke surmised.

I immediately defended myself. "They were Pamela's."

"Don't get your knickers in a twist, Dakota. I was once sixteen. I'm glad you're having fun. Just don't let me ask you to babysit!" Luke teased.

Now I was pouting, but it soon disappeared when he suggested, "Let's go swimming."

Speaking of passed out, Uncle Travis and Mr. Trenton were literally snoring away on cushiony lounge chairs in the cabana. Savannah and Alexis were in Crystal's quarters playing Candy Land, unaffected by us being under the influence. Thank goodness, because before Pamela I had never, ever drunk more than a half of a beer!

It was a warm Bud Lite, half drunk—left over from one of my dad's friends, a work colleague. Hank was his name. He was one of the newer employees Jennings had hired. He had to be around thirty years old. They watched a football game on our new fifty-inch plasma. My dad had been boasting about his new purchase, and Hank had chimed in,

I've never seen a TV that large. My dad, for some weird reason, felt compelled to show him.

Hank was okay-looking but had nothing upstairs, if you know what I mean. Sometimes he was as dumb as a doornail. But then there were times he talked to me about different breeds of horses and sounded so knowledgeable, like he was an expert equestrian.

When Hank left and my dad went to sleep, I sneaked down to watch Alfred Hitchcock's *Psycho*. The can of beer was just staring at me, so I gave it a try. Gross! It was probably better cold. Still, I preferred Pepsi. And no thanks to Pamela, I had a pounding headache. Where was Pamela, my partner in crime?

"So how was the wedding?" I asked

"Very grand," he answered. "I stayed until the photographer was through with the backdrops of the waterfall and fountain, in case it malfunctioned again." Luke boasted in a playful, not conceited, manner, "But of course, my expertise got it working properly."

"Yes, of course. I wouldn't expect anything less of you." I added to his whimsy, feeling so much better now that the cool water had made me come to my senses.

"I'm starvin'. Did y'all eat?" Luke asked.

"We ate lunch. What time is it?" I asked.

"Dinnertime. Let me go see what's cooking and if I can help," he said as he pushed himself up out of the deep end. I couldn't help but notice his defined muscular arms and his six-pack abs. What a complete idiot Janet was for not devouring him.

CHAPTER 11

Legally Separated

The news that their daughter's marriage had failed did not come as a surprise to Constance Powers and Drew Trenton. Drew had no ill feelings toward Luke. Constance was happy to have her daughter back in New York City but was not so keen on the arrangements regarding her granddaughter. She wanted Savannah to be exposed more to the culture and refinement of the upper echelons of Manhattan and to mold her into another Janet, but Janet didn't put up a fight when Luke asked for custody. Uncle Travis was prepared in case she did. Luke offered to fly with Savannah at least two weekends a month to New York, but Janet told him not to bother—she would send a nanny to fetch her when the time was right. And yes, in case you were wondering, she really did use the word "fetch."

Months went by before a British woman appeared at our doorstep to pick up Savannah and take her to New York for a week. Luke obliged without any reservation or criticism, but I personally was disgusted at Janet for making Savannah wait this long to see her mother. Everyone close to Savannah played it cool, giving every excuse in the book to sugar-coat Janet's selfishness. We did it so as not to hurt Savannah, of course—we could give two shits about Janet! The Brit was tall and slender, dressed in a navy blue pantsuit with a crisp white blouse. She wore the classic and practical mahogany penny loafer. Her brown hair was pulled back in a tight bun, and her pale, round face seemed flushed when my good-looking brother answered the door. She probably thought like most women did when they first met Luke—*Why'd his wife let him go?* Her sweet eyes twinkled behind her tortoiseshell glasses when she kneeled down to Savannah's level to introduce herself.

I must say, this was the easiest and most amicable divorce I had ever witnessed. So far, Savannah seemed to be taking it okay. Perhaps it was because I had moved in. I was living in Houston with my brother and his daughter—my new and wonderful family. I hoped I was the positive distraction Luke and Savannah needed to get through this separation. I knew they were what I needed in order to survive being parentless. These synchronicities were rather strange. The death of a loved one and the end to a marriage are negative situations, yet a lot of positives had resulted from these circumstances. The situation had undermined my deeply rooted disbelief in God. I now had faith in Him and was very grateful for that.

Uncle Travis visited quite frequently both for pleasure and for business. He said he found the four-hour drive in his luxury car "therapeutic." He said he missed me a ton, but I think he had become quite smitten with Pamela. She was the pull that got him to Houston.

CHAPTER 12
Independence Day

I had never celebrated the Fourth of July the way I did at Drew Trenton's spectacular BBQ and fireworks show. He must have invited three hundred people—employees, business partners, clients, family, and friends. Everything was unbelievable—the food, the band, the bars, and the entertainment, which included dancers, jugglers, acrobats, and even a moon bounce. He really knew how to throw a party.

As the crowd celebrated, Mr. Trenton walked purposefully to the stage, took the microphone from its stand, and cleared his throat. Every face turned. "Friends," he said in a strong, clear voice that rang out across his estate, "This here is more than just a party. This here is a celebration. A celebration of our great country. the good ol' U. S. of A. Let's never forget the men and women who fight for our country every day, keeping America safe."

The partygoers howled. The band's drummer began to beat a slow but rhythmic chord, allowing Mr. Trenton to finish. "Now, let's show the good Lord we're all happy to be Americans by shaking this here dance floor!" The rest of the band started up as the drummer released its melodic furor and Mr. Trenton hollered, "Thanks for coming, y'all!"

Mr. Trenton handed the microphone to the band's lead singer, and as he walked off the stage the singer yelled, "And God bless you, Drew Trenton!" Then he started to sing his rendition of "One Week," originally by the Barenaked Ladies. As the music escalated to a higher beat, fast-paced and audible for miles and miles, everyone on the dance floor broke free. Wild revelry abounded.

To my pleasant surprise, someone took hold of my waist from behind. As I turned to see whom these strong hands belonged to, I was staring into Luke's brilliant eyes. I smiled but was inwardly disappointed it was my brother 'cause I was feeling aroused!

Luke and I danced. Savannah and Alexis joined us, and Pamela soon followed. She was a replica of J. Lo. All five of us were now in our own little circle, strutting our moves and showing no boundaries.

After the third song I escaped to one of the many bars for an ice-cold Pepsi. Instead, I found myself ordering a cold beer from the incredibly good-looking, maybe twenty-two-year-old bartender. He looked me over in an obviously analytical manner, trying to figure out my age and if he should serve me alcohol. After long seconds he gave a so-sexy, subdued smile. I was trying so hard not to blush and to act more mature than usual. I knew I didn't look twenty-one.

He started pushing down on the keg's pump. He was wearing a tight-fitting, navy blue polo shirt that which accentuated his muscular triceps. And blazed in a white script across his heart was *"Trenton's Bash."* He held a matching plastic cup under the spout and asked me, "How do you know Mr. Trenton?"

I found myself so stupidly distracted with reading his shirt, the cup, and the matching cocktail napkin that it took me longer than it should have to answer, "He's my uncle," I lied. Well, it wasn't really an outright lie. Mr. Trenton did tell me to call him Uncle Drew. After all, I am related to his only grandchild.

Hottie soon smiled a big one and handed me my cool, frothy beer. Before I took a sip I returned the smile and said, "Thanks."

"Do you live here?" he asked.

"No, I live with my brother and his daughter not far from here," I answered.

"Maybe we can get together sometime," he suggested and gave another one of his breathtaking grins.

Holy shit! "Yeah, that'd be great," I said, thinking, *Can we just swap spit right now?*

"I'm due for a break now," Hottie told me. "Wait."

Geez, it was like he had read my mind. He scrolled through numbers on his cell and made a quick call. The next thing I caught sight of was another hot guy taking his place behind the bar. Where in the world did Uncle Drew get them all? Or had Texas been full of them all along, and I was just hiding behind Stephen King and Alford Hitchcock?

Then my free hand—the other one was holding my almost-gone beer—was being taken by his as he led us through the crowd toward the main house. We were inside the foyer. We headed to the den, where another bar was set up. No one was there. He went behind it, opened a large cooler, and twisted open a Bud Lite for himself. He asked if I wanted another beer. I declined but asked for a Pepsi instead. Before he took a gulp, he lightly clinked his beer bottle against my glass of soda and said, "Cheers!"

"Cheers!" I returned with an equally mischievous grin, yearning for a lot more from this hottie. "What's your name?" I asked. I should know it if I was going to jump his bones before the night was over.

"Hubbell, and yours?"

"What? Hubbell, as in *The Way We Were* Hubbell?" I chuckled, completely shocked.

He blushed, looking a little embarrassed. "You know the movie?"

"Of course I do! It's only the greatest romantic drama of all time! My mom and I watched it a trillion times, and each time we cried more—we could've sponsored Kleenex!" I embellished.

He laughed and looked pleased that someone knew the movie and seemed okay with the infamous character, Hubbell. Then he asked, "So what's your name? Don't tell me, it's … Ka-Ka-Katie!"

His impersonation from the movie was adorable.

"Yes!" I joked, "How'd you know?"

"Really?"

"Let me guess … your last name is Gullible?" I teased back.

He smiled and waited.

"Okay, just joking." Why'd I say that—of course he knew I was joking? "It's Dakota, Dakota Buchannan," I answered, trying not to sound nervously stupid.

He smiled. "Dakota Buchannan," he repeated. The way it rolled off his tongue made it sound so sexy. "I like it. What year are you in, Dakota Buchannan?" He seemed to like saying my name, and I definitely liked hearing *him* say it!

I answered, "Senior." Then I inquired, "Your mom's a Streisand fan?"

"No, Robert Redford. Really? You're only a senior in high school? I had you pegged for being in college already. Hmm. My mom, apparently like yours, loved the movie. She was infatuated with Robert Redford, a.k.a. Hubbell Gardner, and promised herself if she ever had a son, she'd name him either Robert, Redford, or Hubbell. Lucky me, she picked Hubbell, huh?" he added, being facetious.

"It's unique, that's for sure. Redford would have been too, for a first name—kinda edgy-sexy." I quickly added to make up for my rambling, "but not as sexy as the name Hubbell."

He smiled again and asked, changing the subject, "Are you looking into colleges around here?"

Initially, I didn't answer his question. Instead I divulged, which I know may seem weird, but I just wanted to get it out of the way. I could hear my uncle's secretary calling out, *TMI, Dakota!* "My mom loved the movie so much its song was played at her funeral, and I played it again at my dad's. My first choice is Rice. What about you?"

His smile faded. "Sorry, that must suck," he said, looking sad.

I shrugged my shoulders and took a sip of my Pepsi, suddenly regretting my morbid mention.

"I graduated from A&M last year. Rice is a great school. You must be smart," he said, smiling again—thank goodness. What was I thinking before?

"A&M's a great school, too. What was your major?"

"Engineering. I interned with Trenton Construction and got myself a job there right out of school. I bartend on the side for extra cash, play money, and ... free drinks," he added, holding up his free bottle of beer. He winked and gave that so-sexy smirk again, drowning me in my own heavenly thoughts of him. I found myself falling back into a deep suede sofa being careful not to spill. He sunk down next to me, close. His knee touched mine. I began to feel overly warm.

Suddenly the sensation was interrupted when two, drunk, giddy couples visited the room. They didn't seem to notice us on the large couch as they headed straight to the bar to top up their glasses. Then one of the females eyed us and obnoxiously announced in a slurred voice, "Look, lovebirds. Hope we didn't interrupt anything?"

Hubbell shook a no to her as he sat up. Then he turned to me, looked into my eyes, and whispered, "Do you want to go somewhere private?"

I nodded. We trailed through the den, leaving our beverages behind, our hands in a tight hold.

CHAPTER 13

Moon Bounce

I decided to walk around and check out all the festivities now that Hubbell had to return to his post. On the dance floor, Uncle Travis had Pamela in an intimate embrace. It looked as if their relationship was evolving with each visit. I was happy for them but a bit surprised Pamela was attracted to him in this way. I had learned she was divorced, and I hoped she wasn't a gold digger. I hoped she realized my Uncle Travis was no one to mess with. I couldn't help but think, wonder, why hadn't she pursued Luke? Pamela and Luke were closer in age and seemed a more likely couple. They were the ones who should be gyrating to "Let's Get It On" by Marvin Gaye.

I spotted Luke with Savannah and Alexis in the moon bounce. He was so much like my dad, it wasn't even funny! I remembered my parents renting a moon bounce shaped like a red barn for my ninth birthday party. It was set up in our back yard along with two real ponies, named Willow and Juniper, and a small petting zoo fencing in two baby goats, three bunnies, and five chicks. It was the best birthday party ever. My parents went all out. It was near the time my mom was diagnosed with cancer. She knew this was going to be the last party of mine she would ever plan. Of course, I didn't know it at the time. They shielded me from the truth, acting as if she just had a bad cold.

"Come on in, Dakota," Luke shouted, jumping with the girls. His wavy brown hair bounced lusciously, looking like he could be in a shampoo commercial.

I took off my purple Converse and climbed in. Immediately I was swept up by Luke's strong hands. Unless I wanted to fall, I didn't have any choice but to start jumping. Smiles, giggles, and freedom took over my entire body. This was so much fun—just like how I remembered from when I was nine.

Even though the machine keeping the moon bounce filled was noisy, like an industrial vacuum cleaner, I could hear that the band had stopped. Mr. Trenton was announcing that the fireworks were going to start very soon. We were to head toward the open field behind the five-car garage, away from the house. Pamela and Uncle Travis had Alexis and were swinging her up and down, back and forth, in between their stride. I remembered how I loved that part of my childhood. Luke and I followed them with Savannah in swing, too. The two girls were giggling and shrieked, "More, more! Again, again!" I was smiling, thinking, *we are all one big, very happy family.* Of course, Hubbell was in my thoughts, too, adding to my merriment!

There were white foldable chairs arranged in rows and blankets provided for the ones who wanted to sprawl out on the grass. We grabbed a few blankets, and as I carried one I noticed "Trenton Bash" embroidered on it just like on Hubbell's shirt. Mr. Trenton had an eye for detail.

We planted ourselves on three blankets (each was the size of a love-seat throw), and within a few short minutes I was pleasantly surprised. Among the vast crowd, Hubbell found me! He didn't ask but scooted beside me rather closely, as if we were already boyfriend and girlfriend. I was a bit taken aback. I blushed and quickly introduced him before Luke said something humiliating like *Young man, I don't think it's right of you to be sitting so close to my sister.*

"Hubbell," I gestured with my hand as I introduced him, "I would like you to meet my brother, Luke, his daughter, Savannah, my uncle Travis, Pamela, and her daughter, Alexis." I suddenly realized I hadn't learned his last name. Was it bad of me to make out with a boy without knowing this? Flashing through my mind was Dad asking, *Hubbell what? What's your last name, son?* I wondered if my uncle would ask.

Luke and Uncle Travis both exchanged hearty handshakes with Hubbell. Hubbell then turned toward Pamela. They traded pleasantries. Alexis and Savannah were already busy making little nests out of the grass they had pulled from the manicured lawn. Luke gave me a wink that conveyed his approval, but my overprotective uncle started in on asking how we knew one another. He hadn't asked Hubbell's surname.

Once Hubbell told him he was one of the bartenders at this party, Uncle Travis had to ask, half serious and half joking, "I'm sure it was only a Pepsi you served to my sweet, innocent, sixteen-year-old niece?"

Before Hubbell had a chance to say anything, I grinned slyly and chimed in like a smart-aleck, "With a shot of Captain."

Pamela rested her head on my uncle's chest and caressed the open area of his button-down shirt. With her manicured fingers, she smoothed his chest hair with those so-sexy, polished red nails of hers. Her touch relaxed him and eased his premature suspicions about Hubbell and me. She then winked at me. She was so cool.

The fireworks began, and they lasted a little over half an hour. They were the best fireworks I had ever seen, and I couldn't have been happier at that moment to be sharing them with the best company, especially Hubbell.

CHAPTER 14

Similarities

On the car ride home, Savannah and Alexis were dozing off to sleep. Alexis was spending the night at our house, and I had a strong hunch that Pamela and my Uncle Travis were planning their own slumber party at the St. Regis. Luke inquired, "How much older is Hubbell than you?"

I answered, sounding rather mousy ... so not like me. "Six years." *And please don't ask me his last name, because I completely forgot to ask him—I was too caught up in the awe of the evening.*

He nodded. "My mom was seven years younger than our dad. She had me at twenty-two. Too young, I think, to become a mom—well, at least a responsible one."

He was implying his mom was irresponsible. Hmm, this was the first time Luke had ever mentioned her to me. He didn't know I already knew a lot about her—runaway, adulteress, and sex maniac. "Were you close to your mom?" I asked.

He hesitated. Then he answered, "Sometimes."

"Why didn't she tell you about our dad sooner?"

"Maybe she was afraid I would leave her and go live with him," he answered.

"What made her finally tell you?" I asked, hoping I wasn't starting to sound like a cold reporter.

"She was dying. She wanted to clear her conscience, perhaps. Who knows? People do strange things, Dakota, when they find out their life is coming to an end."

"Yeah, they do," I agreed. But really, I didn't know. My mom never confessed any life-changing secrets to me on her deathbed.

"When she told me, she finally confessed to running away and hiding her pregnancy from Jethro. She had asinine reasoning—she didn't want to be a wife but was fine with being a mother—something about control. She started rambling on how men control their women once they marry and she hated having anyone tell her what to do. Funny, though, she always told me what to do! She controlled me, in a way—in an overly protective, motherly way. I suppose she was like most mothers, insisting upon me asking her permission for anything I did, whether it was important or not!"

He looked at me for reassurance, as if my mother, too, was controlling about what I could and couldn't do. But I didn't agree this time. I was actually feeling quite peeved at Gerry and blurted, "She really didn't know my dad, then. He never controlled my mom or me—just the opposite, in fact." I held up my pinkie finger and wriggled it as best I could. "My mom had him wrapped around her little finger, but she was never manipulative." I was, of course, implying that his mom was.

He didn't comment or defend her. Instead he said in a conciliatory way, "My mom always looked out for me. And in her own warped, bossy, and selfish ways, I knew she loved me with all her heart and soul. I was her world."

The sentiment—how his mom thought the world of him, like my dad thought the world of me—brought a tear to my eye. Maybe Gerry wasn't so bad. After all, Luke did turn out well. My mom would have called Luke a good egg.

I stayed quiet. I didn't know what to say. I badly wanted to ask him if he knew of his mom's very long affair with Drew Trenton. If my mom were alive, she would have been disgusted with Gerry. Even though she was all about forgiveness, she would struggle with befriending an adulteress, especially one who thought Jethro would, if given the chance, turn out to be a monster! He was the best husband and dad any woman could ask for. But it was a good thing Gerry felt differently, because I wouldn't exist if she had married my dad.

I decided not to pry anymore, at least not for the duration of the car ride home. Perhaps he would disclose more about his mom when he felt ready. I was curious if he would divulge her affairs. Remember, she was also seeing some bigwig political benefactor. I wondered if maybe, just maybe, Luke didn't even know! How embarrassing to have a slut for a mother.

Suddenly he gushed, "She must have apologized a dozen times during her confessional." He startled me even more by literally reenacting the moment, trying to sound like her, "I'm sorry, Luke. I'm so sorry I never told you. I'm so sorry you grew up without a dad ..."

He struggled to hold back his tears, slamming his fist on the steering wheel. He concentrated on the road, not looking in my direction at all.

"Luke, I'm sorry. You don't have to tell me," I said sympathetically. "Guys find it difficult to open up and cry. No worries." Still, I was dying to know.

"No, Dakota, I want to get it off my chest. You're the first person I feel comfortable enough to tell. I didn't tell Janet its entirety. She wouldn't have cared anyway—she couldn't be bothered. My mom begged for forgiveness. She apologized again and again, over and over. She encouraged me to go to him—*Jethro Buchannan*, my dad, the dad I never knew. She told me I might not have had him in my life for thirty-five years, but at least I could have him in my life for the remainder of his life. She believed there was a chance to make up for lost time. So when she died, I fled to Fort Worth. Halfway through my road trip, I took a pit stop. At the register, about to pay for my gas and bottled water, I caught a glimpse of the newspaper."

He spoke more loudly, as if he were a paperboy announcing the headline. "Long-Time Resident of Fort Worth and Dedicated Employee of Jennings Petroleum Dies in Accidental Explosion."

Luke began to sob between his words. "I quickly took hold of a copy and scanned it for the victim's name. It was Jethro Buchannan. I was shocked. The cashier lady asked if I was all right. Supposedly I looked like I'd seen a ghost. She told me to take some water and breathe. I guess I scared her, 'cause she came around from behind the register carrying her stool. She told me to sit and asked me what was wrong, but I didn't tell her. Then she asked if I was feeling any pain in my chest or arm—that would have been a sign of a heart attack. I told her I was all right. I paid for the gas. She threw in the water and newspaper and told me I shouldn't drive just yet. I sat in my car and cried. She was watching me from inside. She looked like she was crying, too. It was really weird how this stranger was so concerned about me—like a mom. I waited a bit. Then I drove off."

"Hmmm, that was nice of her." I didn't know what else to say. I found myself searching my immediate surroundings for a box of tissue. The glove compartment held a few unused paper napkins. I handed one to him. He blew his nose. I handed him another. He held onto it, took a deep breath, and continued.

"I drove to your house and sat in my car across the street and watched, staring at my dad's house. I never saw you, but I knew you were inside, hiding. I knew my dad had a daughter from the article, and I didn't think it was right for me to come knockin' and say, *Hey, I'm your long-lost brother.*"

"Yeah, I probably would've fainted," I said.

"When I saw your uncle arrive and you came out and gave him a genuine hug, I knew he was a man to be trusted. I could confide in him, tell him who I was. So I waited till he left your house and followed him to his. When I approached him, he invited me in, and I laid it all out. He's a great guy, Travis. He encouraged me to attend Dad's funeral and meet you … my sister. He told me how incredible you are."

I reached out my left arm and put my hand on his shoulder. I affectionately squeezed it, rubbing it to soothe him. "It's okay to cry. I'm glad you showed up at Dad's funeral. I'm grateful you're in my life, Luke." Then I teased to break the ice, "Am I living up to 'incredible?'"

He gave a chuckle and nodded. With the back of his hand, he wiped away the tears that rolled down his cheeks. "Just when I finally got the name of my dad, he was gone. I never got to meet him. How weird is that—my mom and dad dying in the same week as each other? I wanted to view him at the funeral home and hold his lifeless hand, but they told me he was cremated."

"Not exactly. Not by choice, anyway. He was charred to death in the accident. The very thought sickens me. What a way to die—fast but disgusting. I have a whole new appreciation for firefighters."

"Yeah, me too," he agreed, sounding less fragile, as if a weight had been lifted from him.

"How'd your mom die?" I asked.

"Cancer. After your dad's funeral, I returned home for my mom's funeral," he answered sorrowfully.

"That sucks, huh? My mom had cancer, too—ovarian," I said rather bluntly. It had been six years since she passed, so I was over the shock.

"Hers was liver … liver cancer."

We both let that coincidence sink in.

"You're a lot like Dad," I said with a smile.

He smiled back. "Yeah? Like what?" He wanted an example.

"Hmm. Well, for one thing, when your wheels are spinning, you slide your hands together back and forth, like this." I acted it out and repeated, "You rub 'em back and forth as if it'll help you to think up the answer to your problem, just like my dad … our dad did when something was puzzlin' him."

Luke smiled again, very pleased, and remarked in a joking weird scientist voice, like Dr. Frankenstein, "Interesting … very interesting."

"And you're a goof ball!" I added, rolling my eyes and shaking my head. "It must run in the family. You're such a goof ball, like Dad!"

We pulled into the driveway. I carried Savannah up to her now-lavender room, and Luke carried Alexis. After her mom moved out, we painted over the pink her mom had picked. Painting walls to look somewhat professional with a four-year-old was nearly impossible, like nailing Jell-O to a tree. That was Mom's analogy for difficult tasks. And even though the drop cloth had as much paint on it as the walls, we had fun, and that's what matters most. Naturally, we painted with the radio blaring, and when "Call Me Maybe" came on, we sang along. Afterward, I carried out my urge to make banana pancakes, and Savannah devoured them, just like my dad had. This made me smile of course, appreciating this little person in my life who evoked happy memories.

I carefully placed Savannah on her bed. I pulled out the trundle for Alexis, and Luke placed her in with ease. They were our porcelain dolls. But then to our surprise Savannah sleepily said, "I need to brush my teeth."

Luke smoothed her hair and softly spoke, "The sugar bugs have the night off. You can brush 'em in the morning. Now go back to dreamin'."

I warmly whispered to Luke as we exited the room, "Just like Dad, Luke … just like Dad."

CHAPTER 15

Belle

Oh my God, I can't believe this. Just when things were starting to look up …

Uncle Travis was hot and heavy with Pamela—the feeling seemed mutual so far, which was good. Savannah had adjusted well to her parents' separation. She was thrilled her bedroom was only a few doors down from mine. I let her help me decide on a color to paint my room. She wanted it to be purple like hers. We went with medieval plum. She had me on a pedestal, and I wasn't complaining. The feeling was a natural high, like when a newbie swimmer has the courage to swim in the deep end. Janet was actually civil toward me. The few times she called the house line and I answered, she asked, "What are you and my princess up to today?" However, if I went into a dissertation, she became curt and asked to speak to Savannah. I had come to accept the vampire. After all, she was my niece's mom, and I knew my own mom would be disappointed in me if I didn't accept someone for who they were and move on. And the next fabulous piece of news—drum roll, please—we were going to move into our brand-new house—some referred to it as a mansion. It was rather impressive. Its swimming pool was tricked out with a cave-like slide and waterfall, and the patio had outdoor speakers, a wet bar, a grill, and a hot tub. It might be a while before every room was furnished. But although furniture makes a house, it's loving people that make it a home.

And you probably think I should be feeling nervous—at least a little—with the start of a new school year fast approaching, but I wasn't. Change was good. At my old school everyone knew I didn't have a mom and had recently learned I no longer had a dad. I would've been the school's sympathy case. Having my peers and teachers take pity on me may have made me take the home-school route. But here in Houston I was given a fresh start, which made me feel almost reborn. And as my all-time favorite inspirational speaker, Reverend Martin Luther King Junior, had put it so eloquently, *Faith is taking the first step even when you don't see the whole staircase.* To begin my senior year in a new high school living in the ultimate party house was downright awesome. Now I just had to work on my brother to let me throw a few! Oh, and yes, of course there was Hubbell. I wasn't sure if it was safe to call him *my* Hubbell yet, but I was beginning to feel giddy like a girlfriend does ... or so I've heard.

Okay, so here was the bad news ... the very sad news. Belle had cancer. And according to curt Janet, it was up to Luke and me to deal with emotional Savannah because we were the so-called "experts" on cancer. Janet couldn't deal. For starters, she hated the dog, even though her daughter thought of Belle as her fur sister. Vampire just did not understand or didn't care to. She warned us that Savannah could not visit until it was resolved. As if Luke and I had a cure for cancer. Janet simply refused to have her sweet daughter spend another weekend in New York because there were too many dogs that reminded Savannah of Belle when they walked Central Park. Every time a Blonde Lab passed, Savannah began to cry and supposedly acted delusional by calling out Belle's name, which Janet found humiliating. I thought it was pathetic how Janet became easily aggravated and mortified over a family pet dying instead of showing the usual compassion and concern a normal person would. I was beginning to think she really was part vampire. She preferred Savannah to be smiling twenty-four seven, as if her daughter were a flavor of ice cream she could choose and place back in the freezer when she was through quenching her palette. Showing Savannah off to the VIPs in Janet's world, who gawked at how beautiful she was—like her mother—was extortion, if you asked me! This was typical of Janet. It shouldn't have come as any surprise, but it still infuriated me. I didn't understand how a mom could act this way—so self-absorbed. I truly was blessed with the most loving mom on the planet. I also loved Savannah, and it hurt me to witness how a mother only saw her daughter out of pure convenience. I prayed Savannah would never realize this.

The year my mother died, my dad and I became somewhat co-dependent on one another. According to the book that our reverend loaned my father from his personal library (but I was the one who actually read it—yes, at age ten) *to aid in coping with loss*, it was very common for a single parent to be dependent on the child—ironically, the roles became reversed. And according to the text, it could be beneficial for both parties if the child didn't feel bothered with his or her new role as caregiver. Feeling needed helped fill a void in a child's heart, and for the grieving parent the child provides a link to the deceased spouse, acting as the component needed to continue sharing memories and making new ones.

I had the tasks of keeping the house looking tidy, doing the laundry, and emptying the dishwasher. I always made my bed before going to school, and on the mornings I didn't have to wash my hair I had extra time to make his. Dad always was appreciative and reminded me that whoever I decided to marry was going to live like a king. My dad cleaned the bathrooms but not as routinely as my mom had. About every three weeks my shower stall would gleam. Dad said the smell of Clorox would warp my growing brain. Due to the lack of a window in my bathroom and my neglectfulness about putting on the vent fan, the mold grew like wildfire. Dad attacked the shower stall and glass door with toxic spray and a ginormous scrub brush while trumpeting repeatedly, *Take that, you scum!* as if he were one of the Three Musketeers in a duel. It was quite comical. He was a genuine goofball—my goofball.

We did the grocery shopping together. He usually let me get the snack items I wanted, even if they were in what mom called the "junk food" aisle. As long as I also ate healthy things, Dad was fine with me having a Twinkie or two while doing my homework.

In the morning I always had a banana with my Fruit Loops, and I snacked on apples and trail mix during the school day so I got my fruit intake. I didn't always spend my lunch period in the cafeteria eating and chitchatting with peers. Depending on my workload, I spent most lunches in the foreign language lab, listening to recorded conversations in French between Pierre and Helene, preparing for the ton of oral pop quizzes Mademoiselle Meyer sprang on us. And we could *never* ask for help in English. The fifty-minute class was entirely in French. It was my own fault, I suppose, for taking AP French and disregarding the many warnings I'd heard about her. But I knew down the road I would have no regrets. Not too far off, in college, I planned on studying abroad in Paris.

For supper I usually had seconds—eating two servings of vegetables, a baked potato, and the meat Dad usually grilled, washed down with a tall glass of cold milk got his stamp of approval, as if I had satisfied the daily food requirement for a growing child. What is it with parents smiling like clowns, watching their kids eat healthy? I could only imagine what it was like when I swallowed my first spoonful of solid baby food. Mom probably cried, *Break out the camcorder, Jethro!* And I bet Dad fumbled figuring out how to work it.

Most nights Dad usually stopped by Nicco's Bake Shop on his way home from work. The Italian bread, so crispy on the outside and so soft on the inside, made it home still warm from the oven, but with a hunk ripped off!

Geez, Dad, couldn't you have waited? I would light-heartedly tease. And his excuses were always different but equally animated. One night it was the little mouse he spotted at a red light, begging for a morsel of bread. *Yeah, right, Dad. Judging from the size of the missing loaf, it's more like a gang of rats!* Next it was the stray dogs that jumped on his car, refusing to leave until Dad threw a big chunk of Nicco's bread at them. *Come see their paw marks on the hood if you don't believe me!* he'd protest. I pictured the hobo dogs from *The Lady and The Tramp* and laughed. My love for movies started at a young age. In fact, I have watched all the Walt Disney classics.

When I got my driver's license, things changed. With my new independence I didn't have to rely on my dad to take me places. But the truth was, I liked it better when I had. We rarely turned on the car radio but just talked instead. We both were happy to hear how each other's days had gone. I especially liked when he asked for my advice to solve a conflict that arose at work. Dad valued my opinion, took me seriously, and treated me like an adult.

But I also liked how he treated me like his baby girl. When he saw a little something at a store that was a tad childish but definitely cute and fuzzy, he bought it for me. My collection of small stuffed animals started growing after my mom passed—all due to Dad. The latest made number eighteen : a furry monkey I named Nealzy, which Dad picked up when he stopped for bananas. Supposedly Nealzy and his cousins were scattered throughout the banana display. I joked, *were their fluffy bunnies by the carrots?* The manager did a great job marketing the merchandise and decorating the store every holiday. But Colby's prices were steeper than those of the big chain, Fiesta Mart, and since Dad was on a budget he only stopped at Colby's out of convenience.

I didn't nearly have as much news to share with Dad. For me, school was humdrum—predictable, really. You studied and earned good grades. You acted polite and earned teachers' respect. You nodded and said, "Hey" to your peers in passing, while shuffling to your next class, and you were considered cool. I had friends but didn't hang out regularly with them, though I had fun when I did.

As time went on, my dad's job was taking a toll on him. He was putting in longer hours and dealing with problems that didn't seem to exist when Mom was around. Maybe I was just too young then to notice, or maybe they spoke of ills after my bedtime. But as far as Mom was concerned, *Home is Sanctuary*—at least, that's what she had painted, in bold black calligraphy, on a plaque in one of her many arts and crafts nights with her friends, which Dad referred to as "girls' night out." Dad was always supportive of my mom's hobbies and complimented the things she made. The plaque hung in the kitchen, over the bay window seat. Home was and will always remain my safe haven.

As far as I can remember, Dad was in the doghouse only once. She forced him to sleep on the sofa, but the irony of it was, in his absence she made the sofa up for him! I tried telling her, *that isn't what an irate wife does when she's pissed at her husband. He has to get his own linens and make it himself!*

Dakota, she hollered, *you quit using language like that!*

Pissed isn't swearing! I retaliated.

In this house it is! Now go on to bed, she ordered. Then she blew me a kiss, adding, *Sweet dreams.* I obeyed, sneering on the way and shaking my head in disbelief. One minute she's hollering at me—the next she's telling me to have sweet dreams.

Dad complained—more like overly exaggerated—about his aching back from just one wretched night on the couch. Mom came around and accepted Dad's millionth apology, and then his back pain suddenly disappeared. The culprit for their spat was Uncle Travis and one measly pitcher of beer, shared over a game of pool. You see, Uncle Travis, won another case but this win was different. It was almost as if he wished the judge had favored the plaintiff. This case seemed to take a toll on my uncle's emotions and made an impact on some of his decisions. In fact, after that particular case he never held another office party at his law firm again.

But Mom's argument was valid. She gave them Fridays, and that fateful night was not a Friday. Friday, after work, was the time Dad could hang with the boys down at Nate's—the local pub. Although he had Mom's permission to return home in the wee hours, he never did stay out that late. He always strolled in before midnight.

Mom would spend her Friday evenings with arts and crafts and the girls. They alternated houses weekly, and I usually accompanied her. I especially liked it when Gloria showed up—another daughter of one of the arts and crafts women. Gloria was the same age as me and drew beautifully—she was an artist. She went to a private school, a Judaic one. She was my only Jewish friend. It was nice having someone for a friend who I wouldn't see at church or school. That gave us more to talk about when we did see each other. She read many of the same books as me, and she was also learning French as well as Hebrew. She taught me a few Yiddish words she learned from her grandma, which in Yiddish is "Bubbe." She always made me laugh during her linguistic tutorial of Yiddish because she could never just teach me the words. There were always stories with them, which were all so funny. Like the time she dragged Bubbe to a store geared for teenagers. At first, Grandma browsed through the racks of clothes with their intentional rips and stain-like marks, especially the blue jeans, but once she saw the expensive price tags she just shuffled through hastily, bellowing, *All dreck! Dreck, dreck, dreck! I'm not spending my money on schmattes, nor are you wearing them!* My assumption that those words implied something negative was right—"dreck" meant "trash," and "schmatte" meant a rag or a worn-out garment. Needless to say, Gloria left empty handed from that particular store but was able to convince her grandma into purchasing an overpriced sweatshirt from Abercrombie & Fitch that wasn't fashionably mangled! I wasn't the least surprised to hear Gloria was in the drama club at her school and got one of the leading roles in *Fiddler on the Roof.* She was a pistol. Or in Yiddish, Gloria had chutzpah!

Gloria always came prepared, carrying her rectangular, wooden case supplied with quality brand paper and pastels, and she always let me use them if I didn't want to do the craft of the week. She had painted the outside of her art case with a prairie landscape and lone horse. You could see the gleam in its eye, the muscles in its legs, and even its nostrils billowing. Seriously, her attention to detail made that horse come alive—and she did it all on twenty-four-by-twenty-four-inch wood. Imagine what she could do on a wall!

As Dad was busier and busier at work, his apologetic calls home to tell me not to wait for him for supper became more frequent. Sure, I was disappointed, but mainly I felt sad for Dad. I knew how much he liked coming home at the regular dinnertime, not after eight. We both cherished our time together over supper. Mom always preached: *A family who eats together stays together.* And we both wanted to carry on her mantra. I never did heat up the frozen meals he had bought. Mom was most definitely rolling over in her grave over those TV dinners! When

Dad arrived home, no matter how late it was, I had a hot, home-cooked dinner waiting for us to eat together. Well, okay, maybe it wasn't all homemade. I had some assistance—Campbell's made it real easy. Just by stirring a can of their creamy mushroom soup with cut-up chicken and frozen peas and throwing it in the oven, I made chicken a la king! Dad was thoroughly impressed. He grinned as I carried it out in one of Mom's casserole dishes. A home-cooked meal with his favorite girl seemed to make his arduous day disappear, making me very happy.

After I learned to drive, my dad expected me to do the grocery shopping, cooking, laundry, and cleaning, which included cleaning the bathrooms. He no longer feared my brain would warp from the toxic fumes of Clorox. How I missed those days of him shouting, *Take that you scum!* as he squirted shots of Clorox into the grout and I stood at the vestibule giggling, still dressed in my Hannah Montana pajamas and so proud my dad was fighting off the enemy with such vengeance. Naturally, he took care of the household bills and any maintenance the cars needed.

After I passed my driver's test and received my license, Dad handed me the keys to Mom's car. They were her keys, attached to a ring with my fourth-grade photo. I was with her in line at Walmart when she spotted the impulse buy—the miniature plastic-framed key ring. She boasted, *once I put you in it, it'll become a priceless heirloom!*

Dad and I buffed Mom's car till it glimmered like new that glorious sunny Saturday. To our pleasant surprise, the interior still smelled of her. With the windows and doors closed tight all those years, Mom's scent was captive. I didn't dare use any cleaning detergents on the inside, only a water-dampened rag to dust down around the dashboard. I wanted to savor Mom's redolence and make it last for as long as it possibly could.

My dad was beaming as he sat in the passenger seat and we drove to Red Hot and Blues for an early BBQ dinner. I think his grin was a combination of many emotions he was feeling that day—his little girl was now old enough to drive, and driving his wife's car. He complimented my astute driving. I thanked him, of course, but then the two of us were content to say nothing more. The balmy day beckoned, but neither one of us put down our windows. We felt at peace with Mom's sweet, loving scent hugging us.

My dad's and my relationship was like warm bread and soft butter. I never thought another person could replace that feeling … until Luke and Savannah came into my life. And now it was up to me to let Savannah know that her Belle had cancer and that it would be less painful if Belle were put down soon so she didn't suffer any longer.

CHAPTER 16

Another Funeral

Savannah and Luke worked together on Belle's eulogy the night before. As Luke spoke, tears streamed down Savannah's face, which in turn made me lose it. "Dear Lord ... I hope you won't get upset if Belle barks too much. She's just telling you she wants to play fetch. She loves to run around, and she licks people who she likes. I bet there are a lot of people in heaven who are nice and will get lots of kisses from Belle, like Dakota's mom and dad. I hope everyone loves her as much as we do ... Amen."

Savannah and her fellow Bible campers, along with their teacher Miss White, Uncle Travis, Pamela, Alexis, Mr. Trenton, Hubbell, and I all said in unison, "Amen."

Belle was laid to rest under one of the sweet acacia trees Luke didn't disturb when the house was being built. Afterward we all adjourned to the pool for a swim and cookout, because that's what Belle would have wanted. Savannah and her friends seemed preoccupied with playing in the pool, which delighted me. I was leaning against one of the pillars of the pool's portico watching the kids when Hubbell leaned into me for a kiss. His groin brushed against mine, and I was overwhelmed with the sensual feeling. I knew at that moment he was going to be the one I would lose myself to. Suddenly, the tingle was interrupted when Luke called, "Chow time!" We shifted. Hubbell tenderly planted a second kiss on my lips and told me he was famished. We smiled at one another as

I gave him the okay to go collect some grub. He pulled me in for one last kiss and told me, "You're so cool. I think I'm falling in love with you, Dakota." Then he strolled away. Now I felt even more breathless, and my legs felt like Jell-O.

I watched him strut over to Luke, who was holding out a cheeseburger on a giant spatula. As Hubbell reached for a plate to take the burger from Luke, Savannah approached and tugged on the back of Hubbell's loose-fitting shirt, which was not completely tucked into his worn-out blue jeans. It was fitted in just the right places. He bent down as she whispered something in his ear. Without delay he had Savannah on his shoulders, and they were strolling toward Belle's grave with the cheeseburger in tow. Hubbell didn't seem to mind Savannah was propping the plate, with his cheeseburger, on the top of his head.

He carefully let her down, and she placed the plate of cheeseburger on Belle's grave. I watched them both giggle and embrace. They returned. I was in awe, and Hubbell said to me while still holding Savannah's hand, "Belle needed it more." Was he amazing or what?

CHAPTER 17

Dakota's Birthday

Everything was going according to plan. The twenty friends I invited over for a pool party had arrived. Okay, so it also happened to be my seventeenth birthday. But really, I just wanted to hang with friends and not be the center of attention. Anyway, one of my really good friends happened to be an amateur but awesome disc jockey—DJ Zach. Did I mention he was cute, too?

Zach arrived way beforehand to set up—very responsible of him. He also knew that I would highly recommend him to Mr. Trenton for when he threw another big party. Hubbell watched as I thanked Zach. My hug lasted a little too long for Hubbell's liking, and I perceived a slight jealousy. It was rather reassuring to see evidence of the love Hubbell had for me.

Luke and Savannah gave us space. They said their congratulatory remarks during cake time, and then since it was well past Savannah's bedtime, they said their farewells. Luke pulled me aside and told me he trusted me to make the right decisions. He also reminded me he was only a shout away. He kissed me on my forehead and told me he loved me and was thankful and blessed to have me in his life. He ended with the infamous quote, "Everything happens for a reason,"

I reiterated similar feelings and returned the kiss. Savannah's head was resting on her dad's shoulders. I tenderly touched her cheek with the back of my hand. She could barely keep her sleepy eyes open, but she managed to give a little smile as I told her, "Good night, sweet dreams. Don't let the bed bugs bite."

I hesitated as I watched them stroll from me but then mustered up the courage to confess. "Wait!" I said as I caught up to them. "Wait. I don't think ..."

They stopped and turned. "I don't think I have told you—I don't think I could have made it, with my dad being gone, if you hadn't come into my life. I don't know what I would have done without you two. People think I am strong—so they tell me—but really ..."

I was falling apart. "Uncle Travis is incredible, but I couldn't have lived with him. He's so busy with work—I would have been a burden. But then you came along. You made me family, and I am forever grateful. Thank you. I love you both so much."

The three of us embraced almost tribally. But then DJ Zach's announcement over the mike broke us apart. "We need the birthday girl up here, pronto!"

Luke told me to, "Git!" with a wink and playfully added, "I've got hidden cameras!" as he carried his daughter off to bed.

I smiled. *Good looks and funny—Janet's an idiot.*

When I returned to my friends, they presented me with a well-wrapped large box topped with a hot pink bow. As I opened it, the smell of leather released into the air. I folded away the tissue paper and saw our high school's letter jacket—black leather sleeves and royal blue bodice in softened wool. The letters "MHS" for "Memorial High School" were boxed and bold on the right breast in matching blue. My name—just my first—was embroidered in cursive on the left breast in an off-white thread, and the number fourteen, which represented my graduation year, was on the upper left sleeve. It was all so incredible. I looked up with a very appreciative smile and expressed my gratitude. I examined it again, teary-eyed. Then I noticed a small bronze square—half the size of a Scrabble tile—pinned on its left collar. It read "A&M"—where Hubbell went to college. Instantly I looked up to find Hubbell, who was right at hand for a kiss. I laid a tender one on his soft lips. Our friends gave a "Woo" sound, and then DJ Zach played "Beautiful" by James Blunt. Hubbell led me to the makeshift dance floor and held me close as our bodies danced as one.

CHAPTER 18

Thanksgiving

"**D**akota, can you help me put in the table leaves when you have a minute?" Luke hollered from the bottom of the stairs.

"Be right down," I called back.

I went under the table to fasten the leaves as Luke pushed them together, transforming the eight-foot-long table to a twelve-foot one to accommodate the eleven people we were having for Thanksgiving—three of whom were the Cavanaughs. Like I was once, Hubbell is an only child. Luke was in his glory. It was his first time being able to host Thanksgiving. Usually the holiday gatherings had been at his father in-law, Drew Trenton's, with Crystal cooking and Pamela serving. And yes, if you haven't figured it out yet, Hubbell's surname is Cavanaugh. I learned it on our first official date, when he took me on a picnic. I know what you're thinking—*so romantic*. Afterward we strolled through the bird sanctuary, acting like lovebirds ourselves.

Crystal and Pamela volunteered to come early to help in the kitchen, but Luke insisted the two ladies arrive only as guests. I wished Luke had taken them up on it, because it was absolute chaos in the kitchen. I had never cooked anything that required four hours in the oven and basting every hour on the hour.

Savannah was a mess. There seemed to be more cake batter on her than in the baking pan. She had decided to make an apple-cinnamon cake because it was the yummiest-looking picture in *The Joy of Cooking*, our kitchen bible. I measured out all the ingredients for her, and she poured them in and stirred. I quickly decided her long locks needed to be tied before we unpleasantly found a few in the finished product, which reminded me of a time when my mom and I were out to lunch. She told the waiter that there was a hair in her quiche when he asked us how everything was. She assured him it was okay because she ate around it, but she just wanted to let the chef know that she needed to tie her hair back before doing any cooking! *Yes, of course, ma'am. You are absolutely right. I will let the manager know, and Chef George.*

Is George her last name? my mom had asked.

No, ma'am … it's his first, the waiter had answered.

Uh-oh! Now my mother was officially grossed out. She had this weird illusion that men who grew their hair long were uncouth and somehow tried to influence them to get a haircut—I'm not joking. It was quite embarrassing. When she met a male with long hair, she'd use flattery to persuade him to change his hairstyle by telling him how much more handsome he'd be with shorter hair. She then would suggest Olivia's Spa. Her very good friend Olivia Nicole was the proprietor of this high-end beauty salon. For ten consecutive years it had been rated four stars. And any customer who mentioned my mom, Loretta, was given a substantial discount on their first visit.

My mom had a 100 percent success rate, and Olivia always phoned her to thank her for the new clients. *You did it again, Miss Loretta!* She was all about building her business and meeting new people, especially cute men. Like Uncle Travis, Olivia was a wicked flirt. My mom actually tried hooking the two of them up, but they were more like brother and sister. To this day, Olivia and Uncle Travis remain good friends, and he is a loyal customer of hers. He actually gets manicures. Guys getting manicures seemed weird to me, but I learned it wasn't so uncommon.

The handsome restaurant manager came over that day to apologize carrying two complimentary chocolate mousses. He also took mom's lunch off the bill, which my mom had said wasn't necessary. We never did return to that restaurant. I think my mom felt uncomfortable when the manager told my mom that her *ravishing* figure wouldn't be disturbed with a little dessert as he closely placed the mousse in front of her, taking in her perfume and winking. She became flustered and told me to *eat up quickly!*

I laughed and thought it was funny that the manager was trying to pick her up. In his defense, he probably thought Mom was divorced because she didn't wear her wedding band that day. She had claimed, *I couldn't get my rings on this morning! Too much salt in that Chinese food we ate last night.* I teased, *I know, Mom. Your fingers are puffy like cheese curls!*

The only man she ever liked to flirt with was Dad. My dad sometimes flirted with other women, but it meant nothing. He was entirely devoted to Mom. And Uncle Travis, as you know, loved the art of it. But since July Fourth he seemed to be falling in deep with Pamela, and he adored her daughter, Alexis.

Oldies but Goodies radio station was coming through the kitchen ceiling speakers. The upbeat, fun-to-sing-along-to song titled "The Weight" by The Band played. Luke sang along to the lyrics he knew, and when he didn't, he swayed to the beat as he worked on the side dishes, which consisted of fresh string beans with slivered almonds, mashed potatoes with cheddar cheese for Savannah, mashed potatoes with garlic for me, and yam casserole adorned with marshmallows for him—a specialty of his mom's but also a nice memory from his childhood—and last, a simple tossed salad with a balsamic vinaigrette. The cooking aromas abounded. Savannah was licking the bowl clean, and I took back what I had said about it being chaotic. It was pure fun, what every holiday preparation should be.

The doorbell rang as I was placing Savannah's cake in the oven. It must have been the Cavanaughs because the others knew to walk in. I quickly wiped my hands, set the timer, and fluffed my hair with my fingers, using the microwave door as a mirror. Savannah shouted playfully at me, "You look boot-a-full!" I giggled and told her, "You, my dear, are a beautiful mess!"

Luke agreed and proposed, "I'll get the door. You clean up my baby girl."

I wiped her down with multiple moist paper towels. Having her take another shower would have been easier! "All right, almost done. Yup." I tapped her button nose with my index finger and teased, "Squeaky clean!"

Hubbell took hold of my waist slowly from behind. He breathed in my hair and planted a tender kiss behind my ear. I turned for those lips of his to move onto my mouth. They did, and he softly mumbled, "You're so gorgeous." I wished for a split second I was alone with him but realized Savannah was still sitting on the kitchen counter, intently watching us. I lightly pushed him off of me and whispered, "Later." I asked in an audible tone, "Where are your parents?"

"Luke's giving them the nickel tour," he answered and playfully snuck in another peck before he turned to Savannah, lifted her off, and gave her a swing around. She adored it when Hubbell played with her—especially airplane.

Then jubilant voices were heard coming from Drew Trenton, Crystal, Pamela, Alexis, and Uncle Travis who entered while talking as usual. Uncle Travis called, "Where's my sweet Dakota?" I practically ran to him. It had only been a few weeks since he took me out for an extravagant birthday dinner, but I had missed him. When I lived in Fort Worth I saw him almost every day.

We embraced. He let go of the hug but took hold of my hands and slowly spun me around like a ballerina. "You're turning into an exquisite lady, Dakota." When he spotted Hubbell coming into the foyer he added, "Just don't grow up too fast."

They greeted each other and moved into the den, where my uncle fixed himself a scotch on the rocks and prepared one for Mr. Trenton as well, knowing he was not far behind them. It would be the first time everyone but me was going to meet Hubbell's parents. I was a tad nervous but really had no reason to be. I just hoped the excessive drinking Uncle Travis and Mr. Trenton tended to do when they got together didn't annoy Dr. and Mrs. Cavanaugh.

"Absolutely beautiful, Luke," Mrs. Cavanaugh remarked.

"And the exquisite craftsmanship shows throughout," Dr. Cavanaugh added as the three of them entered the den. Introductions were made between Drew, Travis, and Ben and Rebecca Cavanaugh.

Soon Pamela and Crystal entered, each carrying trays of hors d'oeuvres even though Luke reminded them they were our guests. I introduced them to Dr. and Mrs. Cavanaugh, which they corrected graciously, "Please, call us Ben and Rebecca." Then Pamela asked, "Where's Alexis?"

I answered, smiling, "She and Savannah are in the new playroom Luke furnished with every toy imaginable." The three of us had fun shopping when Luke played extravagant Daddy Warbucks, which would be an impossible feat for him to top come Christmas. As I bragged to Dr. and Mrs. Cavanaugh about Alexis's and Savannah's adorableness, I eyed Hubbell staring at me more endearingly than usual and wondered what was going through that incredible mind of his.

CHAPTER 19
Christmas

Leave it to my amazing brother to top the day at Toys 'R' Us. It was Christmas Eve when Hank, my father's old colleague from work, arrived. A few weeks after my dad's death, Hank left Jennings's Petroleum because he feared for his own safety. He was there when it happened and saw the whole thing. *Quick as lightning,* he repeated at the reception, almost as if in a trance. Uncle Travis felt sorry for him. Everyone knew he wasn't all there. "Not dealing with a full deck" was the term people often used to describe Hank. But he really had a gift with animals, especially horses. Anyway, leave it to my Uncle Travis to get Hank a job with one of the most reputable horse breeders in all of Texas. You probably could guess what Hank trailered in the night before Christmas.

Luke told me I couldn't come outside. Even though I knew of his present to Savannah, he wanted me to be surprised with what she looked like. "Oh … so it's a girl!" I said, pleased at the slip-up Luke had made in revealing the horse's gender.

"Yes, but that's it! Now get on up to bed before you get coal in your stocking," he teased.

"Well, can I at least say hi to Hank?" I pleaded with a childish pout.

"You can in the morning. He'll be living with us for a few months. I offered him one of the guest rooms, but he wants to stay in the barn—said he'd make the loft his bedroom. He doesn't mind all the smells of a barn … the good and the bad," Luke said with raised eyebrows.

"That doesn't surprise me," I remarked.

"He's going to teach us about our newest family member—get Savannah acclimated to such a large animal, and teach her to ride—on the days I'm too busy with work," Luke explained.

"Luke, I can teach her to ride, too," I volunteered.

"Oh, you will. But there'll be days when you're too busy with schoolwork … and your lover boy, Hubbell. You are still planning on going to college, right? No ideas in that pretty little head of yours of running off and eloping, are there?"

He was joking, but I sensed there was some seriousness to his question. He wanted clarification of how far I'd take my relationship with Hubbell.

I boomed, "Are you crazy? I'm not stupid! Even though I'm not sure what I want to be when I grow up, becoming a Mrs. before I graduate college isn't one of them! So, big brother, you have nothing to worry about! Now, since you won't let me go out to say hi to Hank—without any peeking at Savannah's pony—I am going to bed. You win!" I childishly huffed, teasing him. "Good night. I still love you, even after your ludicrous comment!"

He chuckled. "Good night, Dakota. Sweet dreams. You're going to love me more in the morning."

I don't know what he meant by that last bit, but the way he acted in regard to my love life was so fatherly. Even though my reaction might have sounded aghast, I thought it was special the way Luke took over Dad's role from time to time.

Savannah was practically jumping on me. "Get up! Get up, Dakota! Santa came! Come on, outta bed!"

"All right, all right. Just let me pee first before you make me wet my pants," I begged.

She giggled and pulled me out of bed. She let me head to the bathroom but told me to hurry up as she pushed my bum.

She was running down the stairs in her red-and-white-striped, footed pajamas as I trickled behind, holding onto the railing, still tired. I was not a morning person, and I stopped believing in Santa Claus eight years ago. But it was our first Christmas together, and she was—as usual—so darn jolly and cute, like a performing candy cane in a Christmas special. I did my best to snap out of my lethargic state.

We entered the formal living room where the nine-foot tree stood, decorated to the hilt with all the homemade decorations Savannah had made in Sunday school. Miss Zaftig kept them very busy with arts and crafts. Most of the decorations were crosses made from popsicle sticks and decorated with colored yarn, glitter, pompoms, and stickers. The beautifully wrapped boxes under the tree looked like Crystal's work. She divided her time between Drew's home and Luke's.

"Merry Christmas, girls!" Luke greeted us, handing me my usual cup of coffee with milk and a teaspoon of sugar.

I gratefully cupped it with a smile. "Thank you and Merry Christmas." I smelled the sweet aroma before taking my first sip.

"Merry Christmas, Daddy!" Savannah bellowed.

Within an instant, Luke was on all fours by the tree. "Which one are you going to open first, Savannah?" She didn't answer. Instead she bulldozed him down, sat on his abdomen, lowered her face to his, and gave him a great, big, noisy kiss on his cheek and a tight squeeze around his neck. Luke pretended he couldn't breathe until he found her funny bone, leading the two of them into a giggle fest.

Before Savannah dove into Santa's gifts—typical and expected of most kids—she handed me a box that wasn't so perfectly wrapped. "This is for you, Dakota. I made it in Sunday school with Miss White. I hope you like it."

It was too big a box to be a popsicle cross, but if it was coming from Miss White's tutelage there had to be Jesus somewhere on it, especially on Christmas. I said with the utmost sincerity, looking into her twinkling eyes, "Anything you make, Savannah, I will love."

I carefully ripped off the homemade wrapping paper, which was decorated with tons of gold glitter that showered my sweatpants. Inside, placed in tissue paper, was a bowl. I held it up. It was heavy, made of fired clay, and pinched with her tiny fingers—you could see their prints. It was painted a deep purple with pink polka dots. "It's beautiful," I said, grinning from ear to ear. And as I examined it more closely, noticing how one of the polka dots looked like a heart and asking if she meant to do that, I saw it—there, on the bottom: *"Jesus Loves You"* was written in cursive with a silver Sharpie by Miss White.

"I love it, Savannah!" I gleefully announced. I grabbed her, pulling her in for a super-big hug and kiss, "And I love *you* very much! Do you know every day with you is special?"

She just smiled, dimples and all, at my rhetorical question.

"From now on, when I am feeling the way I do right now, I am going to call it a Savannah Day!" I announced excitedly.

"Okay, but that's silly!" she said with a giggle.

"No it's not," Luke chimed in. "I know exactly what Dakota means. I just didn't know it had a name. It's so obvious, too. Of course, a Savannah Day!" And he winked at me.

When the presents under the tree were disbursed and unwrapped, leaving the ones for Uncle Travis, Pamela, Alexis, Crystal, Drew, and Hubbell untouched, Savannah looked at her dad and asked, "Daddy why isn't there something from you under the tree for me and Dakota?"

"Geez, I must have left them in the barn. That's where I did my wrapping so there'd be no peeking! Let's all take a walk there. They're too heavy to carry."

"They are?" Savannah said, looking surprised, "How will we get it to my room?"

"I think you'll be playing with this toy outside, Savannah," I hinted.

"Yup! Now climb aboard," Luke said, motioning to Savannah to climb onto his shoulders. She shinnied up like a baby orangutan, and off we all headed to the barn.

I was so excited for Savannah. Even though it was her pony, I knew she'd let me ride her. Luke had already done so much for me, but I hadn't a clue what his present for me would be. I hoped he liked the Cross pen I had inscribed, "Number 1 brother and more."

We approached the barn. Hank greeted us. He was slow to recognize me. I automatically hugged him and said, "Hi, Hank. Merry Christmas." He reacted nervously to my hug and said in a monotonous tone, "Same to you. Wait here ... I'll bring her out."

He headed to the farthest stall. Savannah anxiously asked, "Daddy, who's Hank? Did he come with a horse? Is he going to show us his horse?"

"Hank's going to live here for a little while. He was a friend of my dad's." And before Luke could answer her next question, Hank was leading a light brown pony out of the stall, already saddled up and garnished with a velveteen red bow. Luke announced proudly, "Merry Christmas, Savannah! She's all yours."

"Really, Daddy? She's mine? She's really mine? She's boo-ta-full! Can I get on her? What's her name?" Savannah was practically hyperventilating. She was in worse shape than kids shoveling down candy on Halloween.

"You can name her whatever you want," Luke said while carefully getting his daughter off his shoulders and onto the pony.

"What about Merry?" Savannah asked.

"Merry like in Merry Christmas? Or Mary, Jesus's mother? Both represent Christmas."

"Merry like in Merry Christmas," Savannah answered with another one of her contagious giggles.

Then a whinny sounded, but Merry's mouth didn't move. "That's funny, Daddy. How can she do that without moving her mouth?"

"She can't. It must have come from that stall," Luke said as he headed over to it and called to me, "Dakota, come here and take a look."

Now I caught on to what he meant last night when he told me I'd love him more in the morning. I stood still, shocked, and finally said, "Luke, you didn't?"

He said coyly, "Why don't you come see for yourself?" And there standing in the stall was a magnificent chocolate-brown horse—my horse. I started to cry—a happy cry, a no-one-has-ever-done-this-for-me cry. Even though my parents were phenomenal parents, they never surprised me with something this special. Luke took hold of me, wrapped me in his arms, kissed the top of my head, and said while rubbing my back, "There, there, Miss Cavanaugh, you'll be all right."

I lifted my head and let out a laugh. I lightheartedly hit him and said, "I love you, Luke. You're the best brother any sister could ever ask for."

Luke proudly admitted, "I know!"

Savannah inquired, "But Daddy, where's yours?"

"Your dad's horse is coming next week," Hank answered for him.

Savannah eagerly asked me, "What are you going to name your horse, Dakota?"

"Hmmm ..." I sounded unsure. I had never thought of names for horses—never thought I'd get one.

Savannah suggested, "Mine's Merry. Yours should be ... Christmas!"

"That is cute, Savannah," I said as I surveyed my horse's sex. "Well, now that I know it's a he, I think I will name him Christmas!" And I smiled at Savannah as she let out a gleeful, "Yippee! Merry Christmas, everyone!"

"Merry Christmas," a voice called from behind. We turned and saw Hubbell standing at the entrance of the barn, looking rugged with his jeans and cowboy boots. He was all ready to ride. "Hey, did you know?" I asked, having a sneaking suspicion he did—considering his attire.

He nodded with a mischievous smile as I headed toward him. He pulled me in for a hug and told me, "I would never spoil a surprise Luke had worked so hard on keeping from you."

Luke was pleased; Hubbell just scored major brownie points. "All right," Luke said, "Savannah and I are going to head in for breakfast. Hank, you come, too. The gang will be here noon-ish. Don't get lost, you two!"

"We won't," Hubbell and I said in unison.

After Hubbell and I tacked Christmas, we climbed on. I was holding the reins. Hubbell sat straddled behind me. I felt him take a whiff of my hair as his arms caressed my waist, and he whispered in my ear, "I love you, Dakota." I was smiling but didn't return the sentiment. I decided I was going to show him very soon just how much I loved him. This was the best feeling ever.

CHAPTER 20

Stud Muffin

Until this year it had always been a tradition for the three of us—Uncle Travis, Dad, and myself—to bring in the New Year at Red Hot and Blues. Almost everyone we knew went there, and my dad and uncle were always the hit of the party.

It had been eight months since my dad's passing, almost seven years since my mom's, and only one hour since Uncle Travis's dreadful phone call hit me like a ton of bricks. He asked if I objected to his escaping to an island for the holiday—without me. I knew how hard he had been working lately, and his latest case was really taking a toll on him. He was representing a mom-and-pop farm business whose entire crop became contaminated shortly after a chain laundromat was built abutting their land. I hesitated a moment before giving my uncle the A-Okay on his tropical vacation plans, but then I quickly succumbed. I didn't want to sound like a selfish teenaged brat.

It wasn't until a week later I flipped my lid—when I found out Alexis was going to stay with us because Pamela was going with Uncle Travis. I wanted to scream and act like that brat! Just what I wanted to do on New Year's Eve—babysit two four-year-olds playing Candy Land a trillion times.

I wouldn't mind so much if Hubbell were going to be with me, but he was in Jamaica with his parents—they left the day after Christmas. Not being together for our first New Year's Eve made me pout all afternoon in my room until Savannah appeared outside my closed door, asking if I wanted to ride Merry … because it would make me merry! Luke didn't want her with me on Christmas just yet, but her pony could hold both our weight. In Hubbell's defense, he had told me he pleaded with his parents to let me go with them, offering that I'd pay my own way, of course. Although his parents were very fond of me, they had said, *It's a family vacation.*

Wait, it gets worse. Luke had been seeing someone. That wasn't the problem. She was all right—Amber Lee. She was *sooo* into my bro— thought he was God-like. I thought he was a pretty awesome guy too, but did she have to remind us daily at what a "stud muffin" he was? As usual, Savannah giggled her infamous giggle every time Amber Lee called her dad this. However, this time it wasn't contagious. Instead of laughing along, I rolled my eyes. It was a dreadful morning. I became the center of attention, and I was renamed!

Luke strolled into the kitchen all sweaty. He had just worked out— one of the larger rooms in the house was equipped with cardio ma- chines and free weights. He was heading toward the fridge for water when Amber Lee let herself in through the back door and practically skipped into the kitchen, declaring it to be a "Good morning" in her very southern accent. Amber Lee was from Marietta, Georgia, just outside of Atlanta.

Savannah and I were sitting at the kitchen island scarfing our Froot Loops with banana slices when Amber Lee sauntered over to Luke. She slowly slid her long fingers down his chest, admiring the T-shirt that stuck to his body, wet with perspiration, and asked in a sultry voice, "How was my stud muffin's workout?"

Hello, let's keep it G-rated—his daughter's watching. Then as if reading my mind, she squeezed both his biceps and teased in a fun-loving voice, "Hope you have a permit for these guns!"

Oh, please.

She kissed him and disclosed, "You're salty like a potato chip!"

Savannah giggled while I was trying to finish my cereal.

And then Amber Lee turned to giggle-puss Savannah and said,

bursting with enthusiasm, "And you! Well, you are just the sweetest little cupcake there is!" She tapped her lightly on the nose.

There was more giggling, but this time Luke joined in. I was seriously struggling to keep down my breakfast.

Amber Lee looked over to me and then back to Savannah. She made a pouty face. Savannah mimicked her.

"What?" I asked, annoyed and curious as to where this was going.

Amber Lee was on a roll. "Savannah, you know your Auntie Dakota best. What do you think I should call her?"

Oh, please. Please don't conjure up a cutesy nickname for me ... just call me Dakota. I prefer Hubbell to be the only one to nickname me a dessert.

"She's so sweet, like ice cream!" Savannah's voice was as exuberant as when she named her pony.

"Yes, but she's not cold like ice cream," Amber Lee remarked.

I admit, that was nice of Amber Lee to say.

Savannah shook her head, agreeing I wasn't a frigid person, and kept staring at Amber Lee, waiting for her to decide on a nickname for me.

"I know," Amber Lee declared. "From now on, Dakota is ... Sweet Cream!"

Savannah giggled while announcing, "My Auntie Dakota is Sweet Cream!"

All right—now it hurts. I managed a superficial smile at Amber Lee, which she accepted as genuine. She was really clueless, a simpleton. Thankfully she was quite harmless.

Other than that day, Amber Lee left me alone. She was nice to Savannah. which was key. I wouldn't keep quiet if Luke were to date someone who'd ignore my sweet Savannah. But then again, I didn't think he ever would pick another bitchy-type companion.

The problem was, the likelihood of Luke and Amber Lee excusing themselves after only one or two games of Candy Land was very high. They'd offer to bring us a tray of treats—ice cream with all the fixings—but would take their sweet time doing so. They'd share a bottle of champagne and dance over the music Luke had coming through the ceiling speakers. It would all so romantic—like a couple's New Year's Eve should be. Ninety minutes later, they'd appear with the goods as we finished our tenth game and I was practically bald, having pulled out my hair!

Again, I don't want to sound selfish. After all, Luke had been incredible to me. The least I could do was watch his daughter for a few hours so he could have some alone time with his new girlfriend. And Uncle Travis rarely asked me for a favor. I was pretty sure he'd prefer to have Pamela all to himself in Antigua, even though he adored Alexis. Without a doubt, it'd be more romantic if there weren't any daughterly distractions. And Crystal, Alexis' grandma, had already made plans with her bridge group to fly to Vegas for a Wayne Newton concert, so this was the least I could do for my uncle as well as for my brother— without complaining, too! As my mother would say, *play nice, Dakota.*

Janet, Savannah's mom, was somewhere out of the country. If there was such a thing as a part-time mother, Janet was less than that. Some old rich guy was spoiling her. For Christmas, Savannah received a large box from Harrods with a handwritten note from her mom. That was our first clue she was in London. Whether she was still there or not, we neither knew nor cared.

Savannah was thrilled with her new stuffed animal: Paddington Bear, accompanied with its story book and two additional outfits— Beefeater and Bobby uniforms. It was very cute. Every night since its arrival I had read the original book to Savannah and her Paddington.

I really was a positive and grateful person, even though I was sounding the furthest thing from it. If only Hubbell were staying home, I'd be fine. I decided to go and ride Merry, to cleanse myself from acting like such a sourpuss. It helped that smiling Savannah was waiting outside my door.

"Hi Hank," we greeted him.

He nodded a hello and headed to Merry's stall to ready her.

"Hank, I know Luke hired you to take care of the horses, but please don't feel like you have to wait on me. I can tack Merry and even clean out the stalls. I really don't mind. In fact, I'd like to, okay?" I said softly so he wouldn't be offended or become defensive and feel unwanted.

While Hank walked over to where Merry's blanket and saddle lay, he said with a smile, "Let's both do it ... together."

"Okay," I replied, returning his smile.

CHAPTER 21

Gloria

"Dakota, I know you're upset you aren't with the Cavanaugh's in Jamaica. But we'll have a fun time here, the four of us," Luke said, trying to sound convincing.

"You mean the five of us. Isn't your new girlfriend, Amber Lee, joining in on the fun?" I asked, sounding a tad cynical.

"I thought you liked Amber Lee," Luke said while furrowing his brows and beginning to pout as if he were two. OMG, he was so much like Dad!

I scolded, sounding like my mom, "Luke Theodore Lockwood, you wipe that look off your face if you know what's good for you. I'm the one without a boyfriend this week!" Luke obeyed. His pout disappeared. He smirked but stayed quiet, allowing me to finish my ranting. "I do like Amber Lee. I know you're crazy for her. She's nuts about you, and Savannah—well, Savannah's all smiles and giggles at the sight of Miss Southern Belle! It's just … I don't know." I hid my face in my hands and started to cry.

"Is it that time of month?" he asked brazenly.

"Ugh! I'm going to pretend I didn't hear that." I hate it when guys think just because a woman shows any emotional distress, she must be having her period!

"Dakota …" Luke walked over to me and tucked back the hairs that had fallen in front of my face. He totally surprised me with his endearing, motherly touches. "What's really bothering you, sis?"

I wiped my eyes with the back of my hands and looked up to my really incredible brother, confessing, "I miss Fort Worth. I miss the way things were. I miss Dad."

"I've been waiting for you to crack," he softly teased.

I let out a chuckle. He followed.

"You always know how to make me laugh, Luke. I love you, I love Savannah, and I love this house," I assured him.

"Let's not forget Hubbell. You love your Hubbell," he joked again, making me laugh some more.

I then lightly hit him in the chest and told him, "Stop before I hit you again—and this time I won't be so light."

"All right, I will, but only if you stop feeling sorry for yourself. Crying isn't going to bring back Dad. You know you can move back to Fort Worth and live in your old house and return to your old high school, if you want. But Savannah and I won't be a daily fixture ... unless that's what you want?" Luke said with concern.

"No. Of course not. You're my family," I declared. "I couldn't imagine life without you and Savannah. I don't know what's wrong with me." Then out of nowhere I said flatly, "Do you know most suicides happen around the holidays?"

"Dakota!" Luke snapped. "Yes, I have heard that statistic, but it's usually people who feel unloved. And I hope you know you are one very loved girl?" Without hesitation Luke continued with stern but loving reassurance, "Do I make myself clear, Dakota? You and Savannah are my world."

Oh my God. Another sentiment we shared—it was uncanny. "Yes, I know," I answered truthfully. "I know I am loved," I repeated, to calm his worry.

"Good ... so I don't have to hide the kitchen knives?" Luke asked lightheartedly.

And I punched him again in the stomach, but not as hard as I had threatened earlier.

He still played it out. "Ouch! I take that as a yes?"

"Swear to God," I promised, crossing my heart.

"What if you have a few friends over on New Year's Eve? Will that make you feel better?" he asked genuinely.

"Hmmm … I think most of my close friends are away. Their parents planned tropical vacations way in advance!" I said, conscious of trying to make Luke feel a tad guilty for not planning a family trip. Gloria would call this *Jewish Guilt*. Then it hit me! Gloria! Oh my God, I'd love it if Gloria came to visit!

"Well, Dakota," Luke said, clearing his throat like he does when he's about to teach me a lesson. "This here house we live in—with pool and hot tub and the three horses out in the barn, one of them *yours*—doesn't come easy. I've got payments, you know, and a little thing called a mortgage." He returned my guilt with a parental sternness, setting me straight. At that very moment I had the utmost respect for him and felt like a real shit who should stop my whining—or, as Gloria would tell me in Yiddish, *Quit your kvetching, Dakota!*

I announced happily, "Gloria!"

Luke laughed. "Who's Gloria?"

"An old friend from Fort Worth! I met her at my mom's arts and crafts nights. Oh, Luke, you'll love her. She is hysterical. She makes stale bread fresh! Can I invite her to stay the week? Please?"

Luke initially furrowed his brows at my odd analogy of her, but his puzzlement quickly disappeared as he gave a big smile, so pleased with my sudden change of attitude. "Yes! Of course, Dakota, if that'll make you happy. I want you to be happy."

"I am. I am happy, Luke. I'm sorry for acting *mashugga*—that means crazy in Yiddish!" I said, laughing at the crazy word and wondering if I pronounced it correctly.

Luke stared at me, furrowing those brows of his again. He looked perplexed, but he nodded and smiled. I got the impression he had no clue what Yiddish was—it seemed like he had never even heard of the word, let alone knew it was practically an ancient language and on the verge of extinction. How could anyone not know Yiddish?

"Haven't you ever seen reruns of *Coffee Talk?*" I asked him. "You know—from *SNL?*" He shook his head and waited for me to go on, knowing I'd explain it anyway whether he wanted to hear it or not. "Comedian Mike Myers made *Coffee Talk* on *Saturday Night Live* a smash. His hysterical impressions of a Jewish American Princess making quips in Yiddish even got Streisand to pay a surprise visit—his character always referred to Barbara's voice as butter."

I laughed, but Luke just shook his head. "Nope. Don't recall. But it sounds funny."

I assured him, "Not to worry. By the time Gloria leaves, you'll have learned more Yiddish words than you'll know what to do with!" And then I added, "Remind me to set you in front of the boob tube to watch reruns of *SNL*. Right now I've gotta go see if Gloria's even around—to visit." And I hurried off to my room to retrieve her phone number. I was ecstatic!

"Hello, may I please speak with Gloria?"

"Yes. May I ask who's calling?"

"It's Dakota, Dakota Buchannan."

"Dakota Buchannan! Well I'll be. Dakota, dear, it's Ruth, Gloria's mom."

"Hi, Mrs. Gold. How are you?"

"I'm fine, dear. How are you? How do you like living in Houston?"

"I'm great. I love it here! Is Gloria home?"

"Oh yes, let me get her. You take care of yourself, Dakota." Then she shouted away from the receiver, still very much audible, "Gloria, pick up the phone!"

"Hello," Gloria greeted.

"Hi Gloria! It's me, Dakota," I said hoping she'd be happy to hear from me.

"Dakota! Thank God, you're alive! I was starting to worry them Houstonians ate you! What've you been up to? I miss you."

"I miss you too!" I felt very relieved. She was still the fun-loving Gloria I remembered. "Hey, are you doing anything for New Year's?" I eagerly asked.

"Hmmm, let's see. Adam Brody invited me to fly to Paris with him … you know, eat at a fancy, romantic restaurant overlooking the Eiffel Tower," Gloria answered smugly.

I was quiet. Did she really know the actor? Then Gloria broke my silence. She loudly teased, "Hello, Dakota, I'm kidding! I wish. Why? Are you coming to Fort Worth? Do you wanna hang?"

"No. I'm not coming to Forth Worth, but I was wondering if you want to come visit me here, in Houston. We could hang with my brother and his daughter, my adorable niece Savannah? She is such a Shaina Maideleh!"

"Wow, very good! You remember some of the Yiddish I taught you. I would love to visit you! When can I come?" she asked in an upbeat voice.

"Do you remember my Uncle Travis?" I don't wait for her to answer, "He's driving here tomorrow. You can hitch a ride with him, okay?"

"Of course I remember your Uncle Travis. He's a character—a bubeleh! Let me ask my mom." She then shouted away from the receiver but again, like her mother, she didn't hold it tight enough against her chest. "I was still able to hear, "Mom, Mom, can I visit Dakota this week? I can get a ride with her uncle tomorrow."

"Dakota, it's all set!" Gloria cheerfully confirmed.

"Great. I'll let you know about the details ASAP!" I reconfirmed in the same excited way.

"Okey dokey. Can't wait to see you! Bye," she bounced back.

After I hung up I remained fixed on my bed, totally psyched. A really fun friend was going to visit and stay with me. I began thinking of all the fun things we would do! Before I jotted them down in my daily planner, I called my uncle.

"Hi, Uncle Travis."

"Dakota! How'd I get so lucky with this phone call?" Uncle Travis declared in his usual, jovial voice.

"Could you do me a big favor and swing by an old friend of mine's house to bring her out here when you come for Pamela? You met her before—Gloria Gold."

"Oh yes, the Jewish girl," Uncle Travis remembered.

"Yes, the Jewish girl. But really, this is the twenty-first century. Isn't labeling wrong, Mr. Hip Lawyer?"

"Oh, Dakota, you know I am the farthest thing from prejudiced. If I remember correctly, she's a pistol! I would love her company for the drive. Just text me her address, okay? I've gotta go—a client's on the other line. Can't wait to see you—love you."

"Thanks, Uncle Travis—love you, too," I shot back before he hung up.

All right, now I was officially back to my happy self. Thank goodness!

CHAPTER 22

Grungy Bar

Gloria and I went with Pamela and Uncle Travis to the airport. After our hugs and bon voyage wishes, I sat in the driver's seat of my uncle's pristine Jag with Gloria in the passenger's. She instigated, "I've got a fake ID ... let's see if it can fool Houston!"

"Yeah, but I don't," I confessed.

Gloria was surprised. "You don't? But you have a twenty-two-year-old boyfriend. Where do y'all go?"

I shrugged. "He doesn't seem to mind I'm underage."

After I saw her smile melt, I decided to go along with her mischief. "I know a place I think we can get into."

"You do? Awesome!" she said happily. Geez, her emotions were like a faucet.

I pulled into the dimly lit parking lot of a grungy-looking bar a few seniors had told me about. A bright Bud Lite advertisement flashed on and off in the front window. An H was burnt out in the dull metal awning, so only **R** ... **ETT'S** was illuminated in a washed, yellow fluorescent glow in chalkboard lettering. "Heard this place took a Red Cross CPR training certification card as ID!"

She laughed. I couldn't help but think, *I'm in trouble if this is what she has in mind for the six days she's here.*

As we neared the door she instructed, "Walk in like you're a regular."

"Oh yeah, I come here every day after school!" I remarked with sarcasm.

"I'm serious. Just follow my lead," Gloria ordered, strutting in. She was feisty and attractive, reminding me of Katie Morosky—the lead female in the movie *The Way We Were,* played by the incredible Barbara Streisand!

We were in. I was surprised there was no person checking ID's at the door, but the vacant parking lot should have been our first clue. I headed to where the pool tables were. I rested my leather bag on one of the tall round tables. I spotted the triangle and began racking the balls as Gloria went to the bar to order us Bud Lite. She was flirting with the bartender, probably to skirt his asking for some ID from me.

Rhett's was dead … well, almost. It was midweek, two days after Christmas, and around four o'clock in the afternoon—people weren't off work yet. There were tacky holiday decorations scattered through-out, including a row of miniature Christmas stockings employees had written their names on with a black marker in the white part that was supposed to look like fur. They hung above the top-shelf liquors.

The floor felt sticky under the new cowboy boots Savannah's grandpa had bought me for Christmas. It was sweet of him to buy her matching ones as well. I had to pee but was kind of afraid. I could only imagine how gross the bathrooms were. *Be brave, Dakota … especially considering the impending beer.* As Gloria proudly waited for the over-weight, fiftyish-looking, male bartender to finish pouring the second ten-ounce glass of beer, I called, "I'll be right back." I grabbed my bag and headed to the far corner of the L-shaped room, where a plastic Mrs. Claus hung on the door—I presumed it was covering the Ladies sign. Adjacent was the men's bathroom, without a plastic Santa.

When I returned, two guys who had eyed us when we sauntered in approached closer to the pool table, carrying their bottled beers. They leaned into the waist-high counter that separated the bar area from the pool table's room, and watched us. The green felt table was faded, and the outer rims were scarred with cigarette burns.

It was about twenty minutes later when most of the striped balls were pocketed. But I wasn't that far behind, with only three solids to go.

Gloria was bending over, lining up a shot, and called it. Of course, she got it. One of the guys admiring her curvy ass in her skinny jeans said, "Nice shot."

Gloria only smiled. The guy repositioned. "I call next game. You two gorgeous girls against my brother and me, okay?"

Gloria firmly asked with a hint of a smile, "You and your brother have a name?"

"Why, we do." He tipped his Stetson and grinned lightly. He was a little too much of a playboy for my liking, but he was hot! "I'm Cooper, and this here is TJ." He spoke with a different Texan accent—almost like it was half there. It sounded as if he had been raised in a household where one parent was Texan and the other—British, maybe? TJ smiled and also did the old-fashioned gentleman gesture of tipping his hat. He was cute too, but not as sexy as his brother, Cooper.

I smiled, but Gloria said rather curtly, "Can't TJ speak for himself?"

"No, he can't. He's deaf and doesn't talk." Cooper answered. Then he slightly turned his back toward us to summon the waitress, who was sitting on a stool at the corner of the bar with her back facing the open-doored kitchen. "Jingle Bell Rock" was playing from inside.

I felt completely embarrassed for Gloria's brusqueness, and I gave her a glare. But she had the nerve to ask in the same rough manner, "Well, can he read lips?"

Cooper answered smugly, "Somewhat. He's rather selective though. Depends if the company is worth the effort—would you consider yourself worth the effort?"

I actually let out a chuckle, and TJ did, too. The men seem accustomed to stranger's reactions when they learned of TJ's disability. Cooper's way of acting very nonchalant about it and giving Gloria a little taste of her own medicine was well deserved and earned my approval.

"You have to excuse my friend, Gloria. She's exhausted from her long drive. I'm Dakota … Dakota Buchanan." Why I felt compelled to include my last name was beyond me. "Pleased to meet you," I said while walking over and putting out my hand for a shake.

First TJ shook my hand, smiled, and let go. Then Cooper shook it but held onto it longer than protocol called for. Even when the waitress came over and asked, "What can I get for y'all?" Cooper didn't let go. He answered, "Two more Heinekens and whatever the ladies are having … put it on my tab. So, Dakota Buchannan …" He seemed to be tasting my name. "Tell me, Dakota Buchannan, where do you live?"

Then he finally finished the handshake, touching my hand with his other free hand before letting go and whispering, "So soft." I assumed he was referring to my hands—putting lotion on them before bed was one of my routines. Then he winked at me. I found it incredibly sexy when guys winked.

"I'm driving. So I'll just have a water, please … with lots of ice." I quickly told the waitress, feeling flushed from Cooper's actions. I never did tell him where I lived. I knew he wasn't asking for my actual address. He wanted to know what part of Texas I was from. I quickly visualized Hubbell to get me back on track.

"Make that two," Gloria said. "Two waters, please."

I was glad with her decision, but then it turned to disappointment when she added, "I've got to have my wits about me if we're going to cream you two boys!" Then she directed to Cooper slowly and seductively, "Afterward, you can buy me a shot of tequila … I'm not driving."

He smiled and asked, "So what faraway place are you from, Gloria?"

Gloria answered without any cynicism, "Fort Worth."

"How long are you staying?"

"A week."

We beat them, but barely. I glanced at my watch and realized it was near suppertime and Luke was expecting us home. Gloria noticed my worry and declared, "That was one hell of a game. And I sure would love to gloat over a cold beer with y'all, but we're gonna have to take a rain check."

"What's the hurry?" Cooper asked.

"Supper," I answered.

"Then I'll up the ante! Another game of pool, and loser buys dinner," Cooper countered.

"Honestly, that sounds great. But I'm a guest of Dakota's this week. I don't want to start my stay with her brother being pissed at us and all because of me being a bad influence."

"I understand. Can I get your number at least? I'd like that game of pool ... and a free meal," Cooper said with certainty.

Gloria laughed. She then pulled out a pen from her pocketbook and placed it between her puckered lips. She needed both her hands to search her disorganized, oversized bag for a scrap of paper—there wasn't one. She removed the pen from her mouth and said firmly to Cooper, "Let me see your hand."

"What?" he questioned with a grin and his brows slightly furrowed.

"You heard me! I don't think they've got cocktail napkins here. Your hand ... or no number!" she ordered.

He obeyed, still grinning.

She took hold of his right hand and jotted down her cell phone number in the palm.

"Well, that's a first!" he declared, not letting go of that incredible smile of his.

"What, you getting a girl's number?" Gloria wisecracked.

He chuckled. "You're a feisty one all right. You'll be hearing from me soon."

Gloria smiled but said nothing. I looked at TJ and felt compelled to tell him, "I have a boyfriend." God, how I wished I were with him right now in the hot Jamaican sun—his hands all over me, rubbing lotion into me. TJ smiled and tipped his hat again. I really hoped he believed me. I didn't want him to think I didn't want to double date because he was deaf.

Gloria practically screamed once we were in the Jag, "Oh my God, isn't Cooper, like, *the* hottest guy?"

"No. You haven't met my Hubbell yet!"

We laughed.

"Dakota, I am so glad you called me. We always have fun, you and me!"

"Uh-huh—that we do! And this is only day one—we got all week!" I returned with the same enthusiasm.

We giggled some more over our mischievous afternoon, recalling getting into a bar, beating two cute guys in a game of pool, and Gloria's way of giving one of them her number. She then asked me the inevitable. "So, were you totally freaked about Luke?"

"Totally. I fainted when I found out who he was, right in the middle of the floor at the reception. So embarrassing."

"Dakota, I'm sorry I wasn't at your dad's funeral. When my mom called me in Israel and told me, I nearly dropped the phone. I mean, how could this happen to you of all people? God took your mom … and now your dad. I told my mom—*I'm coming home!* She talked me out of it and said she'd share my condolences with you at the funeral."

She looked at me, waiting for me to say something like, *Oh yeah, your mom did.* But truthfully, the funeral and reception was just all one big blur. None of the dozens of genteel *I'm sorrys* comforted me. I got through the funeral and reception by replaying my memories in my mind. Even though I was driving, I could see from the corner of one eye that Gloria was looking concerned as if my response was taking too long. I quickly appeased her, "Oh yes, of course she did. Your mom has always been a sweetheart." I smiled. "A lot of people attended, all telling me the same thing—if there was anything they could do, not to hesitate. Like I would ever call one of them for help. At one point, I just wanted to shout, *Can you bring him back to life?*"

Gloria laughed. "You always know how to make light of things, Dakota."

I wasn't sure if that was a good thing, but I thanked her anyway and let her know, "Luke and Savannah are the best things that ever happened to me—wait till you meet 'em."

CHAPTER 23

Gloria's First Night

"**D**akota's home!" Savannah shouted while running to me. I swept her up and spun her twice around. Her long hair fanned Gloria, who stepped back, smiling at our whimsical greeting.

Luke entered the foyer with a kitchen towel draped over one shoulder. "Great! You're home. We made your favorite."

"Mac 'n' cheese!" Savannah shouted gleefully.

Luke went in for a hug while saying, "And you must be the famous Gloria. Dakota has told me so much about you. Welcome! Make yourself at home. Whatever you need, just let me know. Do you ride, Gloria? We've got a horse and a pony."

Gloria answered, smiling, "Yes I do. Thank you so much for having me. I'm so glad I'm here. And whatever you want me to do—just let *me* know. My mom always reminds me, a good guest pulls her own weight!"

"Great!" Luke repeated. "Dakota, why don't you show her to your room." Then he looked over to Gloria. "Or you can have your own room if you'd like."

"No thank you. Gotta be with Dakota—we've got a lot of catching up to do!"

"That's what I figured. Well, go wash up. Be quick—dinner's ready." He gestured toward Savannah and bragged as he took her from my hip, "Savannah and Alexis set the table all by themselves."

"Where *is* Alexis?" I asked, looking around as if she would pop out from a corner.

"She's in the playroom," Savannah answered. "Playing the piano."

"Okey dokey," I said. "I'll bring her down with us."

And Savannah finished the phrase, giggling loudly, "Art-a-cho-key!" as Luke carried her off into the kitchen.

Gloria chuckled as we headed up the stairs, "You're right, that Savannah of yours is a Shaina Maideleh! Makes me wish I had a baby sister—David's driving me crazy. He's a Mr. Know-It-All even though he's seven years younger than me. I remind him he was an oops baby— that shuts him up for a little while."

"That's so mean, Gloria. David's so cute," I said, remembering her brother as a sweet kid.

"You haven't been with him since he became president of his class," she warned. "And that's easy for you to say—he worshipped you."

"What? He really had a crush on me?" I asked, so surprised at this news.

"Oh, please, like you didn't know," Gloria teased. "Who doesn't have a crush on you is more like it—miss long-legged beauty queen!"

I laughed at her flattery and teased back, "Okay, miss voluptuous." We walked by the playroom. "Hey there, Alexis. That sounds really good," I said, and I actually meant it. Even though it was a toy piano whose keys lit up, Alexis had an ear for music—she was creating actual tunes when she hit the notes. Gloria, who took singing classes, was impressed also and commented, "We've got a little Mozart among us!"

"That was seriously the best macaroni and cheese I think I have ever had," Gloria complimented. After she wiped her mouth with her cloth napkin and placed it beside her plate, she insisted, "Since you cooked, I clean." In three steps, she got up, politely pushed in her chair, and cleared Luke's plate before her own.

"I'm not gonna argue with that," Luke said, stretching his arms above his head and then entwining his hands behind his head, unintentionally showing off his muscular triceps. He looked very content and somewhat proud. "Amber Lee stopped over earlier and brought cupcakes for dessert. Said she was sorry she couldn't stay for dinner, but tomorrow she will."

Savannah and Alexis scurried off their chairs and headed toward the kitchen island. They climbed up onto one stool and reached for the bakery box. They managed to pry it open. As they peered inside, they exclaimed in unison, "Ah! They're boo-ta-full," as if the cupcakes were priceless jewels.

"Who's Amber Lee?" Gloria asked, directing her question to Luke. I interceded.

"She is the ultimate, textbook Southern belle ... and Luke's girlfriend!"

"Daddy, can I have the one with the pink fower?" Savannah asked. Her pronunciation brought back my own memories of having difficulty pronouncing a few sounds—mainly letter combinations. I remembered the three toughest words for me to pronounce as a child: school, wheel, and bagel—all the way up through fifth grade. In sixth grade my parents were so relieved one morning when I had announced *I'm heading to school now*, instead of *skull*. Their glowing faces, clown-like smiles, and *that-a-girl Dakota!* made it sound as if I had been crippled and miraculously could walk all of a sudden! I had my speech pathologist, Mrs. Gordon, to thank. All the mirroring she had me do—my lips looking like a fish's—repeating her dictation a million times had paid off. But to this day my way of saying the word *bagel* supposedly isn't the correct way—according to Gloria. *Maybe, it's a Jewish thing*, she'd remark, making me roll my eyes but also chuckle. This seemed to be her excuse when she didn't have a valid answer.

"Savannah, let our guests pick first," Luke answered.

"That was so nice of your girlfriend. Can't wait to meet her," Gloria said to Luke, eyeing the cupcakes. She told the anxious girls, "Oh, I don't care—they all look so yummy! You two go ahead." Alexis, being a guest as well, even though this was like her second home, picked first.

And Savannah, being the sweetest child on the planet, let her. Alexis carefully lifted the vanilla-frosted one out of the box so the pink flower wouldn't mush. Savannah dove in for the chocolate-frosted one that had a purple flower. The violet-shaded frosting had already made it to the tip of her nose when she began to devour the gourmet cupcake.

After Gloria and I cleaned up, we headed upstairs. I read a bedtime story to Savannah and Alexis. Gloria unpacked, changed into a swimsuit, and joined Luke, who was already in the outdoor Jacuzzi.

"This is such a cool place you've got here. Dakota tells me you helped design it," Gloria praised.

"Thank you. Yeah, I gave the architect a few ideas of my own."

"I am so happy for Dakota. Looks like she is handling the loss of her dad, thanks to you. She told me you're a real blessing."

"I feel the same way about her," Luke returned. "So you're a senior. What colleges are you looking into?"

"I already applied to five ... just waiting to hear."

"Which ones?"

"Yale, BU, Columbia, NYU, and my safety school, Brandeis."

"Oh, all in the northeast. Why so far?"

"I need a change. My mom says I'll be in for a culture shock."

Luke chuckled and agreed, "Your mom's got a point."

"Hey, if I don't like them Yankees, I can always come home—transfer to A&M," she teased.

"Yup, that you can. Dakota's boyfriend graduated from A&M. I'm sure you've heard all about Hubbell."

"Yes, she has," I answered for her as I dropped my towel onto a nearby chair and stepped into the hot tub, easing down next to my brother and across from Gloria. "Amber Lee just phoned ... wants to know what she can bring for dinner tomorrow night. I told her to come early and help make it!"

"Dakota, you didn't, did you?" Luke questioned, hoping I was just kidding about the cooking part.

I answered with an iron voice, "Yes. I did, Luke." Luke shook his head in disapproval, so I softened my approach and explained lightheartedly, "I want to see her in the kitchen, Luke—behind the wheel. Our dad used to say you could tell a lot about a woman by the way she fixes a meal. His first date with my mom was at her place. She didn't want to go to a restaurant. She insisted on cooking dinner, and Dad said by the time she served dessert, her famous peach cobbler, he knew she was the one!"

"I totally can believe that. Your parents were so in love. My parents can't even be in the same room without starting an argument ... over something completely asinine, too," Gloria commented.

"So what did Amber Lee say after you told her that, Dakota?" Luke said with a hint of urgency and nervousness in his voice.

"She said—" I tried to imitate a Scarlet O'Hara–type voice. "*Oh, Dakota, you are just the funniest girl I think I know.* And then I told her, *no, I'm serious. Show me some Southern cooking—there must be some recipes of your mom's you can follow. I'd love it, but you know who'd love it the most?*" I batted my eyelashes to really exaggerate Amber Lee's naivety. "*Who?* she asked. And I said, *why, Luke, of course!*" My last Scarlet O'Hara attempt went, "*You think so?* And she got so excited and told me she had to go and call her mama!"

Luke shook his head, "She doesn't sound anything like that. You need to give her a chance, Dakota."

"Luke, I don't think I was being mean. Gloria, do you think I was wrong?"

"What about if we keep her company in the kitchen—you know, kibitz while helping out?" Gloria replied. "It'll be fun."

I suppose it was right of Gloria to remain neutral and not choose sides.

"Yes. That'd be great. Thanks, Gloria, and keep an eye on your friend. Make sure my sister behaves herself. All right then, I think I've had enough hot water. Good night, ladies. See you in the morning—or whenever you decide to wake up. I remember those teenage years, sleeping till noon."

"Good night, Luke," Gloria said cheerily.

"Yeah, good night, Luke. Gloria and I are just going to soak and kibitz some more," I said with a smirk. I knew he had no clue as to what *kibitz* meant but hoped he had the smarts to figure out its meaning through context.

Gloria waited until Luke was well out of ear's reach before she anxiously confirmed, "You didn't tell me what a hottie your brother was!"

"You didn't ask ... Switzerland," I said.

We both laughed.

"When I first saw him, at my dad's funeral, it was like I was looking at the army photo of my dad. You know, the one hung in the hall of fame? Weird, huh, how things turn out?"

"I'm so glad, Dakota, that you're happy and safe. I know your Uncle Travis would have looked after you, but still, a lot of ... well, bad stuff could have happened. You could've rebelled or became a recluse. I mean, how many kids do you know who turn out okay after losing both parents—before the age of sixteen, with no siblings to share in the misery?"

"Maybe. Well, we'll never know, thanks to Luke and Savannah. They really are a blessing." I changed the subject. "Uncle Travis's dream girl, Pamela, is somewhat of a mystery. We don't know anything about Alexis's dad."

"Huh—why do you care?" Gloria questioned.

"Well, I know how difficult it was for Luke not to know who his dad was for all those years. And then when he found out, Dad was already dead! So I think when Alexis reaches a certain age, she'll want to know who her dad is, and I just hope it won't be too late," I said. And just to clarify she was on the same page I asked, "You see my point—right?"

"Yes. But it's out of your hands, Dakota. I wouldn't be worried if I were you."

"Yeah. But I'm curious."

"You'll be privy—just when you least expect it," she said with experience.

"Probably. That's the story of my life. Hey, do you want to head up for *Rosemary's Baby?*"

"Is that another one of your freaky movies?" Gloria asked

I laughed. "Yes. I can't believe you haven't heard of it. It's a classic ... with Mia Farrow and Ruth Gordon."

She gave me a who-are-they? look.

"Oh, Gloria, what am I going to do with you?"

CHAPTER 24

Cooper Calls!

It was almost eleven in the morning, and Gloria and I were still in our PJs. We lounged in bed, talking about school, music, and of course, the opposite sex—boys! Our stomachs started growling, so we headed down to the kitchen. Luke had posted a note on the fridge—he and the girls were food shopping.

"I feel like a cheese omelet. You want one?" I asked Gloria, who was carefully looking at the framed photo collage I had put together. It was the first piece of artwork Luke had nailed up in the new house.

"Yeah, sure, and bacon if you've got it. Mom never gets the stuff. So when I go to friends', I ask." She was still admiring the collage, "These pictures are great—every one of them. I especially love the one of you and Savannah painting."

"Thanks. You're kosher?"

"No. But Mom said Grandma Ida would have a coronary if she ever bought bacon."

"Isn't your Grandma Ida dead?" I remembered.

Gloria nodded, "Don't ask … it's a Jewish thing. Just be thankful you're Christian."

I laughed as I searched the fridge for bacon. "Every faith has its idiosyncrasies," I mused.

"Got it!" I announced, finding the bacon and carefully balancing the eggs, butter, cheese, and bacon on the trip over to the counter, using my chin to help hold the pyramid of ingredients.

"Dakota, have I told you yet what a really great friend you are? Thanks for calling."

"Thanks for coming," I said, returning her smile. Before I started cracking the eggs into the mixing bowl I pointed to the switches on the far wall, instructing Gloria, "Click that button to turn on the sound system. Luke's got great music."

The rock group Life House started playing "Who We Are." "I love this song!" Gloria cried as she shimmied to the fridge to get the OJ. She poured us two wine glasses full. Even though Hubbell wasn't here, Gloria's visit was a nice way to end my Christmas vacation.

As we sat and devoured my gourmet-looking omelets (they didn't break when I flipped them) the sudden sound of a pig oinking was heard from over by the toaster, where Gloria had left her cell after phoning her mom. I grimaced at the ridiculous ringtone and teased, "You love bacon that much?"

"Very funny! It's that demon brother of mine. David reprogrammed it as a joke, and I can't seem to change it. I told you, he's a pain in the *tukhus!*" she said, sounding exasperated. She quickly pushed a button so it would quit oinking. I laughed as she answered her phone, sounding breathless.

She mouthed, *Oh my God, it's Cooper* the minute she heard who was on the other end. She tried to sound composed but from the look of her, she was ecstatic. "Hey Cooper, what's up? Yeah, I just came in from a three-mile run," she fibbed as I mouthed *Oh my God* back to her.

Her initially out-of-breath answer must have made him guess she was exercising. He must have asked her if I ran with her because Gloria lied again, "No, Dakota stayed in bed." She laughed at whatever reply he gave. I was going to kill her. And why did he care if I ran or not? "Yeah, that'd be great. Can you wait a minute?" Gloria muffled her phone with her overly ripe bosoms so Cooper wouldn't hear, "Oh my God, it's the guy from the bar, Cooper. He wants to hang. Can he come over?" she asked me in a childlike frenzy as if pleading for more candy.

I nervously responded, "Oh, um, I don't know. Luke's not here. Geez, can you call him back in a few? I want to call Luke and ask him first."

"Hey Cooper, gotta get back to you. Give me a half hour, okay? Great! Bye."

I was quick to criticize. "What was that all about? Whatever happened to meeting for a Frappuccino at Starbucks or something else low-key? But to ask to come over … weird."

"No. He said he wanted to come pick me up and take me out, but I don't want to leave you. I want us to all hang out. Maybe he'll bring TJ—he's cute! So what if he's quiet."

"Gloria! I have a boyfriend—Hubbell. And TJ isn't just quiet—he is deaf and doesn't speak. Don't sugarcoat his disability. But that doesn't matter. I already have a boyfriend," I repeated, sounding annoyed at having to convince her that I wouldn't cheat on him.

"Yeah, well, Hubbell's in Jamaica, and you're here! And I think the correct term, if you want to be PC, is *challenged*. TJ's challenged!" Gloria countered.

"Gloria, you are so bad. And don't start. You know what I mean."

Luke, Savannah, and Alexis returned home. They entered carrying the canvas Save-A-Tree/Save-The-World grocery bags that I had insisted we buy. Of course, my environmentally conscious brother had acquiesced. Gloria and I headed out to Luke's pick-up truck to get the rest. Of course, a Prius would be more economical. But it wasn't a practical car for Luke's pool construction business, so we tried to help save the planet in other ways. I inwardly reminisced about the day Savannah had sat on the floor in the mudroom, carefully peeling back the Recycle and Reuse stickers, making sure the letters were right-side-up before adhering them to the plastic bins. Gloria interrupted my thoughts, "So, are you going to ask your brother if Cooper can come over?" she whispered, becoming impatient.

"And hang," I finished with a sardonic smirk.

"Dakota, why are you so mad at me all of a sudden?"

"I'm not," I lied. "And yes, I'll ask my brother." Why would I want to sit around here watching her and Cooper ogling at each other? I wanted to show Gloria Houston. We could go out to lunch and perhaps visit a few art galleries, since she appreciated art.

"Hey, Luke, Gloria and I met these two guys at … at Starbucks on our way home from the airport—you know, after dropping off Uncle Travis and Pamela. One of them just called Gloria, and I was wondering … well, she was wondering if—if he can come over and hang. If it's all right with you, of course?" I asked, trying not to sound as nervous as I oddly felt. I didn't like lying.

"Starbucks, you say? Hmmm …" He eyed us very suspiciously.

"Yeah, Starbucks," I lied—again.

"Well, what's his name? How old is he?"

Gloria answered, "His name's Cooper, and I think he's twenty-three."

"Does Cooper have a last name?" Luke questioned, acting a tad overprotective. But I didn't blame him. Gloria was our guest and his responsibility while she was staying with us.

Gloria looked dumbfounded. She never asked them their last name, nor did they offer it. Come to think of it, I was the only one who offered my last name.

"Ah, I forget." Now Gloria was lying. "Do you remember, Dakota?" she asked me pleadingly.

What—does she want me to make up a last name, too? Well I'm not going to! Instead I tried to sound convincing. "I forget, too—but no big deal. We can ask him later. That's if he's allowed to come over, of course." I caught Gloria crossing her fingers, so I decided to coax. "What do you say, big, amazing brother? Can Cooper come over?" It usually worked.

Luke was hesitant. He busied himself with putting the groceries away. He emptied the bag of apples into one of the fridge's drawers and shuffled a few condiments around so more food could fit on the shelves. When he finally closed the fridge, he spied Gloria's patient stance: excellent posture, hands clasped in prayer form, exaggerated smile, and eyelashes batting.

Luke chuckled, "You're cute—like a puppy in a window waiting to be bought." And then he gave in. "All right, fine. I suppose this Cooper boy—Cooper-with-no-last-name—can come over."

"Oh, thank you. Thank you. Thank you, Luke," adrenalized Gloria repeated a trillion times.

Luke walked toward the pantry and resumed the chore, putting away the nonperishables this time. His back then faced us girls, and Gloria followed. As he knelt down to load a shelf with cans, she squeezed his shoulder blades with each compliment, "You are so cool! Dakota is so lucky to have you! And geez, you're so muscle-y—your girlfriend's so lucky, too!"

"Yeah, yeah, yeah, so I've heard," he said, making to stand up. Gloria stopped her mini massage and stepped back all smiley. "You two best behave," he added. I wondered if it was directed at Gloria. He knows I will, since my lover-boy's in Jamaica.

"Don't worry, we will!" Gloria hollered as she raced with her cell phone in hand up the stairs to call Cooper back. She jumped up onto my bed and just as quickly flopped down with such force I thought a spring was going to burst. I gave an "Oy!" making Gloria giggle. I had never seen her this giddy. It wasn't like this was her first date. She's been around the block a few times, judging from what she's told me in the past.

CHAPTER 25

Cooper Paine

It was about a quarter past noon when Cooper arrived solo. His brother wasn't in tow, nor was he donning that new-looking cowboy hat—it didn't look right on him, anyway. It was probably a Christmas gift he felt compelled to wear. Gloria trotted to his car. It was nothing fancy—a black Toyota 4-Runner. He playfully grabbed her after he shut the car door and gave her a hug and kiss on the top of her head. He was tall—about six foot two—so Gloria came to midchest to him. I followed. He greeted me, "Hey there, Dakota. Some place you've got here."

"Yeah, thanks. It's awesome. It's my brother's. I live with him and his daughter. They're out riding."

Cooper and Gloria were holding hands as I led them to the pool patio. We sat around a round table—shaded by its open umbrella. "Can I get you anything?" Gloria asked.

He shook his head. "No, thank you."

I then asked, "So where's TJ?"

"He's with his family," Cooper answered.

Gloria and I must have looked completely shocked because Cooper explained in something of a sardonic tone, "Yeah. Hard to believe ... he's got a gorgeous wife and two beautiful, great kids."

"How old is he?" Gloria asked. "He looks so young," she said defensively, trying to make it sound like her surprise was due to his age.

"He is. He's twenty-five. Married his high school sweetheart right out of college. They didn't waste any time having kids. She's an incredible girl, Linda. She never looked at his handicap as a problem, only a challenge. Her ambition to learn to sign was because of him."

Gloria and I were quiet. I couldn't read Gloria's mind, but I knew I felt like a complete nincompoop. I was ashamed at myself for thinking TJ wasn't marriage material.

Cooper interrupted my thoughts, continuing their love story, "The very first day Linda saw him trying out for the football team in the ninth grade, she looked into a signing class. She was one of those high school students who were nice to everyone. She befriended anyone regardless of what group he or she fell into. She desperately wanted to be able to communicate with TJ. She was the *only* kid at our school who signed with him. They fell in love. He became the star quarterback and got himself a full four-year scholarship at Texas State University. Linda followed him there, also earning a scholarship—not in football, of course," he ended with a chuckle.

I was totally taken-a-back and it must have shown because Cooper commented, "Yeah, I know. Pretty amazing, huh?"

"Yeah, really great!" Gloria and I agreed almost simultaneously. She added, "I'd love to meet her. How old are their kids?"

"One and almost three. Shoot, that reminds me—I've got to get him a birthday gift. He's into cowboys and Indians. In fact, those ridiculous-looking cowboy hats we wore last night were a gift from him and his grandpa—Linda's dad. He's a fifth-generation Texan, born and bred. My nephew emulates him. TJ and I couldn't leave the house without wearing them. He had us squat down to his level so he could reach our heads to put them on." Suddenly Cooper's voice changed. He spoke, imitating his toddler nephew, "And don't take 'em off, Daddy and Uncle Cooper! You gotta wear 'em the *whole* night!"

I was enamored with his cute impression.

He finished, "Naturally, we couldn't disappoint the little fella, so we wore them into Rhett's."

See, I knew there was a reason.

"What's his name?" Gloria asked.

He answered in its entirety. "Brigham Charles Paine. But we call him Charlie."

Okay, so we had learned the last name—Paine. Luke would be happy. "And the one-year-old ... boy or girl?" I asked.

"Girl. Summer Anne," Cooper answered.

"No way. My middle name is Summer!" I said, surprised.

"Great name," Cooper commented with a smile.

"There's a cute toy store downtown on Main Street. I think it's called Noah's. Why don't you two head down there and get Charlie something for his birthday? Take your time. Go out to lunch, even. I'm gonna go riding ... I need to exercise my horse.

Cooper and Gloria looked at each other. They smiled, pleased at my fun suggestion. Gloria didn't hesitate. "Okay!" Then she added whimsically, "Sounds like a fabulous plan ... Mom!"

"Great. Let's go," Cooper summoned as he stood up. His shadow towered over me, as I remained sitting. Gloria gleefully announced, "You rock, Dakota!" She kissed me on the cheek.

They left. I took my cell from my back pocket and scrolled down to Hubbell's number, praying he had reception there in the blue hills of Jamaica.

"Hey there, beautiful," Hubbell answered. I smiled at the sound of his voice, but it melted into a pout as I whined, "When are you coming home?"

"In five days. Why, do ya miss me?"

"You have no idea."

He consoled me, "I miss you too, baby."

CHAPTER 26

Amber Lee Cooks!

I was watching Savannah and Alexis swim when Cooper and Gloria pulled in almost simultaneously with Amber Lee. He parked his car next to hers—an almost spotless white BMW convertible. I was within earshot and could survey the scene over the newly planted hedges, which obviously weren't mature enough to hide the driveway yet. Gloria jumped out of Cooper's car and scurried over to Amber Lee. With jubilance in her voice she declared, "You must be Amber Lee" and offered her hand. "I'm Gloria."

"Why ... yes I am," Amber Lee answered while returning the handshake. "What a beautiful name—*Gloria*—one of my favorites! And who is this mighty handsome fellow you got with you?"

"Oh, this is my friend, Cooper Paine."

Cooper shook Amber Lee's hand and smiled down at her petite frame. They exchanged pleasantries.

"Do you mind helping me with the groceries?" she asked while motioning toward the trunk. "I hope y'all are planning on staying for dinner. I've got a ton of good stuff I'm cookin', thanks to my mammy. She had me on the phone half the night jotting down a dozen recipes!"

They all laughed, and then Amber Lee confessed while handing Gloria and Cooper each a grocery bag, "Can I let y'all in on a little secret?"

"Sure," Gloria answered, taking the bag. Cooper bent to retrieve another.

"This here night ... well, it'll be my first time—my very first time—cooking! I mean, really cooking, cooking up a full-course dinner. I'm a little nervous. I really want to impress Luke ... and his family," Amber Lee said anxiously. Then she bent to pick up the two remaining bags and closed the trunk.

"If your cooking's anything like your hospitality, I bet you'll do just fine—not to worry. Thank you for the invite, but I've got to head back. I can't stay," Cooper said.

I summoned the girls out of the pool, wrapped them up in plush blue towels, and rubbed my hands up and down their bodies to warm them. Alexis ran inside, hollering her reason why: "I've gotta poop!"

I laughed. Savannah stayed with me as I continued to rub her down. I repositioned her towel so I could carry her and headed toward the walkway that joined the driveway to greet our guests. "Hey guys! Did y'all have fun?" And before Gloria and Cooper could answer, I was introducing Savannah to Cooper. When he made reference to her being such a cutie, I gave him the heads-up: "There's another one in the house. We're watching Alexis while her mom's on vacation with my uncle." I then redirected myself to Amber Lee. "Hey, Amber Lee. I can't wait to have some of your Southern cookin'!"

Amber Lee laughed and then lightheartedly warned me, "Just you wait, Sweet Cream—I've got a few surprises up my sleeves! And how's this cute little cupcake you're carrying?" She managed to kiss Savannah's button nose even with the cumbersome load she was balancing in both arms. And as usual, Savannah giggled and returned the kiss.

Amber Lee and Cooper cut in front, allowing Gloria to quietly whisper to me, "Sweet Cream? Cupcake?"

"I know. I told you," I whispered back. "She'll be calling you Sugar before the night's through."

Gloria shushed me. "I think it's endearing."

We all headed through the back door. I was still carrying Savannah, as the rest were toting the groceries. Luke was sitting at the kitchen island, intent on his laptop. He looked rather pensive. I hoped nothing was wrong. He looked up from it and joyfully greeted us. "Hey, welcome!" He quickly logged out and folded down the screen of his computer.

Cooper set down the bags and went over to shake Luke's hand while he introduced himself. Naturally my brother, being the gregarious person he was, invited, "We'd love to have you stay for dinner."

My peripheral vision detected Gloria's excited look again—the please-say-yes look!

"Well, I don't want to *intrude* on any special family dinner," Cooper said, sounding like whatever priority he had before—just seconds ago in the driveway—had suddenly disappeared!

"You're not," Luke confirmed.

"See, you're not," Gloria double-confirmed, beaming from ear to ear.

I wanted to shout, *yes he is—go home, Cooper!* But I didn't want to be rude in front of Savannah.

"Well, if it's not any trouble, I'd love to," he said, smiling over at Gloria. She looked like she was about to burst with joy and was holding back from jumping into his arms.

"Great! It's settled. What are you drinkin', Cooper? Do you shoot pool?" Luke asked as he gestured Cooper out of the kitchen and toward the billiard room.

I hoped Cooper knew not to say anything about meeting us at Rhett's.

Like in the olden' days, us girls remained in the kitchen, fixin' dinner. I released Savannah. Her towel dropped as she scurried like a little mouse up the back stairs to change out of her wet bathing suit and into some dry clothes. I picked up her damp towel and walked it to the washroom just off the kitchen. I hung it on her princess crown hook for a later swim and called as I headed back into the kitchen, "All right, Gloria, spill it!"

"Oh my God, I had the best time! Can you believe he bought his nephew the entire cowboy fort—two hundred dollars!" Her ecstatic voice lowered to a dreamy one reminding me of Pepe le Pew. "Then we sat outside at some really quaint restaurant, ate a little, and talked and talked. He is *sooo* incredible, Dakota!"

Amber Lee was smiling at us, relishing in our adolescence. She tightened her apron around her twenty-six-inch waist and then fixed her loose hair into a ponytail. My mom would have been thoroughly impressed.

I couldn't hold it in. "Well, you're mine tomorrow!" I added playfully, even though I was serious. "*I* want to show you around Houston— *not Cooper*. I thought we could visit the Museum of Fine Arts—there's a contemporary art exhibit I think you'd like. Are you still interested in art?"

"Yeah! Absolutely! You got it, sis-ta! This is gonna be one of my best vacations ever—maybe even better than my time on a kibbutz, and that was *a lot* of fun! Let's just say, what happened in Israel stays in Israel!" she guffawed at her own punch line.

Amber Lee followed, "You girls are somethin' … makes me want to be a teenager all over again. Well, you're in good hands, Gloria. This is just one of the nicest families I know. It's so much fun, and there's so much love to go around."

Right at that moment, my mind started racing back to what Bible-thumping Miss White, Savannah's Sunday school teacher, had told me. *So much love to go around* was one of Mom's sentiments. It was as if Mom had been reincarnated as Amber Lee. And Luke resembled Dad in so many ways. His mannerisms and some of the things he said were just like Dad's. It was as if God really was watching over me, just like Bible-thumper told me.

"Dakota, is something wrong? You look like you've seen a ghost!" Gloria exclaimed. I shook my head no as I watched Amber Lee organize all her ingredients before starting to cook, just like Mom did. I was glad Amber Lee was oblivious to my staring. Unexpectedly, Amber Lee's idiosyncrasies didn't annoy me anymore. They disappeared into the wind like tumbleweed. My sudden change to accept her, and actually like her, overwhelmed me. I found myself fishing for my mom's apron.

I gingerly put it on and positioned myself close to Amber Lee—right by her side, in fact. I decided to happily assist her with this cooking endeavor she was wholeheartedly undertaking, just to impress us and get our approval—and all because of my pushy rudeness. I could be such a jerk sometimes.

She put both her arms around my shoulders and complimented my very worn embroidered apron. "I bet that beautiful apron of yours was your mama's. It fits you perfectly, Dakota." She smiled. I returned the smile, and we both began following the recipes she had neatly copied from her mammy's instructions last night.

Gloria was taken aback by our rather touching moment and perceived we could manage without her. She proposed, "Looks as if you two have everything under control. Why don't I just go see what the girls and boys are up to?" She didn't wait for a response as she hustled out of the kitchen, heading upstairs to Savannah and Alexis. Something told me she also wanted to freshen up for lover boy!

CHAPTER 27

The First Supper

"**W**ow! This is ab-so-lute-lee-de-lish!" Gloria embellished each syllable, making us laugh. "And I love the salad—the lemony dressing and the hearts-of-palm—so much better than artichoke hearts. Artichoke hearts are overrated. Hearts of palm kick ass." Then, looking at Savannah, she apologized and corrected herself. "Butt. Hearts of palm kick butt!"

Savannah giggled. "The mashed potatoes are so cheesy and yummy!"

Immediately we all concurred and were compelled to give Amber Lee our list of likes.

"Mmm," Alexis hummed, agreeing with Savannah and asking for seconds.

"I love these little baked spinach-and-goat-cheese thingamabobs wrapped with bacon," I added.

"The pork chops are cooked perfectly," Cooper remarked. "And the sauce over them—sweet, with a little kick!" he added whimsically.

Amber Lee divulged, "I added cinnamon to the Cajun rub." She was beaming.

Luke was thrilled with everything, from the food his girlfriend had prepared to the fact that all of us were sitting around the table complimenting her. I think my suddenly optimistic attitude toward her surprised him even more. He looked over at me and winked as if to say *thank you*. Then he stood up and walked around refilling our wine glasses with the Merlot Amber Lee also had selected. He remained standing and proposed a toast. "It's not often a man is so lucky as to be surrounded by five beautiful girls, making this dinner a real special one. Gloria, thanks for making the trip out here to be with our Dakota. And Cooper, thanks for joining us. Food alone isn't what makes for a great meal. It's the company as well."

He then took a few steps over to Amber Lee and kissed her softly on her mouth. He whispered loudly enough that I could hear, "You're incredible."

I smiled and thought, *Just like Dad*.

She beamed like a fluorescent light. "Wait till y'all see what I've got for dessert."

"I already know what I want," Luke teased as he resumed his seat. I blushed at my brother's sexual innuendo. Gloria looked over at Cooper, who seemed to have had his eyes on me.

"So, Cooper, are you still in college?" Amber Lee asked.

"No. I graduated last year."

"From where?" she continued her questioning.

"Harvard."

I guffawed and blurted out, "No way!" Cooper just didn't seem like the Harvard type.

Luke, embarrassed at my rather rude reaction, defended Cooper by saying, "Dakota thinks everyone born and bred in Texas doesn't ever leave!"

"Most don't, but I've got New England roots," he defended.

"Paddington Bear is from England," Savannah chimed.

Then Cooper did a ninety-degree turn toward Savannah and conducted a conversation with her in a lively voice, sounding as if he were a preschool teacher. "You have Paddington Bear? I do, too! You know, he's not really from England. He's originally from a place called Peru."

"I know that!" Savannah replied, giggling, "My Auntie Dakota reads me the story every night." Savannah then looked at me, asking for permission. "Can Cooper read it with us tonight?"

This time I didn't blurt out *No way*, but I wanted to. And I must have looked opposed to Savannah's suggestion, because before I could come up with a polite excuse to exclude him from our special reading time, Cooper chimed in. "I would love to, Savannah, but I've got to get up very early tomorrow morning and head to Dallas—maybe another time."

"What's in Dallas?" Luke asked.

"My grandparents."

"Will you be back for New Year's Eve?" Gloria eagerly asked.

No way is he coming over on New Year's Eve. Nor are you leaving me!

"No, I spend it with them." Then he discreetly looked at his watch. "I'm sorry, but I can't stay for dessert." And he got up, pushed in his chair, and was about to clear his plate when Amber Lee told him to leave it. "Don't you lift a finger. Any man who spends New Year's Eve with his elderly grandparents is a saint!"

Cooper remarked with a laugh, "Oh, they are the spriest seventy-five-year-olds you'll ever meet. Seriously, they still play tennis and golf, ski, and sail. They're in better shape than I am!" he teased.

He then walked over to Amber Lee, who was now standing up from the table about to clear the dinner dishes. Before she picked up a plate, Cooper took her hand to shake it. Then he lightly pulled her in for a kiss on the cheek and told her again, "Thank you so much. Everything was just perfect. Didn't I tell you you had nothing to worry about?" and he winked.

She blushed, and Luke playfully reminded Cooper, "She's taken!," making Amber Lee blush some more.

Cooper repeated his thank-you to Luke, minus the kiss. They shook hands and gave each other friendly but hearty hope-to-see-you-again slaps on the back.

Gloria volunteered to walk Cooper to his car. But before he exited the dining room with Gloria, he swung Savannah up into his arms and whispered loudly enough for me to hear, "Your Paddington Bear is one lucky little bear."

Savannah then loudly whispered back, "Do you sleep with your Paddington Bear?" This time Cooper whispered into her ear so no one could hear. Savannah threw back her head and giggled hysterically.

All right, what did he say? I wasn't too worried—I knew Savannah would tell me if I asked. Cooper was quite the charmer. Already, he practically had Gloria eating out of his hands, had made Amber Lee blush, and had been included in Luke's toast. But wait—just when I thought it was over, my niece was holding Cooper's face between her tiny little hands. She looked into his eyes and said endearingly, "Will you be my friend?"

No way! She had said those exact words to me that infamous night I met her mom.

He mimicked Gloria's "ab—so—lute—lee!" and gave her an Eskimo kiss.

Hey, only family have that privilege, I wanted to warn him, but I remained speechless. I was taken aback by this stranger who seemed to have already worked his way into the circle of trust.

He then put her down next to Alexis, who was standing now, waiting for her friend.

He half-tousled Alexis's wavy brown locks and told her it was nice meeting her, too. She was more the shy type, especially around men, maybe because she didn't have a father figure.

He looked over toward me. Before he had a chance to grab my hand and pull me in for a good-night kiss, I quickly busied myself with clearing the table. I grabbed a stack of dishes that required both my hands and told Amber Lee, "Don't you clean a thing! Gloria and I got it!"

I then looked over to Cooper. "Have a safe trip, and Happy New Year!" I said as I pushed through the butler door with my butt.

Amber Lee hollered as the butler door closed behind me, "All right. Thank you. In a little while I'll whip some cream up to go with my peach cobbler."

I couldn't believe it—peach cobbler, just like Mom!

CHAPTER 28

Brunch

Gloria and I decided to pull together a nice brunch for Luke and Amber Lee. It was January First, the New Year—time for new beginnings. Savannah and Alexis were drawing at the kitchen island in the new coloring books that Gloria had bought them at the museum gift shop. Savannah joyfully admitted, "That was *sooo* much fun last night!" Alexis agreed with her friend, not letting up on her coloring. Of course, they were referring to all the card games we played, baking chocolate chip cookies, and then watching my favorite Walt Disney movie, *Beauty and the Beast*. Amber Lee served us vanilla ice cream with our still-warm cookies, and I wasn't upset when she and my brother left the movie early. I understood and accepted the love they had growing for one another.

Luke sashayed down the back stairway into the kitchen, all bright-eyed and bushy-tailed. "Good morning, girls," he announced. "It smells so good."

"It must be the challah French toast I'm making," Gloria responded, feeling proud of her culinary talent.

"Hell-a-what?" Luke questioned, not sure if Gloria was exaggerating her words again. She rolled her eyes, enunciated slowly for him, "Chal—lah," and explained playfully and slowly as if Luke were a small child, "a loaf of white leavened bread, typically braided and traditionally baked to celebrate the Jewish Sabbath. Of course, it's not limited to

Jewish people. Many restaurants use it for making French toast. You've probably had it before and didn't know it."

"Oh, cool," Luke said. "Can't wait to try it. Amber Lee's in the shower. She'll be down soon." Last night was the first night Amber Lee had slept over—or at least, it was the first time they were open and honest about it.

"So what time is Uncle T. coming in today?" Luke asked while sitting next to Savannah, quietly admiring her coloring. He rubbed her little back and planted a peck on the back of her head.

"Gloria and I are heading out at about three. Their plane lands at four-fifteen."

"Do you want me to go get 'em so you two can do something more fun than driving to the airport? I don't mind," Luke offered.

"No thanks. Thanks anyway," I said, taking the plate of bacon from the microwave.

"Yum, bacon. Have to get my fix before heading home," Gloria relished.

"You can't get bacon in Fort Worth?" Luke questioned.

"Oh my God, Luke. You live such a sheltered life, but I still love you!" Gloria teased. "Even though we're not kosher, you won't find many Jewish homes serving bacon."

Luke then gave a quizzical look and asked, "What's kosher?"

Now I interjected, "You really did live under a rock growing up!"

Gloria chimed, "No worries. It's an ancient Jewish thing. It's hard to explain. It has to do with certain foods—dairy and meat—and rules. Rules," she repeated, ending with a humph. "The Jews invented them! No worries." And she gave him a wink. "But you have heard of the Holocaust, right?" she added, looking somewhat concerned.

"Of course," Luke answered. "I read *Night* by Elie Wiesel when I was in high school ... gave me nightmares."

"All right, just checkin'. Cuz if you hadn't, I'd be worried," Gloria admitted.

The phone rung, and I headed to get it.

"Hello, Happy New Year!" I greeted whoever was on the receiving end.

"Hey Uncle Travis. Yeah, everything's great. Can't wait to see you. Oh, okay … but I really don't mind staying up that late and waiting. Well, do you want me to ask Luke? All right, all right, fine. I'll see you tomorrow. I love you, too. Bye."

I hung up the phone and turned around to find Luke and Gloria both staring at me eagerly waiting for the latest news.

"Their plane is delayed and won't get in till one in the morning. He doesn't want me, *nor you*—" I directed to Luke—"on the highway that late. He started going into a dissertation about it being a holiday and people partying, drinking, and driving when they shouldn't be. When I was nine he won a case defending a drunk driver who killed a couple. It happened around this time of year, and ever since, he wigs out." I shook my head. "Always around this time of year he acts more nervous with me driving than any other time of the year."

"Well, he's only looking out for us," Luke defended Uncle Travis.

"So, he'll take a cab—no biggie. That means another day of driving in his sweet Jag. Maybe we'll head back to that Starbucks we met Cooper at," Gloria said brazenly while snagging another slice of bacon.

That's what I loved about Gloria. She was a go-with-the-flow type of friend. I was really going to miss her, but now that she had met Cooper I figured I'd be seeing a lot more of her around Houston.

"You mean the Starbucks that has a pool table and serves beer?" Luke questioned with both sarcasm and parental sternness in his voice. Cooper must have blown it—what an idiot. Luke quickly dismissed my too-late apology with a wave of his hand and said, "Save it, Dakota." He looked over to Gloria and chided her, "You too."

Thankfully Amber Lee entered just at that moment, allowing Gloria and me to turn with our tails between our legs to finish the last touches of our brunch. "Good morning, everyone! That was so much fun last night, playing all those old card games I haven't played since I was a child. Seems like ages ago!" Amber looked about twenty-seven—I haven't asked Luke her age. I smiled. It was pretty funny how we secretly conspired for Luke to always end up the Old Maid—and even more funny how he didn't catch on to us. I think the champagne bubbles went right to his head.

"So what do you girls have planned today for Gloria's last day?" she asked but then pouted to Gloria, "I'm gonna miss you, Sugar. I hope you come back and visit real soon."

Savannah then looked up from her coloring and said loudly, "Don't go, Goria!"

"Oh my God, you make me melt, Savannah. I wish I could take you with me." Gloria snapped Savannah up, carried her to the seat next to hers, and called, "Brunch is served. Let's eat!"

I didn't want Alexis to feel left out, so I carried her from the kitchen island to the table and planted her beside me, opposite Savannah.

"This holly French toast is delicious, Gloria," Luke declared. "Mmm, mmm, mmm."

Amber Lee chuckled and said to Luke, "I believe it's pronounced *challah*."

Wow. Gloria and I looked at one another, impressed.

The phone rang. This time Luke answered it, since he was already up for a coffee refill. From the sound of it, Cooper was on the other end. Gloria leaped from her chair, almost spilling her glass of juice. Why'd he call the house line instead of Gloria's cell?

"I'm not sure if she's here ... let me see," Luke said, teasing Gloria, who was practically on top of him trying to grab the phone from him. "Oh wait, she just came in. Good talkin' to you, Cooper. Happy New Year!"

As he handed Gloria the phone, she whispered, "Very funny, Luke," before greeting her Cooper with a jovial but cool-sounding "Hey there."

The rest of us found what Luke did very amusing, but we calmed our laughter so we wouldn't irritate her any further. She playfully stuck her tongue out at us as she exited the kitchen with the cordless phone. Her gleeful "Really? Really?" was soon out of our earshot.

When she returned, Luke teased again, imitating her, "Really? Really?" But he quickly returned to his regular voice and asked her seriously, "What's so really, Gloria?"

"He decided to come home tonight instead of tomorrow, but he wanted to make sure I would still be here so he could see *me*! And now that Uncle Travis's plane is delayed, we won't leave for Fort Worth until tomorrow. Yes!" she cried, doing a gung-ho arm-thingamajig-move—usually what men do when the sports team they're rooting for scores. Jealousy came over me—there went my last night with my best friend. And it didn't help, I inwardly pouted, that Hubbell wasn't here.

CHAPTER 29

The Accident

I knew something was wrong when the doorbell rang at three in the morning, just like I had known something was wrong when Mr. Jennings came to my house after school. Why would the CEO of the oil company my dad worked at stop by our house when he knew Dad was at work? Those thoughts were just as clear to me today as they had been eight months ago.

The doorbell rang again. I felt afraid. "Gloria," I whispered, feeling for her next to me. Oh my God, Gloria wasn't home. She was still out with Cooper. I wanted to kill her. I went to get Luke, who was already up out of bed slipping on his pants. Amber Lee was a sound sleeper. The doorbell's ringing didn't startle her, nor did Luke's movement and the sound his belt buckle made when it accidentally clanked against the nightstand.

As we hastened ourselves to the front door before another chime rang, I noticed cop car lights flashing through the foyer windows. I panicked, falling back on the third bottom stair. I clasped my head in my hands. I didn't want to look up when Luke opened the door to the police officers—but I did. One officer had a buzz cut, and the other was very tall—about six five.

Buzz Cut asked, "Is this the home of Dakota Buchannan?"

I immediately prayed out loud quietly, shaking in disbelief, "Oh my God. Please, dear Lord, not again."

Luke nodded to the officers but remained quiet. I could see sweat forming on the back of his neck, just below his hairline.

The other officer said, "There's been an accident. A Mr. Travis Bernard Kenwood was rushed to Memorial Hospital. You can come with us in the cruiser—or we'll escort you in your own car."

"How bad … what about his girlfriend?" Luke asked, sounding almost breathless.

"The female in the car." He hesitated, "She seemed to be—well, she was able to talk and sit up when we left, but that's all I observed," Buzz Cut confirmed.

The tall one added, looking at his notes, "A Miss Pamela Mendez, also taken to Memorial. We are trying to get in contact with her mother and daughter."

Luke informed them, "Her daughter's four. She's with us. Her mom's in Las Vegas. She doesn't have a cell phone. She's staying at the MGM Grand."

I finally spoke. "How bad … how bad is my uncle?"

"I can't really say. It looked as though he has sustained injuries. He was rushed to Memorial. That is all I know. I'm sorry, ma'am," Buzz Cut formally stated.

Ma'am! Do I look like a ma'am? I'm seventeen years old, for God's sake! I wanted to scream, just like I wanted to scream at the funeral directors: *Open that casket and let me see my dad!* But it wasn't their fault my dad was burned to death, just like it wasn't the officers' fault for being the bearer of bad news—they were just doing their jobs. Instead I asked, "And the driver—what's wrong with him?"

Buzz-cut looked down at my bare feet and then back up and reported solemnly, "He didn't make it."

I quickly got up from the steps, afraid I would break down and cry, drowning myself in my own puddle of tears, if I sat any longer. I hastily slipped on my nearby cowboy boots—the ones Mr. Trenton bought me for Christmas—and hurried out the open door, ordering, "Let's go!"

I've never sat in the back of a cruiser before, nor have I ever had the desire to. It's true how they're portrayed in movies as being crammed—how the arrestee's legs are squished and body is hunched over. Even though I am not a large person, I could see how someone who was could perform the Heimlich on himself with his own two legs! *I never want to see you in the back of a police car, Dakota,* my dad had preached to me the time I was acting rebellious, around the age of fourteen, and hanging out with a girl named Dixie. Dad and I happened to be at the mall the day Dixie was put in a police cruiser after she was found shoplifting. But it wasn't the valuables she stole that made the mall security get the county police involved—it was her accosting the clerk who caught her and then supposedly breaking the young man's nose when she punched him in the face trying to get away. She didn't seem like such a brute the Sunday prior to her arrest, when we both snuck out of church to smoke. Skipping the sermon to cough up Virginia Slims, which I later found out Dixie stole from a parishioner's opened purse, seemed harmless. Besides, I wasn't about to train my lungs to inhale and become addicted to nicotine. I knew smoking was and still is a disgusting and dangerous habit. I just hung with Dixie just because. Of course, looking back, I was an idiot.

When Dad took away my movies, I quit acting rebellious. But he still grounded me some more. I was forced to be at the reverend's beck and call for an entire month. The reverend passed me along to the old lady churchgoers, whose list of tasks seemed endless. A few would declare, *Dakota, dear, we're just watching out for you. It's not easy on your father since your mother died.* Another prune-lady wearing a wig whispered into my ear as I poured her third glass of sticky-sweet iced tea during their game of Hearts, *If you ever want to talk about the birds and the bees and you don't feel comfortable talking about it with your dad, you can come to me. You know, I've been married six times. I have a lot of experience.* Once she saw my exasperated look, she added, *widowed—never divorced.* I wanted to joke back, *Yeah? What, did you kill 'em?* Instead I found myself fixing her lopsided wig and thanking her for offering advice. Another one of my chores was to call out the numbers during Saturday's bingo. And even though the senile elders were methodical in searching for the numbers on their card, the task was very mundane, like watching paint dry. I vowed never to get out of line again—or at least to be smarter about it and not get caught!

Once we pulled into the emergency room wrap-around and before the police came to a complete stop, I shouted, "Let me out" as I banged on the interior of the door. Another truth—the rear doors of police cruisers can only be opened from the outside. It was understandable, but I had no mercy at this point. They abruptly came to a stop, and Buzz Cut got out to let me out. I hastily brushed past him and ran without a measly *Thanks* escaping my mouth. I ran right through the automatic sliding doors, which didn't open fast enough as I screamed, "Open!" Immediately my look of sudden urgency attracted the attention of one of the nurses.

"Who are you looking for?" she asked quickly.

"Uncle Travis—Travis Kenwood."

"Are you his daughter?"

Lady, I just called him uncle. "Yes," I lied, remembering emergency protocol—that immediate family were the *only* ones allowed access.

"Come with me," she said assertively.

I was hurtled into an elevator. I didn't pay attention to the floor number she pushed. I watched the middle-aged, husky nurse with salt-and-pepper hair fiddle with a charm on her bracelet. Then the door opened, and I was taken to a small waiting room. "Wait here," the nurse told me. And then she vanished.

A three-seated sofa adjacent to four small chairs with a barren wooden table separating them was the entire waiting area. There wasn't any reading material—no outdated magazines or even pamphlets advertising good health were showcased. What else was I supposed to do but wait? I don't bite my nails, but I found myself intently looking at them and contemplating, should I? But I quickly remembered Mom's scolding words, *Biting nails is a disgusting habit.*

I hoped Luke was on his way. He probably first had to rustle Amber Lee up to tell her what had happened and that she would be in charge of the girls in the morning. Of course, she would have to sugarcoat the situation so they wouldn't become scared, which I knew she would be able to do quite well. Luke probably thought Gloria was a sound sleeper like Amber Lee, since she hadn't come down the stairs, and that Amber Lee would fill her in when the kids were out of earshot. Little did Luke know Gloria was sleeping at Cooper's.

I didn't have my cell to call her. Do pay phones still exist? I looked around but didn't see one. What was I talking about? I didn't have any change on me anyway. I was in the Hello Kitty pajamas Uncle Travis' secretary, Candy, had bought me for Christmas. The kitties were decked out with Santa hats. Since Mom's death, Candy had taken the liberty of buying me pajamas every Christmas—no joke. Were fathers not good at buying girly-pajamas? I think she got more of a thrill shopping for them than I did receiving them. She had five sons—*always tried for that girl,* she used to joke. She wanted a daughter in the worst way—a girl to shop for, to shop with, and to go to the hair salon with. All of the above she tried with me. Buying PJs was as far as I let her get. If you saw how she wore her hair, you'd run the other way too—unless you needed a pen! She would stick at least three in her tornado-like, meticulously coiffed bouffant. She was an aerosol hairspray fiend. Environmentalists could fault her personally for aiding in the destruction of the ozone layer.

I was still waiting alone. My legs were propped on the table—something I would never do if others were present. I felt scared as I anxiously waited to find out if I was I going to be uncle-less? I began fiddling with a loose string on my pajama bottom hem, which reminded me of sewing with Mom. *Dakota, hurry up. We're gonna be late, honey, if you don't hurry,* Mom sweetly had hollered at the foot of the stairs. I had to fish for the bag of sewing stuff I had pushed under my bed months prior. Everything and anything I got bored with went under my bed—the black hole. Mom had signed us up for a "creative sewing" course at the community center, and it was highly suggested to bring a project on the first day of class. Project? I had never sewn before, so really, I needed to start from scratch. But Mom reminded me of the decorative pillow I started to sew at one of her weekly arts and crafts meetings eons ago and never finished. I could still hear her voice, encouraging me, *Pull it back out, honey, and finish it—from what I can remember, it was adorable. You were sewing a little bird in turquoise-blue felt surrounded by pink flowers.*

Mom had an incredible memory and an incredible outlook on life. She was always positive and always going. But she knew how to slow down, too. She knew when people needed help, and she always volunteered her time and services—big and small. Sometimes it was watching a child of an acquaintance so the overworked single mom could put in a double shift to pay her mounting bills. Or she would run a week's worth of errands for an elder in just one day: grocery store, pharmacy, post office, even a pet groomer. This one old lady had the cutest little poodle. When Mom picked me up from school that day, I thought it was a stuffed animal sticking out of a new purse of hers. Its name was Slippers. Cute, huh?

And no matter whose home it was she visited, she never arrived empty-handed. Usually it was a homemade casserole, and she'd say, *Keep the dish when you're done. I have plenty.* Our kitchen cupboards held at least two dozen. Mom sort of had a fetish for buying them. Whenever she'd see one on sale, she'd grab it up, even with my plea, *Another one, mom? But we've got a trillion at home.*

Yeah, but this one's different, she'd say, holding it up under the light. *Just look at those little pretty scrolls—and the color—and the handles.* She was right. Each casserole dish was different. But the real reason she bought 'em was to give them away with her famous shepherd's pie. She never gave away the ones she made in pottery class, though. Those were for our family, and they didn't live in the cupboard with the temporary ones. They were out on our hutch for all to admire. Her nickname was Casserole Loretta, and Mom loved it—she smiled every time she was greeted with it. Dad and I got a chuckle out of it, too.

Another noteworthy cause of Mom's was donating blood for the American Red Cross and then staying afterward to recruit other individuals to do the same. Mom was mentioned in the community paper so many times Dad used to kid that her name was part of its layout. Then he'd say how he was going to call *Star-Telegram* and suggest a column exclusively for Loretta's deeds. My mom would warn, *Don't you dare, Jethro Theodore Buchannan!*

CHAPTER 30

Blood Donor

"Miss Buchannan," a male voice called. "Dakota Buchannan," he repeated, since I was not responding the first time. No one ever calls me *Miss Buchannan*. "Excuse me, Miss Dakota Buchannan," he said louder as he walked closer toward me.

"Yes," I answered, practically jumping up from my chair. "I'm Dakota Buchannan."

"I'm Dr. Pauling, Joel Pauling." He offered his hand.

I put my moist hand out to shake his while urgently asking, "How is he? Can I see him?"

"He is unconscious. He lost a lot of blood. I had to remove his spleen."

"What?" We simultaneously let go of each other's hands, allowing me to put mine up to my mouth as I uttered "What?" again, shocked. It sounded horrible—removing a body part.

"He ruptured his spleen. We removed it. People survive without their spleens—don't worry," the doctor assured me.

Don't worry? I hated those two words. Usually when people said *don't worry*, it means, *worry*.

"Dakota, it's his liver. People cannot survive long with a sick liver. Part of his liver ruptured. I closed him up temporarily and put him on a dialysis machine, but we will need to operate very soon."

"Is he going to live?" I asked. He looked at me. Rather, he looked down at me. He was almost a giant. I felt as if I were an ant about to be stepped on, awaiting the inevitable. "It's hard to tell right now. We'll need more of his blood type before we can operate."

That's easy. Call Red Cross. Tell them Loretta Buchannan's daughter sent you. They ought to remember her. "Yeah. Don't you have blood?" I asked curtly.

"Your father has a rare blood type. Not many donors carry this. Close to three percent of the people in the United States have AB-Positive type blood, and your dad's one of the three percent."

I muffled an irritated laugh. Leave it to my Uncle Travis to have rare blood—how apropos. He is one of a kind. I gave a heavy sigh trying to wrap my head around this. Doc was looking at me strangely. I tore both my hands through my tangled hair and began to cry. I couldn't believe this.

He continued, "We already put it into immediate circulation—our database—requesting this blood type. All we can do right now is wait."

That was easy for him to say. I felt like I was suffocating. My breathing became heavy and audible.

"Let me give you something that may help," he said while placing a hand on my shoulder. "To calm you down," he finished in a soothing tone, as if he already wanted to commit me to the psych ward.

I looked up, shaking my head, and wished I had the nerve to say, *I'll tell you what will fucking calm me down—you getting a donor! Get movin'! Make phone calls! Announce it over the intercom—hospitals still have these, don't they?* Instead I let out a huff and returned to my seat. Doc left.

I heard the sound of an elevator door opening. Luke arrived and rushed over to me. I remained seated. I was emotionally exhausted.

"How is he?" Luke asked with urgency.

"He needs surgery, but they're waiting for blood."

"Huh?"

"I know—hard to believe. They need more of his blood type."

"Did you bring your cell or mine by chance?" I asked, changing the subject.

"Yes, here," he said, handing me my cell. "I stupidly left mine on the kitchen counter."

My hands stopped shaking but were clammy. A different nurse than the one who originally brought me to this waiting area approached me holding two small plastic cups, one containing a pill and the other filled with water. She said while gesturing for me to take them from her hands, "Here, Dr. Pauling ordered this for you."

"Oh yeah? What is it?" I asked, even though I had a strong suspicion that the pill was a sedative. I was agitated. Doc wanted me calmed, a.k.a. loopy!

"A mild sedative," she answered sternly. Even though I appreciated her honesty and I knew she was just following orders and doing her job, my reply was sarcastic. "Nice, but no thanks. I want to have my wits about me." And I rudely started scrolling down for Gloria's number on my cell.

"You can't use that here," she said with authority, turning her head to the picture sign on the wall that conveyed her message. "It'll interfere ..."

"Well, where can I use it? It's important," I asked, still not letting go of my obnoxious manner.

"Take the elevator to G, ground level. Pass through the lobby, and you'll see another waiting area on your right where cell phone use is allowed. Or you can head outside to use it," she instructed me in a bitchy tone.

Okay, so I deserved it. But still, I didn't thank her. I just nodded and said to Luke, "Wait here. I'll only be a little while."

"When you get back, I've gotta do the same and try to get in touch with Crystal. She needs to know about her daughter," Luke conveyed urgently. "I don't know if the cops got a hold of her at the hotel."

I nodded and pushed the elevator button. It opened right away. I had to call Gloria. I had to call Hubbell—maybe his dad could help.

"Gloria, where the hell are you?" I yelled into my phone.

"We're on our way," she answered.

"We?" *Not Cooper, too,* I silently prayed.

"When Cooper drove me home, I saw the note on the back door telling me you were at Memorial Hospital because Uncle Travis was ..." She stopped regurgitating Luke's note and asked, "How is he?"

How did Luke know Gloria wasn't asleep in my bed? My cell. He probably tiptoed in to get my cell, knowing I would want to call Hubbell, and saw my bed empty. "I don't know," I answered curtly, not bothering to fill her in.

"We'll be there soon. Cooper's driving like a maniac."

"Yeah, well, tell him to slow the fuck down. I don't need my best friend getting into an accident, too." I clicked End before she had a chance to respond and scrolled down to Hubbell's number. Shit, what time was it? Too late—it was ringing.

"Dakota, it's five in the morning," Hubbell said in a sleepy voice.

I talked hurriedly. "Uncle Travis has been in an accident. They need to perform surgery but can't because they need more AB-Positive blood. Can your dad help?" And I begin to cry hysterically. Maybe I should have taken that sedative.

"Oh my God, Dakota. I'm so sorry. We leave today at ten. I think that's the first flight out. We'll go right to the hospital. Which one?"

"Memorial. Hurry, please," I pleaded.

"Dakota, he's going to make it. Don't worry."

Don't worry. God, I hated those words.

I began to head back upstairs so Luke could call Pamela's mom, but before I did, I looked for one of the emergency ward nurses. My manners returned as I remembered one of Mom's life lessons, *You can attract more bees with honey than with vinegar.* "Excuse me. Could you please tell me what room I can find a Miss Pamela Mendez in?"

She looked at the enormous dry-erase board on the back wall of the nurse's station and answered, "Mendez has been moved to 708. Take the elevator to the seventh floor."

"Thank you," I said with a smile.

Suddenly my name was being called. I turned to find Gloria rushing toward me. Cooper was following but not running like Gloria was. She embraced me. I started to cry again. She coaxed me, "He's going to live, Dakota—don't worry."

I pushed her off of me and freaked. "Geez. Everyone is telling me not to worry, and I hate it!" Gloria looked hurt, but I ignored it and filled them in, "He needs AB-Positive blood, and this stupid hospital doesn't have enough."

Cooper questioned, "How much does he need?"

"Huh? Enough for him to live," I snapped.

Cooper ignored my tone. He usually had good comebacks, but this time he let me slide and volunteered, "I'm AB Positive."

"Oh my God. We've gotta tell 'em!"

I grabbed his arm and pulled him with me to the elevator. It coincidentally opened up when we got to it. All three of us entered. It closed. "Oh my God, I don't know what floor." I started to freak out again. "I didn't pay attention to what floor Uncle Travis is on!" I was hysterical.

Gloria was soothing my hair like the crazy lady had at my dad's funeral. I rolled my eyes. She didn't see, but Cooper did. The elevator door opened again. People getting on were surprised we were not getting off, considering it was the ground floor. One of the people getting on happened to be the salt-and-pepper-haired nurse. "Oh, thank God. Do you remember me? What floor is Bernard Kenwood on, please?" I begged, hoping she would remember. I knew my uncle wasn't her only patient.

She smiled nervously when she recognized me and said, "I believe it was five." Cooper pushed five. It lit up. The other passengers pushed higher numbers. An express—good. We'd get to Dr. Pauling quicker.

I rushed out. Luke was pacing back and forth, waiting for me, and loudly called, "Dakota!"

I frantically said, "Luke, Cooper has the same blood type. Where's the doctor? Where's the nurse? We have to let them know. And Pamela's in room 708."

"Okay. Let's find the doctor," Luke said with assertiveness as all four of us rushed to the nurses station.

I grabbed Cooper, practically pushed him onto the counter, and blurted, "He's AB Positive!"

"Come with me," the nurse said, leading Cooper into a room. The door closed behind them.

Almost two hours passed, and nothing happened. Luke was with Pamela. Gloria stayed with me in the dreadful area they called a waiting room. She had fallen asleep looking very uncomfortable, sitting up with her head slouched down.

Cooper appeared, looking somewhat disheveled, and said groggily, "I fell asleep ... after giving blood. It wiped me out. How is he—your uncle?"

I shrugged, feeling utterly hopeless and helpless. A fresh set of tears started to run from my already-swollen eyes. He eyed Gloria, who was still asleep. He put his arm around my shoulders gently but securely and led me down the corridor. He stopped at its dead end and gingerly leaned me into the wall, putting both his arms on the wall with me in the middle, like I was his captive. My face was very near his chest. His shirt was wrinkled but smelled clean, as if fresh from the clothesline. I could feel the warmth of his skin. His chest rose and fell slowly. I could hear his breathing. He raised my chin. I found his eyes brimming with tears. He spoke softly. "Dakota, I lost my parents, too."

"How old were you?" I asked solemnly.

"I was sixteen," he answered sadly.

"Who?" I asked, wanting to know which parent had died but forgetting that he had spoken in the plural.

"Who? My parents," he answered, sounding slightly baffled that I didn't catch on.

"You lost both of them ... at the same time?" I asked, confused and surprised. Then suddenly I felt stricken with grief, as if it had just hit me on the head.

"Yes," he reiterated, looking puzzled.

"How? That's impossible. That's terrible. Holy shit!" I rambled like a crazy person. "That's just not right."

"They were coming home from a weekend getaway when a drunk driver crashed into them, killing them instantly." He snickered. "The asshole was coming from an office holiday party." I shook my head in disbelief.

He continued, "My parents had a slew of Christmas presents in their trunk to put under the tree." He sighed and ran his hand through his thick, wavy hair as if it would stop him from crying. He averted his glossy eyes from mine. "My grandma still wrapped them, but it took months before TJ and I felt like opening them," he said, teary-eyed.

"Cooper, I'm so sorry. I didn't know. My mom died when I was ten. My dad … when I was sixteen."

"I know. Gloria told me." He spoke softly as he moved closer, letting go of the wall. He lightly touched my chin with his hand, lifting my bowed head. Oh my God, was he going to kiss me?

CHAPTER 31

Safe ... Maybe

An apprehensive "Dakota" sounded. It was Hubbell's voice. "What's going on?"

Shit. I pushed Cooper away and ran to Hubbell. I began sobbing again, this time in my boyfriend's chest—a heavenly aroma, a combination of coconut and aloe. He held me tight, kissing the top of my head. After breathing me in, he said, "God, I missed you, Dakota."

"Me too," I mumbled into his chest. I didn't want to move, but he gently eased his tight embrace, moving his hands from my back to my arms. He squeezed my biceps, looked into my teary eyes, and confirmed, "My father has talked to the surgeon and checked on your uncle himself. Your uncle's going to make it. He got the blood."

"I know. Cooper donated it," I said and turned to quiet Cooper, who was keeping his distance. His hands were tucked into his front jean pockets, and he looked very solemn. Hubbell released me and strutted with confidence to Cooper with his hand extended. They shook, and Hubbell said, "Thank you, man." He had completely dismissed the idea that Cooper was coming onto me, realizing I was in a vulnerable state and needed coddling ... if that's what it was.

I realized I hadn't even thanked Cooper yet. I was properly introducing them, letting Hubbell know that Cooper was Gloria's friend and that they drove together to the hospital, when Dr. Cavanaugh, looking very tan and casually dressed, appeared. He spoke, sounding somewhat cold, as if I had ruined his vacation, "Dakota, you can see your uncle. He's unconscious, but you can see him. Come with me."

As Dr. Cavanaugh led the way to my uncle's room, I felt compelled to ask him, "How was Jamaica?"

"Great," he answered as he opened the door and gestured me in. Then he left as quickly as he had appeared.

When I entered the room, the same feelings I had felt when Mom was in the hospital overtook me. Mom had surgery, but it didn't do any good. I walked over to my uncle's bed. The room was dim. Only a small light shined on the wall behind his bed. He had tubes in both his hands, and his nose had one joining tube for both nostrils. The bed sheets seemed whiter than ever against his bronzed skin. What a way to end a week in Antigua. I gently smoothed away his longer-than-usual hair from his forehead and kissed it, telling him, "You need a haircut. You're too old to be sportin' this do."

I pulled up the one chair in the room to sit beside him, holding his hand carefully, and continued to talk to him. "How did this happen? I'm not letting you out of my sight. Gloria's new—" I hesitated. "A friend of Gloria's had your blood-type. He saved your life—Cooper Paine." Suddenly Uncle Travis' right hand twitched a little.

Luke entered the room quietly. "Dakota, can I talk to you outside?"

"Tell me here. I don't want to leave him. His hand moved. Maybe his eyes will open up soon," I softly said.

"All right." He then whispered, "the police are up with Pamela, questioning her."

"So what? Isn't that protocol with any accident?"

"Yes, but … you aren't going to believe this. It might not have been an accident."

"What?" I asked, shocked.

"There was another vehicle involved. It crashed into the taxi driver and sped away, according to witnesses."

"What?" I asked. I tried to stay calm, but my blood was starting to boil, and my voice was rising. "Who would do that? Why?"

"There's something else you don't know."

"Oh my God, what?" Luke was hesitant. I asked again, sounding more aggravated. "Luke, what?"

"Well, it's about Alexis's dad."

"You know her dad?" I asked, distressed.

"Not exactly. Her dad's in prison. He's getting released soon."

"What?" I said, appalled.

"There's the possibility he's coming after Pamela—for his daughter."

"This is crazy. Why's he in prison? When did you learn about this? Alexis's dad is in prison. Oh my God, why didn't you tell me? Why didn't Uncle Travis tell me? He used to tell me everything! Geez, I hate secrets!" I rambled hysterically.

"Dakota, try to calm down, please. Pamela didn't want you to know. It's nothing that she's proud of—having an ex-husband who's a drug dealer—so calm down," he repeated. I took a deep breath.

Luke continued, "She didn't know, of course. She would never have married him and had a kid if she knew, and Alexis doesn't remember her dad. She was too young."

"Luke, our house—Amber needs to know right away. They need to stay inside, with the windows and doors locked. No matter how much pleading Savannah does to go swimming—she can't! Get a cop there too— to watch over them!" I ordered. Luke gave a hint of a smile. "Why are you smiling?" I asked, completely pissed off. "And don't tell me to calm down!"

"It's the first time you've referred to the house as ours," Luke answered. "Amber Lee's been informed. A police unit is already there. Don't worry. I'm going to go check on Pamela again. Don't worry, Dakota," he repeated and then exited the room. I wanted to scream.

Later, Luke returned with a cup of coffee. "Fixed just the way you like it," he said, handing it to me. He then gestured me to move away from my uncle so he could tell me something, but I didn't budge. I was still holding my uncle's hand as my other held the weak, lukewarm hospital coffee. Why couldn't hospitals learn how to brew a good cup of joe? Of all places, hospitals should have the strongest coffee. Luke saw my stubbornness, so he began to whisper, "I've got some more bad news to tell you. Reporters are here."

"What?" I think I shouted this time.

"Well, your uncle is well known. A lot of cases he won got publicity, good and bad. Some people wanna see him live ... others want him dead. I'm sorry, Dakota. Outside the hospital there are a slew of them—camera crews, too."

Suddenly I felt flushed with anger. My blood had reached a hundred degrees Celsius. How could my uncle have enemies? He was so incredible in so many ways. I loudly whispered, "What? My uncle only defended the good—the innocent—and put the bad—the guilty—away! You don't know what you're talking about. They don't know what they're talking about. They're stupid reporters."

Then my uncle's hand twitched again. "Uncle Travis, Uncle Travis," I cried, squeezing his hand. Then he closed his fingers. I turned to Luke and whispered, "Do you think he heard?" Then my soft voice turned to a low bark and I ordered, "Can you just leave? I want to be alone with him. And don't return with any more bad news."

"I'm sorry, Dakota." He started to walk away.

Shit. Luke didn't deserve that. I gingerly released my handhold and hurried to Luke, who was already at the door. "Wait. I'm sorry, Luke. It's been a long night. I'm a little crazy."

"Yeah. Speaking of crazy, your friend Gloria has major apologizing to do. I believe I gave her a midnight curfew."

I chuckled. "You're right. Give it to her good, Luke!" I had a strong feeling he wouldn't be able to, though—it wasn't in his nature. I once saw him easing a spider onto a piece of paper and then gingerly carrying it outside. He set it free and told it, *Don't come back!* He didn't know I was witnessing this humane act of his, and I preferred to keep it that way. It made me love him even more.

CHAPTER 32

Brigham vs. Kenwood

The nurse entered my uncle's room carrying a tray. "I thought you'd be hungry. Seeing you haven't left your dad to go get some food, I took the liberty," she said, setting the tray down and lifting the plastic lid from the dish. "You're in luck. It's one of the better ones: chicken potpie." She recovered it.

"Thank you. That's very nice of you. Are you my uncle's nurse?"

"For the next eight hours I am. I thought he was your dad?" And she walked to all his apparatuses to check his status. "All good," she reassured me.

"My dad was killed at his job eight months ago. He's really not my uncle—no blood relation, that is. He and my dad were best friends since the third grade. He's more like a godfather, but from the time I could speak he taught me to call him Uncle Travis."

"Where's your mom?" The nurse asked curiously.

"In heaven, too. Cancer killed her. I was ten."

"Geez. You've had it rough, girl. No wonder you went a tad berserk."

"I'm sorry. You nurses must hate me and think I'm a brat."

"Yeah," she answered without any hesitation but then added kindly, "but I'll set them straight." She winked. "And who were all those good-looking boys surrounding you?" she teased.

I blushed and answered, "The oldest one is my brother. The

brown-haired guy was the blood donor, and the cutest one, the tan blond, is my boyfriend, Hubbell."

"Hubbell? Like in *The Way We Were* Hubbell?"

I smiled and nodded.

"One of my favorite movies," she admitted. "Well, he sure is cute—and crazy for you. Go on and eat. You need more meat on those bones of yours. I'll be back in a little while."

"Thank you again. Hey, what's your name?"

"Penny."

"Thanks, Penny."

"You got it, kiddo!" She exited the room, saying, "I'll be back" as the door slowly closed behind her.

I decided to eat. I put on the television as I uncovered the chicken potpie and took in the smell. *Not bad*, I thought, or I was too famished to be picky. The *O'Reilly Factor* came on. Good. I liked him—well I liked how Uncle Travis had befuddled him a year ago.

"Good evening, America. The topic tonight: Boy saves lawyer—who defended the drunk driver—who killed his parents." Bill O'Reilly spoke in his usual cutting voice.

"What?"

"One of most controversial law cases is reborn. Seven years ago parents Walter and Jennifer Brigham filed suit against the law office of Bernard Travis Kenwood for the murder of their only child, June Brigham-Paine." Three photographs were shown—one male, two females. "Young office intern Willet Mathews—not of legal drinking age, inebriated from the office holiday party—crashes his car, instantly killing June and her husband, Eric Paine." More photographs were shown—two males, one female. "Mr. Mathews leaves the accident unscathed. And sons TJ and Cooper Paine are left parentless, just days before Christmas." Two more photographs were shown—both male. I recognized Cooper and TJ. They hadn't changed much—just gotten better-looking with age.

"Due to 'tampered' evidence and 'technicalities—'" Bill made the quotation-mark gesture with his fingers and gave his usual sinister smirk—"about not following the arrest protocol, the judge sided with the law office of Bernard Travis Kenwood. Mr. Mathews served some community service, had his license suspended, and attended AA meetings. Was that enough? Had justice been served—or did Attorney Kenwood spin the system? Now, folks, here's the irony."

Bill repositioned himself in his stationary seat and began talking in his usual monotone. "Mark Cooper Paine—the boy who lost his parents in that car accident seven years ago—came to Travis's rescue, donating blood for Mr. Kenwood's operation just yesterday when he was a victim of a fatal car accident. Did he know whom he was saving? Why was he even there at the hospital when this happened? Did fate bring them together?"

Oh my God. I quickly shut it off and announced, "I hate you, Bill O'Reilly!" Did I dare flip to another channel? I did.

A local news anchorman reported, "Former wife of notorious drug dealer Carlos Sanchez, Pamela Mendez-Sanchez, fell victim to a hit-and-run car crash while leaving the airport at one o'clock this morning after a week-long vacation in Antiqua with infamous attorney Bernard Travis Kenwood, who is on life support at Memorial Hospital with Pamela by his side." Then the idiot added his own halfwit questions. "Were they the victims of a former plaintiff gone berserk or the drug cartel?"

Oh my God! I felt like puking. Remind me never to work for a news station—they're full of shit! "You imbeciles, I'm by his side, not his girlfriend!" I spewed to the TV. "And he's not on life support. He's going to wake up any minute."

I continued to channel surf. Somehow I felt compelled to—it was all so surreal. All of a sudden a photograph of the taxi driver was shown. Oh my God, that was the guy who delivered Paddington Bear. Luke walked in and saw the horrid look of shock on my face, "Dakota, what is it?"

"Luke, he's the UPS guy who came to our house. He brought the big box for Savannah. He was so nice." I replayed the scene for Luke almost in a daze. "The guy knelt down to her level. He told Savannah, *I have a daughter around your age. Let me guess … you're four.* And he put out four of his fingers and smiled. Then he said, *let me guess,* and he acted Houdini-like. *Your name is Sa—Sa—Savannah!* Savannah's eyes widened, and she nodded as if she really believed he had magical powers. Then he told her, *I've got a big package for you … all the way from England!* He seemed like a genuine, sweet guy, Luke, and now he's …" I cried. "Now he's dead."

"Geez," Luke said, almost breathless. "He worked two jobs so he could support his family … his poor wife and kid." He took a deep sigh and shook his head sadly. "Why do bad things happen to good people?"

I flipped off the TV and rested my face in my hands but didn't cry. I was feeling as if this couldn't really be happening. I was utterly exhausted and drained. It was as if my tear ducts had dried up. Luke walked over to me and rubbed both my shoulders from behind. "Dakota, let me take you home. A hot shower, some rest, and a little something to eat will do you good. And then we'll come back later. Everyone's gone home … Gloria, Cooper, and Hubbell. They didn't want to disturb you. I thought it was best, too. Pamela's asleep. They gave her something. They're keeping her overnight to run some more tests. You can see her and Uncle Travis when we come back, okay?"

I shook—at least three nos. "Please, Dakota. You can't help your uncle right now, and when he does wake, he'll want you awake. Look at you. You're a mess, and you're beginning to smell," Luke teased. He moved his hands from my shoulders to my mop hair, tousling it, and added "Pew … ee!" Even though I knew it didn't smell—I had washed it the day before—I muffled a chuckle with a quick elbow jab to his ribs. He gave a fake "Ouch!"

I knew Luke was right. I succumbed to his suggestion. I bent over to kiss my uncle good-bye, telling him in a soft voice, "I'll be back. I love you." Luke and I headed to the door. His arm was around my shoulder as I told him, "I did have some chicken potpie—wasn't bad for hospital food."

"Good. When we get home you can have some chocolate cake, brownies, pie, muffins … Amber Lee kept 'em busy with baking. And you thought she didn't know her way around the kitchen."

"She's great, Luke. I mean it. You have my permission to marry her," I said sincerely.

"Yeah? Marriage? I haven't known her very long, but I'm glad you approve, kiddo! I think she's pretty special, too."

We managed to bypass the reporters and drove home.

CHAPTER 33

Back Home

Savannah ran to me the minute I entered. I bent down to hug her, but her charge was like a bulldozer. I was pushed down to the floor onto my bottom. She tightly embraced me and planted herself in my lap. She loudly asked with a pout, "Where have you been? I missed you!" She didn't let me answer. "We made *sooo* many choc-o-it-tee yummies, Dakota. Wait till you try 'em."

"Okay, but can I take a warm bath first?"

She nodded. "I'll bring some to you in the bathtub," she said as she got up from my lap. I pretended she was strong enough to pull me up. Once I was to my feet again, Amber Lee walked over to me and gave me a hug, rubbing my back. She softly said, "My prayers are with you, Dakota, and your uncle and Pamela."

I smiled as she released her hold on me and was greatly relieved she didn't tell me not to worry. "Thank you," I said. As if one wasn't enough, I repeated, "Thank you, Amber Lee" as I headed up the back stairs. Gloria was in my room packing. She stopped what she was doing to give me a welcome-back hug. She immediately volunteered, "Is there anything you want me to do?"

"No. No thanks. I'm going to take a hot bath, slip on some clean PJs—these smell of hospital—and climb into bed. I'm so exhausted."

"Yeah, I bet you are. Just think, if we had picked them up at the airport, we would've been part of the accident. Scary, huh?" Gloria said, shuddering at the thought.

"Yeah. Unbelievable. I didn't even think of that. I was referring to the shock of who Cooper is," I replied.

"What? What do you mean? He donated blood—he's a blood donor," she said in a duh-no-kidding kind of way.

"Gloria, you didn't hear?"

"Hear what, Dakota?"

"My uncle defended the drunk driver who killed his parents! Cooper's grandparents sued my uncle's law firm."

"What? Why?" she asked, acting in the same shocked way I had when I learned of it.

"The driver was a college intern at the firm. He was underage, but that didn't stop him from drinking at the firm's Christmas party. He left drunk. No one took his car keys from him. No one drove him home. Cooper's grandparents believed it was my uncle's responsibility. That it was his fault … their daughter and son-in-law were killed."

"Oh my God, Dakota. I don't think Cooper knows who your uncle is."

"If he watched the news tonight he does. When you two left the hospital, weren't there reporters waiting outside?" I asked, surprised she and Cooper weren't bombarded with questions.

"Yeah, but we thought it had to do with Pamela. Her ex-husband is Carlos Sanchez—the notorious drug dealer. Did you know about that?"

I nodded. "Didn't the reporters recognize Cooper? He hadn't changed much. How'd you two skirt them?" I asked, mystified.

"We left through the service entrance. Cooper overheard someone calling to a custodian, *Your shift's up, Juan—go home.* So we followed Juan. Cooper's so clever."

I smirked. *Yeah, you don't know the half of it,* I thought, thinking back to our dim corridor moment.

"This is so, so surreal, Dakota," Gloria said, taking a seat at the edge of my bed.

"Tell me about it," I said, completely agreeing with her.

"Cooper's driving me home tomorrow. And seeing that Dallas is only a half-hour drive from Fort Worth, he's stopping over at his grandparents. Geez, wait till his grandparents find out who he donated blood for." As if this was the worst thing he could have done. If only she knew he came on to me at the hospital when she was passed out.

I became defensive. "It makes no difference. It was a long time ago, and I'm sure my uncle had a very good reason to defend the driver and save his law firm. He built it from nothing Gloria. He grew up very poor. Maybe it wasn't entirely his fault. Maybe Cooper's parents ran a red light." Although I felt that was highly unlikely, I felt even more strongly that I had to defend my uncle, especially as he lay helpless in the hospital.

Gloria heard the sharp tone in my voice and dared not defend Cooper's parents, or grandparents. She only shrugged her shoulders and busied herself with nervously stuffing more unfolded clothes into her monogrammed duffle bag. I now wished I had that sedative to calm me down. I really shouldn't be upset with Gloria. If it weren't for her, we wouldn't have met Cooper, and he wouldn't have been at the hospital to donate blood and save my uncle. I remembered I had never thanked him. To change the subject I asked in a much nicer tone, looking at her bag, "What's the M stand for?" The funeral hanky flashed in my mind.

"Miriam—my dad's grandma," she answered solemnly.

"Pretty," I said with a smile. Yeah, I bet the hanky lady was a Miriam, too. I headed into the bathroom. "I'm going to go drown myself right now—not literally, of course." And I began filling the tub. I undid the cellophane from the basket of aromatherapy goodies Mrs. Cavanaugh had given me for Christmas and chose a mauve-colored ball that immediately fizzed when I plopped it into the tub. Already the lavender scent released into the air.

It only felt like a few solitary minutes before I was recaptured by my niece's company. She wasn't carrying a basket of goodies like I had expected—she and Little Red Riding Hood fit the same mold. Instead, and just as practically, Savannah utilized her oversized cardigan sweater pockets that were shaped as mittens. From the left mitten pocket she

171

released a brownie wrapped in a paper napkin and from the right mitten pocket a mini-muffin also wrapped in a paper napkin. She saw my what-flavor-muffin-is-it? look and joyfully exclaimed, "Boo berry. They're so yummy and cute-looking."

"*You're* yummy and cute!" I teased back. "Little muffins are my favorite. I think they taste better than the big ones." Savannah giggled some more. How I loved hearing her laugh. If it could be bottled and sold, the world would be a happier place.

"Is it okay to come in?" Amber Lee called from my bedroom's vestibule, just outside the bathroom door. "I've got a cup of tea I thought you'd like." She really was a gem, like Mom.

"Yup. Come on in," I answered, making sure the suds were covering my private area as I placed a face cloth over my chest. She carried over the vanity stool to place the mug of tea on and asked, "Would you like anything else? Perhaps something a bit healthier?" She eyed the brownie I had placed on the bathtub caddy. I had already downed the mini muffin. "There are the leftovers from dinner—spaghetti and meatballs. I can make you a meatball sub—you can eat it in the tub." The three of us laughed at her spontaneous rhyme.

"What time is it?" I asked. "Time has completely escaped me."

Looking at her watch, she answered, "A little after eight."

"Where's Alexis?" I asked.

"Her grandma, Crystal, took the earliest flight she could out of Las Vegas. Mr. Trenton picked her up at the airport, and they hurried over here to get Alexis before heading to the hospital to see Pamela." Amber Lee then picked up the mug of tea and handed it to me so she could utilize the vanity stool. She sat herself down and asked, "How long has Crystal been working for Drew Trenton?"

Before I answered Amber Lee, I looked to see what Savannah was up to. She was sniffing the perfume Hubbell had given me for Christmas. We watched as she gave her neck a spritz while looking into the mirror. She was so innocent. "Savannah, thanks for the goodies, cutie." I motioned her to come closer to me and said in a hushed voice, "I've got a good idea. Since it's Gloria's last night, I think she'd love it if you asked her to read *Paddington Bear* to you. Wouldn't that be nice? I bet she'd love it. She's going to miss you."

Savannah nodded and kissed me and Amber Lee good night. She then scurried out of the bathroom smelling of Estee Lauder's Beautiful and called in her usual adorable voice, "Goria," which immediately made Amber Lee and me chuckle.

Sounding concerned, Amber Lee asked, "Do you think she ought to see a speech specialist for that—she can't pronounce her L's —or will it come with age?"

I shrugged and said, "I'll ask Luke what he thinks." Then I told her to close the door so I could answer her initial question about Crystal's employment with Mr. Trenton.

"Crystal became a full-time employee of Mr. Trenton's after her husband, Hector Mendez, suddenly died, leaving her in major debt with their five-year-old daughter, Pamela, to raise. She had very little money saved and no family to help her out, so when Mr. Trenton made an addition to his home, he set Crystal and her daughter up with one of the roomier suites. He made them feel like they were a part of his family."

"I have heard about what an incredibly generous person Drew Trenton is—humble, sincere—the best kind, really," Amber Lee said. But then her voice suddenly changed from sounding enthusiastic to sounding suspicious. "Still, there is something mysterious about him, too, don't you think?"

"I don't know if mysterious is the right word ... more like strange. For the entirety of his marriage he had a mistress—Luke's mom, Gerry. And his wife knew about it. Supposedly everyone knew about it. Constance, Janet's mom, finally left him after a tumultuous ten-year marriage. She put up with his infidelity for that long—crazy! And even stranger, Gerry didn't want to marry Drew. She sounded like a major wacko, but Luke told me she was a loving mom."

"Well, it's a good thing she never wanted to marry your dad either—or else you wouldn't be here," Amber Lee declared.

"Yup. That's how I look at it too."

"Luke told me all about his mom's confessional on her

deathbed—how she fled to Houston in her first trimester and refused any persuasion of your dad's when he found her, not knowing the real reason why she left." Amber Lee rushed, knowing I had heard the story before. I appreciated her for that. It really bothered me when people talked just to hear themselves talk. My grandma called it *diarrhea of the mouth*. Grandma was a hoot who called it like it was.

"I don't understand why Gerry chose to be a single mother. She may have thought she was being independent, but I think it was downright selfish of her not to let my dad know and not to tell Luke until he was thirty-six. I think she revealed Jethro's identity because she didn't want to die with guilt. If she hadn't died when she did, our paths might never have crossed, at least not at my dad's funeral. My life would be so different." Then the thought of not having his daughter in my life scared me. I shuddered. "I don't even want to imagine my life without Luke and Savannah. Because of Savannah I'm happier than I have ever been."

Amber Lee smiled. "I believe everything happens for a reason, Dakota."

"Funny, my brother says the same thing," I said, returning her smile. I was happy they shared the sentiment.

"Well, I'll let you relax by yourself. I've babbled on long enough. Do you want me to fix you anything ... a sandwich?"

"No thanks. No sub in the tub for me!" I joked, making Amber Lee chuckle. "You've done a lot already. Thanks for being so good with Savannah and for keeping her and Alexis occupied all day. I know how tiring that can be."

"Are you kidding? It was my pleasure—we had so much fun, under the circumstances. They kept me from thinking the worst, even though I felt God was going to help your uncle pull through." And she looked up at the ceiling and said in a Hallelujah-type way, like Mrs. White would, "Thank you, Lord!"

"Yes. Thank you, Lord," I worshipped aloud, looking up as well.

"It was a miracle Cooper was there," she added.

I wasn't sure if I should confide in her about Cooper's approach—maybe another time. "Yes. It was definitely a coincidence," I said.

"It was more than mere coincidence, Dakota. Cooper didn't have to divulge his blood type. We would never have known unless he volunteered. And thank God he gave. I knew I liked the boy the minute I set eyes on him," Amber Lee said adamantly.

"Yes," I said again. "You're right. I'm sorry. I didn't mean to sound ungrateful." I was reminded again of how I hadn't thanked Cooper and prayed he understood my negligence—I wasn't thinking clearly in the hospital. "When Cooper was having his blood drawn, before Gloria fell asleep on me, she told me a Yiddish proverb that rings so clear: *Coincidence is when God chooses to remain anonymous.*"

"I like it," she said. "That Gloria is something else, too. So full of life! They make a cute couple."

I took a sip of my tea and a bite of the brownie. "Delicious," I complimented.

"Thanks," she said. "If I ever have a daughter of my own, I'd want her to be like Savannah. But I bet God broke the mold when she was born," Amber Lee boasted.

I said, smiling, "Maybe you and Luke will ..." Then I stopped myself, thinking it was premature. I wouldn't want to give her hope—my brother had only just divorced.

"Will what?" Amber Lee said curiously.

"Get married and have more kids of course!" I said with obvious conviction.

"That'd be my dream come true," she said with a heavenly sigh and an angelic smile. I swear it sounded like she was singing. "Good night, Dakota. Sweet dreams," she trilled as she waltzed out of the room, reminding me of Cinderella dancing at the ball. My brother really was her Prince Charming.

I turned on the hot water to warm the bath again and sunk under. I thought about all the circumstances—were they coincidences or fate? I had never really understood the cliché *it's a small world* until now. And having learned Gloria's Yiddish proverb I knew, just as Mrs. White had reiterated to me, God had my back.

CHAPTER 34

Cooper Returns

I glanced at the clock when the doorbell rang. It was ten in the morning, and Gloria wasn't beside me. I couldn't remember if she was there when I went to bed. Had she fallen asleep with Savannah after reading to her? I traipsed down the stairs and heard Cooper's voice coming from the kitchen. "We should get going soon."

"But I want to wait until Dakota gets up," Gloria said with assertiveness.

"I'm up," I said flatly while entering the kitchen. Cooper looked down at his shoes. "Where's everyone else?" I asked.

"They should be back any minute. The note said they went riding at eight," Gloria answered.

And sure enough, Luke, Amber Lee, and Savannah headed in through the back door almost seconds later. Luke came and hugged me while asking, "Have you had breakfast yet?"

"Just got up," I answered.

"As soon as you get something in your belly, I'll take you to the hospital," he said, sounding fatherly. "Crystal and Drew called. They both said Pamela and your uncle are doing much better. Pamela may be coming home today. Your uncle's awake and talking, supposedly giving a few nurses a hard time." Luke chortled, "That's a good sign—he's on the mend."

"That's great news! Well, we're headed out—my parents are expecting me home by midafternoon," Gloria explained.

Amber Lee walked over to hug Gloria and tell her, "It was so nice having you here with us Gloria. On your next visit, which won't be far off—" She looked over at Cooper. "We'll have a party—everyone can be here," she said, sounding like a cheerleader.

Savannah hugged Gloria too, with Luke following. I was next in line.

Cooper took her duffle bag and slung it over one shoulder as Gloria and I walked to his car with our arms around each other's waists. "I'll call you as soon as I get home," Gloria said.

"It was great being with you. I'm sorry I snapped. I'm at a breaking point with death—or near-death situations. These past two days were so surreal. I just wanted to close my eyes, count to ten, and imagine this was all just one big scene from a movie. You understand, don't you?"

"Of course I do. Was I in the movie?" she kidded.

"Yes. You were the damsel in distress," I joked back.

"Who was rescued by Prince Charming?" she said, looking over at Cooper.

"No. You used your fake ID to save yourself," I quickly improvised.

She laughed. "I like it—women have to fend for themselves!"

"I'm going to miss you," I said.

"Dakota, you're more than a friend. You're like a sister."

"Same here," I happily concurred as she sat herself down in the front passenger seat and I buckled her in like a mother would a child. We chuckled at this, and then I gave her another kiss good-bye and shut her door. Cooper stayed stationary after putting Gloria's bag in the back and shutting the hatch. I assumed he was giving us girls "our space." I knew what I had to say to him. I walked over. He was leaning against the back as if waiting for me. Hadn't he heard Gloria's door shut? "Thank you," I blurted.

"Thank you?" he said, sounding hurt.

"I never told you in the hospital, and I'm—I'm sorry." I could feel tears welling up in my eyes. *Dakota, hold it together. Don't you dare cry!*

"I'm sorry," I stupidly repeated but said no more. I felt sorry for what my uncle did, felt sorry Cooper was parentless, and felt sorry I had behaved curtly toward him. I began to feel tears releasing. *Hold them back, Dakota!*

He hugged me as if he could read my mind and spoke softly in my ear as if it were our secret, "I know. You didn't know about my parents—my grandparents—and your uncle. I didn't know who he was, and I'm glad."

I motioned so he would release me. His embrace loosened, but he still held on to my arms and looked at me thoughtfully as I conjured up the courage to ask, "If you had known, would you have donated blood?"

He hesitated. Then he said, looking directly into my wet eyes, "For you, yes." At that instant he let go of my arms. He walked to the front of the car and climbed into the driver's seat, and that was that. I was left with "for you" weighing on my conscience. My best friend's new boyfriend had just implied something heavy. Dear Lord, why did life have to be so complicated?

Gloria gave me an is-everything-okay? look.

I nodded and smiled at her to reassure her that it was. However, I couldn't help but feel Cooper was completely falling for me. I just hoped he wasn't using Gloria to get to me. I had read about twisted romances like that before, and right then I wanted to pretend it was all make-believe.

CHAPTER 35

Hospital Visit

Before I visited my uncle, I told Luke I wanted to see Pamela first, since I hadn't yesterday. Room 708 was actually bigger than my uncle's ICU room. Pamela was sitting up eating. She had a large bandage on her forehead, and even through her tan I could see her right cheek was already forming a large bruise. Her left wrist was wrapped in a bandage. "Dakota," she immediately greeted me, putting down her fork. She lifted her arms for me to come in for a hug. I did. She said, "I'm so sorry, Dakota. How is he?"

"I heard he's rattling the cage, so I guess he's on the mend," I said lightheartedly. "I wanted to see you first since I couldn't yesterday—you were asleep."

"I have a concussion, and the meds they gave me for my pounding headache wiped me out."

"Today how does your head feel?"

"Heavy but better—the migraine's subsided."

"Good," I said and waited for her to explain more.

"It all happened so fast, Dakota. That poor taxi driver—his family, his wife and kid," she cried. "They haven't caught the driver of the other car yet. They suspect foul play. My ex may have something to do with it. I just can't believe it. I thought I was safe from him."

I added to ease her guilt and worry, "Or some other crazy person. Maybe someone my uncle had put away. They don't know yet."

Just then a nurse walked in, which I was glad of. I just couldn't begin the morning with tears. I'd had enough crying to last me a lifetime, and I wanted answers. I wanted to get to the bottom of this notorious case of my uncle's. I deserved an explanation, especially since I held him in such high esteem.

"Time to wheel you into radiology—doctor's orders. You're having another CAT scan." The nurse spoke with reverence.

"I'm gonna go see my uncle now. I'll be back. Perhaps later I can wheel you in to see him. I'll ask, okay?" I said, sounding hopeful.

My uncle had been moved out of the ICU. There wasn't any private rooms left, so he had a roommate. When I walked in, the roommate practically shouted, as if he were on a game show and I was the answer, "Hi-ya, kid!" I jumped a little, startled. He laughed. I grinned and stepped quickly to my uncle's bed, which was behind a drawn curtain separating him from this slightly strange roommate. My mom would tell me, *it's too early to judge,* but my first impression of him was—wacko!

Uncle Travis immediately declared when he eyed me coming around the curtain, "It's about time my sweet Dakota decided to show up! I thought you'd be here when I woke." And before I could conjure up an excuse without blaming my brother, Uncle Travis said in his good ol' bossy, Texan way, "Get over here and give your uncle a kiss!"

A big smile of relief spread across my face. The sound of his jovial voice was all I needed. I squeezed him and didn't want to let go, but he said, half teasing and half serious, "Be careful now. They've got more wires and tubes in me—don't want to set off any alarms!" So I released my hold and found a spot on his bandaged face to plant a gentle kiss.

"All right, now I am as good as gold," he said. He tried to give me his usual big smile, but I could see him grimace and wince. It pained me to see him like this. "How is Pamela?" he asked.

"Good. I just came from visiting her. She was sitting up and eating." I didn't mention her leaving for a CAT scan. There was no need for him to worry about a precautionary measure. "I'm gonna ask the nurses if I can bring her to you."

Just then, Nurse Penny entered from behind the curtain, "Well,

I see you have company. Does this mean you'll behave yourself?" she teased.

"Oh, I was just having some fun! No harm done," he said lightly. Usually a wink followed his foolery. For a brief second I was worried he had lost his ability to wink. *Impossible,* I thought. And what did he do exactly that got the nurses all riled up? "Penny, this is my niece Dakota—more like a daughter, really," my uncle introduced me as Penny checked his vitals.

"Oh, I know Dakota." And she gave me a wink and asked me, "How ya doin', sweetheart? I see that you went home and changed out of those cute PJs!"

"You're still here." I smiled. "Would it be all right if I wheeled in another patient to see my uncle—it's his girlfriend?" I asked, feeling relieved Nurse Penny was in charge.

"Yup, I'm picking up another shift. Someone called in sick. I don't foresee a problem with it, but clear it with her nurses first."

Penny checked my uncle and the apparatuses he was hooked up to. "Looking good, Mr. Kenwood," she said. Just like that, she left. The roommate asked her, "Am I looking good, kid?" I guess everyone was a kid to him, regardless of age.

"Like Fred Astaire!" she teased as her voice trailed off.

My uncle and I both smirked at Penny's whimsy.

Roommate hollered, "I'm better-looking!"

"Have you watched TV?" I asked my uncle, prompting him for my next question.

"No, but I got hold of today's paper." We both sighed simultaneously. He continued, "Dakota, there's a lot they're leaving out. Don't believe everything you read or hear. It's a real shame, though, about the taxi driver—a real shame."

"Terrible." I said, shaking my head. I looked down at the linoleum floor, starting to count the squares. After some silence between us I blurted, "Cooper donated blood for you."

"I know. Where is he? I want to thank him in person."

"He's driving Gloria back to Fort Worth and then staying with his grandparents in Dallas. How weird is it that my friend meets *him* at a bar?"

"Dakota, it's not easy being a lawyer. There are times when I have to do some things that aren't … well, things that don't seem right to others. But the choices are limited, and people's lives—their livelihoods—are at stake. That case was one of my toughest cases, Dakota. Please believe me. I did what I had to do. Do you understand?"

I nodded. Not because he was my uncle and I loved him like a father. I did understand. He wasn't a heartless lawyer. He did what he was taught to do—in law school, no less.

"What about Pamela's ex? Do you think he had something to do with the accident?" I inquired.

"He's so close to finishing his jail term. Four years in the slammer and he's out in ten days. I can't imagine any prisoner being so stupid as to set up a hit just before his release."

"Yeah, but maybe that's what he wants people to think. Being in jail could be his alibi?" I countered.

"Listen to you, miss future lawyer. You have a valid point, but I don't buy it. Let the investigators investigate. You—well, you go get Pamela."

"Okay." I planted another kiss on the same spot as before and had just started walking away when he spoke in a stern parental voice. "Dakota, did you say Gloria met him at a bar?"

Oh shit. "Don't remember … did I say that?" I mumbled as I quickened my footsteps and made it past the separation curtain.

"Dakota, you come back here!" he hollered.

"I'll be back with Pamela!" I bellowed and scurried to the open door. Weirdo roommate called out, "Kid, bring me a donut … a glazed."

CHAPTER 36

Normal Again—Maybe

The phone rang. It was Gloria. "Hi Dakota. Finally, I'm safe and sound in my own room—away from my parents, thank God! You should have heard them with Cooper—it was like the Spanish Inquisition! Of course, when he left, my mom said, *What a nice boy ... too bad he's not Jewish!*"

I laughed, picturing the scene.

"Oh Dakota, I miss you already. I'll be back in Houston soon."

"Hmmm, you will? For me or Cooper?" I teased.

"Both."

"Now that Hubbell's back we can double date," I said, sounding enthusiastic.

"You were right—he is a major cutie pie," she said, sounding bubbly. "And smart, too."

"Yeah, I know, right? I'm so lucky," I boasted. "Good looks and brains!" But I was curious as to what he did that gave her that smart impression considering the brief and strenuous circumstances they had met under. "What'd he do that was so smart?" I asked.

"Got into med school, duh?"

I must not have heard right.

She continued, "Isn't it funny? My Cooper's in Houston with you, and your Hubbell's in Connecticut with me. That's if I get into Yale, of course."

"What?" I said quietly, feeling very fragile all of a sudden. Inside my head I was screaming. Gloria must have misunderstood. I couldn't deal with any more drama.

"Yeah, Hubbell told me he had been accepted to Yale Medical School—where his dad went," she clarified in a where-have-you been? way.

I was quiet. Mad thoughts ran through my mind. Why didn't Hubbell tell me? I didn't even know he wanted to become a doctor. I couldn't believe Gloria knew this before me. Did Hubbell want her to break the news to me first? I was so mad I could ...

"Dakota, are you still there? Are you okay?"

"Yeah. Yeah," I mumbled, but I most definitely was not okay. I felt like I couldn't breathe, like when my mom's casket was being lowered into the ground. My thoughts were abruptly startled when my phone clicked. "Hold on, Gloria. I have another call."

"Dakota," Cooper's voice chimed.

Oh my Lord, it was Cooper. "Hi, I can't talk right now," I said curtly.

"Hi, it's Cooper," he said, ignoring my request. "How are you?"

"Yes, I know. What's up? I'm fine." I didn't let up on my briskness and was annoyed at this unexpected small talk. Who was I kidding? I was annoyed at Hubbell and taking it out on Cooper.

"Just wanted to let you know your friend's back home. I'm at my grandparents."

"Great. Thanks," I said flatly. What was he really trying to tell me? His stay at the Golds' had been brief. He met Gloria's parents and then fled to his grandparents to play prodigal grandson.

"Dakota, I just thought you'd want to know ... my grandparents don't hold any animosity anymore. It took 'em some time, but they ..."

"Great," I interrupted. I was sounding like I didn't care, but the truth was, I was still in shock about my Hubbell moving halfway around the world to go to medical school. Okay, so it wasn't halfway around the world, but you know what I mean. My mind raced. Maybe I should have applied to Yale. I could have gotten in. I had the grades. I just didn't apply to any away schools—I wanted to be close to my family. Rice was an excellent school—like an Ivy League. Yale's deadline had passed. I couldn't go to Yale until the following year. My inward rambling ceased with Cooper questioning, "Dakota, are you still there?" Shoot—Gloria was still on the other line, too.

"Yes. I'm sorry, Cooper. I've got to go. Thanks for calling. Bye."

I clicked over. "Hi, Gloria."

Ah shit—she hung up. Geez. I knew I should call her back but I really wanted to call Hubbell and scream! How could he do this? How could he not tell me? Who should I call back—Gloria or Hubbell?

"Hi Gloria. I'm sorry about that. It was Uncle Travis," I lied.

"No worries. Is everything all right with him?"

"Yeah, he just wanted me to bring him a few things to the hospital tomorrow. I'm beat. I've gotta go. I'll talk to you later, okay?" I finished with a heavy sigh.

"Of course. I'll call you tomorrow. Bye, Dakota."

We hung up. I really felt like the wind had just been knocked out of me. And the reason I didn't tell her about Cooper phoning me was that I thought she'd feel the same way I felt about it—a tad weird. Why'd he call me? I know it was nice of him, under the freaky circumstances. His grandparents were no longer feeling animosity, thank heavens. Oh dear Lord, I was so exhausted from this. And to think it still wasn't over—who was the other driver? Where was he?

Just then Savannah ran into my room and plopped onto my bed. Well, for her it wasn't exactly a plop. It was more of a climb-up-onto and then plop! She had Paddington Bear in tow along with his book, both of which made it on the bed before her. Ah yes, escape to storyland. The three of us were nestled together under my fluffy down comforter when I smelt Beautiful on him! "You sprayed my perfume on your teddy bear." My rhetorical question was answered with a giggle. "You rascal, you!" I teased, tickling her sides. I thought, *thank the good Lord I've got this slice of heaven right beside me, my sweet, sweet Savannah.* Because of Savannah, my glass was always half full.

CHAPTER 37

Dr. Cavanaugh Phones

Well Hubbell and I had officially gotten into our first argument. I had every reason to be upset with him. Was I being unfair? My boyfriend applied to med school, and I learned about it from my friend! Gloria met Hubbell briefly at the hospital, and he decided to divulge this life-changing move to her rather than to me. Well, I suppose if he had told me then, when my uncle was practically on his deathbed, I would have … I don't know what I would have done. Perhaps I would have shouted for that sedative. The point was, I was pissed at Hubbell.

Luke called from his bedroom, "Dakota, pick up the phone. It's Dr. Cavanaugh."

What in the world did he want? I prayed nothing was wrong with my uncle. I said, "Hello," hoping I didn't sound as nervous as I felt.

"Hello, Dakota. It's Ben Cavanaugh."

"Hi, Dr. Cavanaugh. Is everything all right? Is something wrong with my uncle?" I think I sounded a tad panicky. Well, can you blame me?

"Oh no, dear. Mr. Kenwood is recuperating well—right on schedule. It's my son, Hubbell."

I cried, "Something happened to Hubbell?"

"No, Dakota," he said, sounding rather annoyed with me. "He has just come home very upset. I asked him … Well, he told me you two had a quarrel about him becoming a doctor."

What? I thought it was great he wanted to follow in his dad's

189

footsteps. That most certainly wasn't the reason why we argued—it was about how I was the last to know. "Yes sir, we did," I said respectfully, though I also wanted to tell him it was none of his business. "But it's not because I don't want him to become a doctor. It's just that I didn't know. I didn't know he applied to med school."

"Yes, my alma mater no less," he stated proudly. *Big F-in deal!* But I remained quiet, allowing him to go on. "Dakota, I know it's far away. It's in Connecticut, you know?"

Okay, now he was pissing me off big time. "Yes. I know," I said trying not to sound like I wanted to wring his neck. *Does he think I'm an idiot?*

"Well, I think he didn't tell you because he wasn't sure if he was going to get in—he didn't want to stir up any unnecessary anxiety between the two of you. He just applied to the one. And when he recently received the letter of acceptance, well, he was very surprised—the wife and I were, too. I do hope you'll remain the sweet girl you are and be supportive of our son. I wouldn't want any unexpected surprises."

Oh my God. Did he just imply what I think he implied—that I might be trapping his son with a pregnancy? If he thought I would be capable of jeopardizing his son's career with a human life, he didn't know me very well. I would never do that. And what about *my life?* Did he think I was that stupid? I had dreams and ambitions, too, that didn't involve being a mom—yet. I thought everyone knew of my Paris plans. Hubbell may be my first boyfriend, but he would definitely not be my last! And now that he was off to Connecticut, our end was nearer. "Dr. Cavanaugh, I think it's incredible Hubbell got in, and I won't get in his way—I promise. Well, I have to go now. Savannah's waiting for me," I lied.

He chuckled. "Oh yes, that precious little niece of yours—she's something else. You tell her I say hello. I'll stop by your uncle's room the day of discharge, which should be soon. Dakota, I do hope you understand the reason I called—I only want what's best for my son."

"Uh-huh," I mumbled, rolling my eyes.

"Well, good-bye Dakota." Click—he was gone, thank God. I could not believe how condescending Hubbell's dad had sounded. Gloria would have a cow. The jerk didn't even try to sound encouraging by saying how long distance relationships are trying but can work if both are willing. That was something my dad would have said. Hasn't he ever heard that absence makes the heart grow fonder? Now not only was I pissed at Hubbell, his father infuriated me! I had thought Dr. Cavanaugh liked me. Come to think of it, Dr. and Mrs. Cavanaugh rarely included me when they had family celebrations. Like the time Hubbell's grandma came to visit for her eighty-fifth birthday. They threw a little gathering but neglected to invite my family and me, even though Luke *always* asked them over whenever we had any party. Sometimes they came, and other times they seemed to have valid excuses why they couldn't, but now I was second-guessing their excuses and their sincerity.

The only reason I had met his dear, sweet granny was my impromptu visit to Hubbell, who was still living with his parents. I slaved over making him homemade chicken soup because he was complaining of a cold. When I arrived he was up and about. He told me he took Nyquil the night before and it worked wonders. I believed him. Even my own mom swore by it whenever she got sick. She said she could never afford to stay in bed for more than a day—she had too much to do. She took the over-the counter nighttime cold medicine and praised its miracle cure. Of course, Hubbell was appreciative of the soup and my efforts making it, and he seemed excited to introduce me to his grandma. His parents were cordial and told me it was a spur-of-the-moment family gathering. Yeah right. Having an elderly parent fly solo from Massachusetts wasn't an everyday occurrence. It took planning and precision to make sure she was properly cared for.

I knew this from experience. My mom's grandma, whom I called Nana, came to visit when I was seven, all the way from Anchorage, Alaska. And my mom was adamant with the airline, making sure the skycap was right there at the terminal with a wheelchair for her. He wheeled her to us. His two front teeth were capped in gold. I asked if I could push her—it looked fun. The skycap gave me a big shiny gold smile, nodded, and stepped aside. After about ten yards I relinquished the task, though. It was a lot harder than it looked to push a person in a wheelchair, especially for a seven-year-old.

When my mom thanked him and shook his hand, she slipped money into his palm. Unfortunately, he lacked subtlety. He unfolded the ten-dollar bill and was so surprised, as if this was the first big tip he had ever received. His thank-yous to my mom seemed endless. He even helped my mom get Grandma settled into the front passenger seat and buckled her in, which later Grandma said made her feel uncomfortable. With his big, smiley head still in our car, he wished us a Merry Christmas and a Happy New Year. Then he closed her door and was on his merry way. I swear when he sprinted away, pushing the empty wheelchair, he had kissed Alexander Hamilton before slipping the bill into his pants pocket. A little trivia—he and Ben Franklin were the only two nonpresidents stamped on money.

Nana complained almost for the entirety of the trip home—first about how unfounded it is for airlines to charge for food when it should be included in the price of the ticket and then about tipping the skycap. Although the skycap was appreciative he didn't acquire decorum. Mom preached that it was in poor taste to count money in public—which was not to be mistaken with counting your change. Mom was in charge of teaching me manners. Although she loved my dad immensely, she said if she left it up to him, I'd be using my shirtsleeve as a napkin!

Loretta, I paid them enough money—they shouldn't get more. My mom tried explaining that the skycaps didn't get any percentage of the airline ticket sales, that they depended on tips, and besides, that it was Christmastime—the season of giving! But Nana kept shaking her head until I interrupted and told her all about the potholder I had just crocheted. I knew she'd like that, since she was the one who introduced me to crocheting. She asked me what color yarn I used. My mom gave me a wink in the rearview mirror, thanking me for changing the subject.

Oh Mom, I need you more than ever now—dealing with boy troubles. If my dad were alive, he'd set Dr. Cavanaugh straight. I'm not the type of person to hold anyone back and certainly not the type of girl to get pregnant to trap a guy. "Leave. Go!" I hollered, imagining Hubbell, as I dove face-down into my pillow and cried.

CHAPTER 38
Pamela Confesses

I was waiting for the day Pamela would come clean to me. After all, she did like gossiping with me—divulging the scandalous lifestyle of Gerry and Mr. Drew Trenton and describing the nonchalant attitude Constance carried throughout her husband's infidelity, as if it were normal marriage behavior. But Pamela's marriage was marred with lies, too, so in my book that made her a hypocrite. That is, of course, if she knew and turned the other cheek.

Even though I was only seventeen and some statistics claimed teenagers were naïve about the logistics of real-life issues such as marriage, I didn't think I fell under that category. I had good role models and knew what true love was thanks to my parents, who had the ultimate marriage. So I wondered, how could a woman in her thirties not know that the man she decided to marry wasn't what he appeared?

His job as a narcotics officer at George Bush Intercontinental Airport was really a front. He worked for the drug cartel, smuggling in drugs. He had a good run with it until the day he was stupid and careless. When Pamela found the small suitcase in his car, she thought he was surprising her with a romantic weekend getaway—a little break from their routine of raising their baby girl, Alexis. But then when she opened it to spy on what clothes he packed for her, she was shocked to find it contained cellophane-wrapped bricks of white powder. She had seen enough movies to know it was cocaine.

"Dakota, I was scared. He threatened me to stay quiet or else I was going to jeopardize our safety. He told me the drug cartel would come after Alexis and me if I stopped his dealing. I didn't know Carlos was involved. But Internal Affairs knew, and they watched his every move. Internal Affairs suspected him for years, way before we were married. They were waiting to close in once Carlos led them to the distributers."

I was speechless.

"I was at a playground, pushing Alexis on a swing, when a man approached me. He discreetly showed me his badge. He guaranteed our safety if I testified against my husband. Why couldn't they have approached me when we were engaged? Our marriage would never have come to fruition … although it's hard to imagine my life without my daughter."

I still remained quiet. I really didn't know what to say. She seemed annoyed with this. Her voice went from explaining gravely to acting defensive. "Dakota, are you following? Do you understand the sacrifice I had to make and the danger I was in? I was guaranteed he was going away for a long time. The feds didn't even know there was a loophole in his trial. The high-powered lawyers he hired found one and ran with it."

I finally said, "I'm really sorry, Pamela."

"He is out in five days." She nervously laughed. "Supposedly he was a model prisoner." Then her voice softened. "I'm scared, Dakota. And I'm sorry, too."

"Pamela, why are you so sure it was one of his men who clipped the taxi?"

"I'm not positive, but I just have that feeling," she said, shaking her head.

"Well, presumably my incredible uncle has put away a few convicts who could want revenge, too—according to the media," I said, trying to ease her guilt.

Both of us gently lowered ourselves into Mr. Trenton's Jacuzzi. Pamela and Alexis were staying with Crystal for safety reasons because Mr. Trenton's had a security system and Pamela's apartment didn't.

"Remember the first time we met here? It seems like ages ago," Pamela said, letting go of a smile.

"Yes, I remember. And you made me those sweet drinks—what were they called, Cosmopolitans?" I asked, feeling better. I was pleased that we were both smiling and reminiscing.

"Yes, you remember correctly," she teased. "And it wasn't like I poured them down your throat, Missy!" she added cheekily.

We laughed.

"I'm glad you and Alexis are safe here and relieved that my uncle decided to recuperate here for a few days as well."

"It wasn't easy convincing him—he can be so stubborn! Once he realized he wasn't able to dress himself without Nurse Penny helping him, he came to his senses," Pamela explained in a motherly fashion.

I recalled, "Yeah. That Nurse Penny made it seem harder than it was, though, just so he'd abide by our rules. I saw her wink at me. She's a tough cookie but a sweetie."

"I'd rather have nurses like that than meek," Pamela said. "Anyway, your uncle's upstairs sleepin' like a baby. The doctor prescribed pain-killers that knock him out. I'm going to make us those drinks again." And she sauntered out of the tub, looking even thinner from her recent hospital stay, and headed toward the wet bar.

"Make mine a virgin—I'm headed home soon," I said loud enough for her to hear me.

"One cranberry juice on the rocks comin' up!" she fired back.

CHAPTER 39
Hubbell Apologizes

I returned from a ride on Christmas. I was taking off his saddle when Hubbell appeared. "Luke said I could find you in here."

I ignored him and continued untacking Christmas, taking off the bridle and hanging it over the peg. I grabbed a brush and began stroking Christmas while talking to him—my horse, that is—goading Hubbell. "You are so handsome. I bet you'd never keep secrets from me—would you, Christmas?"

"Dakota, I already told you a million times, I'm sorry," he said while combing his own hair with both his hands, seeming frustrated and desperately trying to win back my heart.

I ignored him some more, driving him crazy! I balanced the brush on two pegs, walked Christmas into his stall, and slowly turned him around so his large, beautiful eyes stared out. He nuzzled me as I slid the lock on his stall. I took the sugar cube from my pocket. He gently mouthed it from my open palm as I petted his forelock, kissed him on his star-marked, velvety-soft muzzle, and told him, "Love you."

When I turned around, Hubbell, looking like a lost puppy, longingly proposed, "What do you want me to do, beg?"

"Maybe."

He laughed and actually got down on his knees with his arms out, gesturing me forth. He looked so darn cute. I desperately tried not to smile and give in, but he cooed, "Please, Dakota. You know I'm crazy for you."

I took baby steps forward, shaking my head while telling him, "You are so bad!" And as quick as lightening I was pulled into his apology hug. Hubbell was still on his knees, with my crotch near his mouth. As he rested his head on my pelvis, he teasingly began to nuzzle.

"All right, easy there, cowboy," I said while petting his head.

Then I was suddenly lifted—my chest over his shoulder and my butt at his head. "Put me down!" I cried. "Where are you taking me?"

He walked to the ladder that led to Hank's loft. "Now hold on tight," he said as he began his climb up the six rungs. He threw me down onto Hank's bed.

I slightly bounced and laughed, "Hey, Hank can show up at any moment."

"I know he's away—you told me so. He's visiting family in Austin," Hubbell reminded me as he slowly lowered himself on top of me and softly kissed me on my neck. I melted, of course.

He whispered in my ear, "I love you, Dakota," and kissed behind my ear. "And I'm sorry I didn't tell you about my plans sooner."

His breath was warm and heavy as his mouth moved to my mouth. He gently kissed me. Then, surprisingly, he eased off of me, onto his side. His head was on his arm, resting on Hank's plaid flannel pillow. Okay, I thought, very big of him to want to explain before our passion exploded. I eased on my side, too. We were looking into each other's eyes.

He divulged, "I didn't tell anyone … in case I didn't get in. My mom got the mail and saw the letter with the Yale Medical School insignia. She was surprised when she saw it was addressed to me and not my father. She asked me about it. I was kind of trapped to open it in front of her. You were the person I wanted to tell first … really, Dakota."

"So then why'd you tell Gloria?"

"I didn't. My dad did. He bragged about it to everyone that night at the hospital. You should have heard him in Jamaica."

"What? You knew before you left for Jamaica?" I shouted, motioning myself up. I was almost off of Hank's bed when Hubbell quickly pulled me back. He clasped his arm firmly over my stomach, acting as a seat belt, so I couldn't escape as he continued to explain.

"The day we left, I swear. The mailman arrived at the same time the car service pulled in. Dad told my mom to leave the mail, but she said she just wanted to check it to see if there was anything urgent. She scanned the lot, since we didn't get any the day before—it being Christmas. Mom threw the late holiday cards with the red and green envelopes back in the box and then said, *Hey, there's something addressed to you, Hubbell, from Yale Medical School.* I got so nervous, Dakota. Naturally my dad thought it was meant for him and my mom didn't read it right, but my mom corrected him: *It doesn't say Dr. Ben Cavanaugh. It says Mr. Hubbell Cavanaugh!'* She kissed him anyway while handing me the letter. My dad, eyeing my reluctance, said, *Well, what are you waiting for, son? Open it!"*

I remained quiet, pondering. I couldn't help but think, *What else does he keep from me?*

"Dakota, I knew you were upset you couldn't come to Jamaica. If I had called you from the beach to tell you, you'd have been even more depressed. I was going to tell you when I got back, but then the accident happened. And again, it wasn't the right time to break the news. Gloria overheard my dad bragging about my acceptance. I'm sorry, Dakota. I didn't mean to hurt you." He finished, sounding utterly sincere, and kissed me.

A minute of French kissing went by before I took a breather to ask, "What's going to happen when you go to Connecticut and I'm here?"

"A lot of studying," he answered.

"I'm serious, Hubbell."

"I am, too," he whispered back, kissing behind my ear.

Our kissing led to more. His hand cupped my breast, massaging my nipple, as he moaned, "I want you so bad."

"Hubbell, I can't do this and then lose you," I pressed breathlessly.

"Come with me," he whispered. "You can get into Yale."

I didn't respond to this absurd suggestion—was he serious? Did he really mean it? I was feeling overheated. He didn't relent massaging his hardness on my privates. His hands pushed up my shirt. His kisses moved from my mouth to my breasts. One of his hands slid down my torso and into my pants. Then Dr. Cavanaugh popped into mind, ruining the fiery moment. "Hubbell, I ... I can't get pregnant!" I blurted, thinking of Dr. Cavanaugh's warning, threat, and asinine phone call!

"Dakota, don't worry."

Should I tell him how I hated those two words?

He pulled out a foil packet from his front jean pocket. I smiled, relieved.

He returned the smile. "What can I say? I've been waiting for this day. I love you, Dakota."

"I know you do. I love you, too ... doctor!"

CHAPTER 40

The Proposal

A three-day weekend was approaching, thanks to Dr. Martin Luther King Jr. His widow, Coretta, strived to get her husband's birthday on the docket to be recognized as a holiday for Americans to pay tribute for all he accomplished in the civil rights movement. Surprisingly, even though President Ronald Reagan signed off on it back in 1988, it wasn't until 2000 that all fifty states recognized it as a federal holiday. If my mom were alive today she'd be thrilled about having Obama for president—we were finally at an age when race had receded and color was no longer a barrier to achievement at the highest levels.

The phone rang, Gloria bellowed, "I'm taking the bus!"

I laughed.

"Both my parents need their cars this weekend. School gets out at two thirty, and there's a three o'clock bus. It gets in at seven thirty, okay?" Gloria said, all bubbly. Naturally, I knew her *okay* was rhetorical—she added, "Don't be late!"

She hadn't wasted any time. "I'll be there with bells on!" I assured her. "Can't wait!"

When the bus pulled in, we embraced. And a few miles later, rolled into Rhett's for old times' sake! But this time Hubbell met us there with Cooper not far behind. TJ was at home with his wife and kids. Gloria still hadn't met Linda, Charlie, and Summer. Gloria and I played against Hubbell and Cooper in a game of pool. The boys seemed to be bonding nicely. In between turns, Gloria hinted she wanted some juicy detail about my *first time*.

"I won't divulge until we're home in PJs and in bed!" I said in a hushed voice. Like I was really going to discuss losing my virginity at Rhett's—and with Cooper, no less! I spotted Cooper giving me looks of admiration a few times and couldn't help but think he was actually looking forward to Hubbell and Gloria heading off to Yale while he and I remained in Houston. I also grew suspicious. Had Gloria told him, as if my sex life were any of his business? Or had Hubbell? My dad warned me how boys boast among one another—supposedly, according to Dad, keeping score among sports *and girls* is a pastime for the male species!

We were awakened by our sweet Savannah. Luke halfheartedly warned her not to get us up until ten, but my digital clock read 9:10—she got part of the number right. She climbed up onto my bed, pulling on the covers, shimmied between Gloria and me, and giggled. "Welcome home, Goria!"

"Thanks, Savannah. It's good to be back. I missed you *sooo* much!" Gloria exaggerated as she tickled her.

"Aunt Dakota, will you make your yummy banana pancakes for breakfast?"

"Hmmm, that all depends," I answered cutely.

"Depends on what?" Gloria asked.

"Depends if Savannah is going to sing and dance to 'Call Me Maybe.'"

"Hey, that's *my* favorite song!" Gloria announced.

"Ours too ... huh, Savannah?"

Savannah giggled. "The best!"

"Any girl who doesn't love that song is crazy!" Gloria declared as she jumped out of bed and skipped to the bathroom, singing the first verse. "I threw a wish in the well ..."

"Uh oh, you've got competition!" I warned Savannah teasingly.

Minutes later in the kitchen, Amber Lee and Luke were chiming in and strutting some dance moves to our song. We could be cast as the corniest family in America for a reality show! Soon the song ended. Another good one came on, but Luke lowered the volume so he could be heard.

"So I thought the boys and I would go shooting today while you girls tended to the home and put out a spread on our return," Luke said in a John Wayne voice. He was trying to be funny, but I think he was half serious—about the meal part, that is! I was actually embarrassed for him and couldn't help but ask facetiously, "Do you want us to darn your socks, too?"

"Okay, can I hit him and send him back to his rock?" Gloria asked.

"No, let me!" Amber Lee said with furrowed eyebrows.

Simultaneously the three of us let out an evil laugh, walking toward devilish Luke with wooden spoons and spatulas in hand (I was actually holding a whisk) as if the kitchen tools were swords. It reminded me of a scene in the Hollywood version of John Updike's *Witches of Eastwick*. Luke backed away, comically scared we'd resort to sorcery! He grabbed the closest dishtowel, shimmied it back and forth as though it were a machete, and defended himself. "Girls, girls, girls, I didn't mean anything bad by it, I swear. Y'all just seemed like you had a grand ol' time cookin' together last time. And Amber Lee, I doubt you learned how to hold a rifle at Sweet Briar?"

Oh dear brother, you shouldn't have added that last part!

"Ouch," Luke hollered as Amber Lee whacked him with the wooden spoon.

"Luke Theodore Lockwood, if you want my pork chops again, all you have to do is ask!"

"Amber Lee, make him *beg*," Gloria ordered in a roguish tone.

"Gloria, you stay out of it if you know what's good for you," Luke warned lightheartedly, looking around for something more tangible than a dishtowel to defend himself.

Savannah was oblivious. She was still eating her banana pancakes bathed in maple syrup. She had turned on the TV that fitted tightly below one of the cabinets on the counter and was mesmerized with the animated show *Dora the Explorer*. I wished I still had my *Dora* nightgown to hand down to her.

In one quick swoop Luke grabbed Amber Lee's slender waist and firmly but lovingly hugged her pelvis against his. He took the spoon from her hands, placed it on the counter, and stated mildly, "Miss Amber Lee, I didn't think you had it in you." He asked adorably as if they were the only two in the room, "Do you still love me?"

She ignored his rhetorical question and said rather leniently, "You don't know a thing about me." She ended with a huff, trying to maintain a tough stance, but it was hopeless—there wasn't a mean bone in the woman!

"Yeah, like what?" he asked, smiling at her, totally entranced with her adorable assertiveness.

"I placed first in a turkey shoot," she answered firmly but with a hint of playfulness.

Luke exclaimed, "You mean, *you* shot and killed a turkey?" He put his hand to his heart. "I don't believe it!"

"Yup!"

Luke confessed, "All right, now I'm even more in love with you—if that's possible."

He got down on his knees. Oh my God, was my brother about to propose? His hands were holding hers. He lovingly looked up into her beautiful, dark brown eyes and continued, "Miss Amber Lee, will you do me the honor of becoming my wife?"

Amber Lee began to cry. Shedding happy tears she answered, "Yes." She knelt down, cradled his head, looked into his deep blue eyes, and kissed him. Another "Yes" escaped her mouth, as she confessed, "I'd be honored to be Mrs. Lockwood."

For a moment I selfishly wished Luke had changed his last name to our dad's, especially since he was all Dad. Amber Lee was just as cool as my mom, and it'd be nice to have another Mrs. Buchannan.

They stood up, kissed again, and then faced us, holding hands.

Gloria cried, "Mazel Tov!"

"Congratulations," I said sincerely. "I'm so happy for you two." I set the whisk down to embrace them. The three of us shared a bear hug that felt right at home.

Sweet Savannah was still captivated by the television. She was answering to it in Spanish, *"Uno ... dos ... tres,"* unmindful to our excitement.

CHAPTER 41

Wedding Planning

It had only been one week since Luke's proposal, and already Amber
Lee had begun planning for the big day. She insisted that I help her,
telling me she valued my opinion and it just wouldn't be as much fun
if *I* weren't a part of it. "The planning and all" was how she worded it,
and she asked in such an animated, excitable way that it was hard to
refuse! So one day after school I headed over to her condo—she worked
out of her house.

She was an interior designer, and boy did her condo exemplify it!
Every square inch of her ginormous two-bedroom home was beautifully decorated—better than Mr. Trenton's. I got excited thinking she
was going to make our home look like a showplace soon enough! Her
furniture was upholstered in clean patterns and straight lines, and she
had a mixture of antiques and practical, contemporary furniture. The
large, beveled glass coffee table displayed three books depicting colored illustrations of Europe. The book on top I had browsed through
at *Barnes and Noble* before. Its jacket depicted a French man wearing a
beret, riding a bicycle toting baguettes in its basket. I just couldn't wait
to experience the French countryside myself when I studied abroad.

She told me to have a seat in her dining room where the long, mahogany table was nicely set for two on one end. On the other end lay
an array of bridal magazines, note pads, and fabric samples.

"I made us chicken salad and mango iced tea—okay?" she called from the open kitchen.

"Yup, sounds good," I answered as I smoothed my finger over the delicately painted blue and yellow flowers on my fine china plate.

She eyed me. "That's my great-grandma's wedding china—pretty, huh? They don't make china like that anymore. You have to go to auctions for it."

She carried out the glass bowl containing the chicken salad she had made. "Hope you like grapes and walnuts. I think they give chicken salad that extra oomph!"

"Looks great, Amber Lee—I'm starving."

"Oh good," she said while serving me a hearty spoonful of salad. "I remember you telling me you don't eat much lunch at school."

She also poured me a tall glass of iced tea, letting me know, "It's not sweetened." She passed me a little crystal bowl with mini silver tongs. "Here's sugar cubes if you want." I imagined Mom calling this a true ladies' luncheon and reminding me to use my manners. I placed the linen napkin on my lap and politely said, "No, thank you."

"Oh Dakota, I am so glad you came over. I hope I didn't pull you away from any after-school activities. Oh wait, I bought a baguette!" She got up and scurried to the kitchen for the long bread. "Hope you don't mind—they're clean!" she said, breaking off pieces for us both with her hands.

"Merci beaucoup," I said in French. I was relieved she wasn't all that proper. But she seemed slightly perturbed at the mess she just made, and with her hands she swept the table bare of crumbs and scurried back to the kitchen, probably to toss them in the sink.

"So are you going to wear your mom's wedding dress?" I asked on her quick return.

"I wish."

"Why can't you?"

"On their wedding night there was a fire in their room—the dress perished!"

"Really? Were they okay?"

"Yeah, they were. They went out for a midnight stroll, forgetting they had left candles burning. Thank goodness the fire was contained to one room and the bathtub was still full of water. It was a chambermaid who smelled smoke and let herself in. She used the champagne bucket and tub full of water to douse the flames. My mom's dress was hanging on the back of the bathroom door in the plastic, zippered-up bag, and the metal from the hanger and the plastic were like tar on the once-beautiful silk fabric. None of the dress could be salvaged. Isn't that terrible?"

"Terrible!" I concurred. And then as quick as lightening I offered excitedly, "You can wear my mom's!"

"Dakota!" She seemed just as surprised as I was at my offer. She warmly smiled, "That is so sweet of you. Thank you. But I think your mom would want you to be next in line."

I smiled, thinking that my mom wouldn't have minded. But maybe Amber Lee was more traditional than I thought.

"That's for you to wear on your special day. I'm sure it's beautiful. Thank you so much for offering it—it means the world to me," she said so endearingly that for a moment I thought she was going to shed a tear.

I returned the smile. "Okay, but if you change your mind, just let me know!"

"Okay." She shrugged almost giddily and asked, "How's Hubbell?"

Huh? Wasn't I too young for her to correlate my mom's wedding gown with Hubbell? "Great!" I lied. I mean, he was great, but I was sad he was moving to Connecticut, and I wanted to avoid talking about him and his impending departure. "So are there any dresses you found in those magazines?" I asked, to change the subject. I gestured to the stack. "I'd love to see them!"

"Well, there is this one that is just so gorgeous." She anxiously got up to retrieve *Modern Bride*. A number of yellow sticky notes were sticking out of the pages. She found the right one and showed me.

I exclaimed, "Wow!" and looked just as ecstatic. Amber Lee lit up like a Christmas tree as I continued with my honest opinion. "That is beautiful, Amber Lee. I can totally see you in it."

"And this … well, this dress I thought you would look beautiful in," Amber Lee proclaimed as she flipped to the page where a brunette model was wearing an emerald green evening gown. It was strapless with a straight, tight bodice and slightly flowing skirt. "She looks kinda like you, although you're prettier!"

"Yeah right! But thanks anyway. The dress is pretty, though."

"Dakota Summer Buchannan, you have to show a little more self-esteem when it comes to your looks. You're a natural beauty!"

She remembered my middle name! Her tone and mannerism reminded me of Mom. I curiously asked, "What are your bridesmaids going to wear?"

"Emerald green, of course—I just showed you."

"What? You want *me* in your wedding?"

"Why of course! Dakota, I want you to be my maid of honor!"

"Don't you have a sister or best friend you want for your maid of honor?"

"I have a sister-in-law and good friends, but I want you, Dakota. Why do you seem so surprised?"

I remained quiet. I was touched and flattered but couldn't express it quite yet.

"My sister-in-law, Suzanne, is pregnant with her second child. She wasn't too happy with the emerald green color—she thought she looked like a tent. But considering she's quite big, I think she'd say that about any color dress. She also isn't feeling up to par—she's in her last trimester, so I told her she was off the hook but her five-year-old son wasn't. My nephew, Timmy, is going to be the ring bearer. He and Savannah are going to look adorable walking down the aisle together, aren't they?"

"Totally. Savannah will make a perfect flower girl. They'll look adorable. And I'm honored to be your maid of honor, Amber Lee. Thank you." We embraced as I asked, "Does Luke know you wanted me for your maid of honor?"

"Are you kidding? He wanted you for his best man!"

I laughed, feeling touched and pleasantly surprised with his forward thinking.

"That wouldn't go over too well with my traditional-type Southern parents. They already expressed their disappointment in Suzanne for not being in the wedding. And they're still having trouble accepting the fact that the new, young pastor rides a Harley and bares a few tattoos, even though one is a crucifix. They're thinking of changing churches, but I told 'em I wanted to be married in the same church they dragged me to every Sunday as a child. He's a cutie, too, like my soon-to-be husband! My mom has this stupid belief that men of the cloth aren't supposed to have tattoos and be good-looking with muscular physiques."

"And drive motorcycles," I added.

We laughed some more. After lunch she showed me the color of the table linens she was thinking of, the dinner menu, the flowers for the church, reception, and bouquets, the cake, and last, the invitations.

"So much to do! What's the date?" I asked.

"Well, we were thinking about making it around your schedule. When's your spring break?"

"Huh? That's only three months from now. Isn't that so soon—I mean, how can you do all this? Doesn't it usually take a year to plan a wedding?"

"I am very organized and efficient and can pull it off," she said with certainty and then looked away from me and studied her shoes. This peculiar act of hers propelled me to ask, "Amber Lee, are you pregnant?"

She quickly looked up. "I'm not showing, am I?" she said in horror.

"Oh my God!" I let out an enormous laugh and said again, falling back into one of the plush sofa pillows, "Oh my God!" And to ease her mind I answered, "No, you're not showing ... yet."

"Thank heavens. All right, all right, quit your laughing. It's not funny. You won't tell anyone, will you?"

"Amber Lee, I thought you knew me better by now," I teasingly chided as I propped myself up, stuffing the pillow on my lap under my loose-fitting shirt as a joke. "Well, it's not like people aren't going to figure it out soon enough," I said as I patted my pretend baby.

"How far along are you, anyway?" I asked, feeling very giddy.

"Very funny!" She took hold of the pillow fringe that was sticking out from my shirt and yanked it out.

"No, my baby!" I teased.

She hit me with it and answered, "Only five weeks."

"Does Luke know?"

"Of course! But he proposed on his own before I even knew I was late." She beamed, relieved he wasn't marrying her because she was pregnant.

"Why the big wedding? Why not just get married now … go off and elope?"

"My parents would die! My father dreamed of the day he'd walk me down the aisle."

"What will they say when they find out you're already pregnant before getting married?"

"Dad would get out his shotgun!"

I chuckled. "Really?"

"He wouldn't kill Luke—just scare him a bit. And threaten that if he didn't take care of me and my unborn child, he wouldn't miss in the next round of shots!"

I laughed some more and finally answered the question that began all this. "My spring break is the second week in April."

"Great!" And she reached out and opened a leather-bound calendar with her initials embossed in gold on the cover. She flipped to the month of April. Already there were a number of entries, each one in perfect cursive. She ran a finger down the page, examining two Saturdays. She slipped the gold Cross pen out of its sleeve and circled the thirteenth while saying, "My lucky number! Great—now I've got to call the church and caterers. We're having the reception at my parents'."

"And I have to head—I have a lot of homework."

"Oh, I remember those days—staying up late struggling with homework. I wasn't smart like you. I bet it comes easy for you," she complimented, walking me to the door.

"Some classes yes. Others no. Thanks so much, Amber Lee, for lunch. It was delicious. Hey, where are y'all going on your honeymoon?"

"I don't know. He won't tell me. He wants it to be a surprise, but a girl's gotta know what to pack! Will ya do some snoopin' for me?"

"Well, it won't be a booze cruise, since you can't drink!"

"How do you think I got pregnant? Two margaritas and I forgot my diaphragm!"

"Lightweight," I retorted as she closed the door, laughing. I smiled and felt truly blessed to have my new family growing ... literally!

CHAPTER 42

The Private Investigator

Drew Trenton hired a PI because the legal authorities of Harris County weren't working fast enough. Drew was a jovial and generous man, but patience wasn't in his cards. Like all of us, he wanted answers! Who was the driver of the big, black SUV that had slammed into Uncle Travis and Pamela's taxi, killing the innocent driver and then speeding away? Was it a planned hit-and-run, an illegal immigrant—there were plenty of them in Texas—or a confused drunk who didn't know what hit him? Of course, the possibility the driver was female shouldn't be dismissed, even though statistics show more males as criminals.

It could have been a number of people, and not knowing was killing us. It was very nice that Drew was making this case his priority—but why? Amber Lee told me she thought he was mysterious, and now I could see her point. Was he getting agitated that Pamela and Alexis were still residing at his estate, in Crystal's apartment? Had they overstayed their welcome, becoming a nuisance? I couldn't imagine that, since he allowed his employees to use the pool and grounds and ride the horses. They needed exercising—an impossible feat for him to accomplish on his own. He was slightly annoyed when Luke got his own horses. He told Luke we could've taken three of his, especially for Savannah, his only grandchild. Come to think of it, she had two, a horse at her gramp's and a pony at her dad's. When I was her age I only had hamsters …

My first one I named Pumpkin Pie. Then when it died I got another—Blueberry Muffin. When he died I got Strawberry Shortcake, who lived the longest. When she died, I didn't want another hamster. I wanted a dog, and I promised my parents if they got me one I wouldn't name it after a food. But that didn't make any difference—having a dog for a pet never came to fruition. I did, however, become the proud owner of a kitten unexpectedly. When Mom stopped for gas at Buddy's garage, she heard excessive crying meows. She followed the heart-wrenching sound to a large cardboard box by the clothes donation bin. Inside was a teacup-sized ball of fur. Buddy knew nothing about it and told my mom to take it home before his German shepherd, Alfonse, sniffed the little critter out and made it his snack. We named the kitten Buddy. He grew into a big, fat tabby. Sadly, he followed my mom to heaven only a few days after her funeral. I wanted to bury Buddy next to Mom, but my dad said the cemetery wouldn't allow it. So instead Buddy was buried under the elm in Fort Worth.

Although it wasn't common for a seventeen-year-old to own a house, I had been bequeathed my parents' home back in Fort Worth after Dad died. However, my Uncle Travis became responsible for all the undertakings, like paying the property tax and maintenance and seeing to any repairs the house needed. He hired landscapers to keep the grounds tidy so they wouldn't start looking haunted—this also kept the neighbors from complaining.

Inside it was just how I had left it—untouched. I wasn't ready to pack, sell, and give away any of my memories. The home was full of treasures—my treasures. Uncle Travis assured me I could leave it indefinitely. I trusted him, of course. But I also had the inkling that my house would be safe and sound as long as old Mrs. Turner lived next door. She was the nosiest neighbor you could imagine—a true busybody.

My mom rarely used profanity. She referred to it as colorful language that didn't need a voice. But one day my mom stormed into the house, intentionally slamming the door, and yelled with clenched fists, *I swear, that Angela bitch even knows when I get my period!* But her fury turned to remorse within lightening seconds. She suddenly gasped, putting her hand to her mouth and looking ashamed. She stared at us with the saddest eyes and began to cry. My dad dropped what he was doing and held her for a long time until her tears ceased. There was a wet mark the size of a grapefruit on his shirt, now slightly stained from her mascara. After she noticed it she fussed with it using her bare hand, apologizing profusely and promising him she'd get the stain out. Dad tried to hush away her silly concern. *It's just a shirt. Who cares?* he said while gently grabbing hold of her hands, causing the bag to drop to the floor. That's when I saw what was in it and figured out why she had said what she did. It was the time when my parents were trying to conceive a baby, and when I glimpsed the box of tampons in the plastic bag I could only imagine what Mrs. Angela Turner had spewed to my mom, doubtless in front of other patrons without lowering her voice.

Mrs. Turner practically had x-ray vision, supersonic hearing, and a memory like a steel trap. If she could fly and do good deeds, she'd be a superhero! At first she came across as a sweet, little old lady, but once she reeled her victim in, she talked the hopeless person's ears off and pried out every little personal detail, right down to his social security number!

At church that Sunday Mrs. Turner indiscreetly brought the subject up again. Other parishioners couldn't help but listen, for Mrs. Turner had a vehement voice that was hard to ignore. Even though she spoke with sternness, there was something of a melody to it, and her facial expressions were exaggerated, almost like those of a Baptist preacher giving a sermon. But in this instance, Mrs. Turner's approach was too zealous. *Just last month, Loretta, I saw you at the drugstore buying a home pregnancy test. And then yesterday, I saw you buying—well, you know what you bought.* My mom was speechless, looking discombobulated, as Mrs. Turner continued, *Is it a good thing, Loretta? Do you even want another baby at your age?* My mom was frozen, like a bag of peas, and ol' Mrs. Turner was waiting for an answer. *Well?* she repeated. Before Mr. Fisher, one of the ushers, steered her away, she light-heartedly threw in, *I'll host you the best baby shower, Loretta!* as if her prior remarks weren't insulting. Mr. Fisher pushed the hag along as well as he could without making her fall down as she cried, *Just don't let the cat out of the bag until it's safe—at least three months. Before then, you can miscarry, you know!*

Yeah. I inwardly laughed at this impossibility—not at my mom getting pregnant or miscarrying, but that it could remain a secret from Mrs. Turner for so long! I wanted to wallop her with my rolled-up church program, but Mom stopped me and told us—there were at least a half dozen ladies standing by, some even lightly rubbing Mom's back as if they could smooth away the chagrin—*She means well.*

She means well? I had snapped back, not believing what I just heard my mom say.

But Mom repeated, sounding as cool as a cucumber, *Yep. You heard right. She means well. Now let's hurry in. You know how I don't like to be late for church!*

And just as quickly as the storm blew in, it blew out. Later that day, Mom explained to me why Mrs. Turner was the way she was.

She and Mr. Turner had only one child, a son who went missing in Vietnam—MIA was the military term. Sometimes when I saw Mr. Turner tending to his garden I'd see him endlessly shake his head and repeatedly mumble *MIA* pausing in between each letter. He didn't seem to care if anyone were watching. He was in his own world. I suppose it's almost natural for a parent to act this way when their child dies. It's just not right for parents to outlive their offspring. A few years later, Mr. Turner had a stroke and became brain dead. Mrs. Turner always held hope that her son would return home, that her husband would wake up from his coma, and that things would be normal again. But they never were. After he effortlessly sustained three months on life support, she pulled the plug, and her world changed. From that moment on she busied herself with everyone else's lives to fill her own empty days.

Deep down I knew my mom felt sorry for her. On days when Mom made her famous shepherd's pie, she made extra for *me* to bring over to old Mrs. Turner—always in the aluminum, throw-away dish, though, so Mrs. Turner wouldn't have an excuse to stop in to return it and over-stay her welcome. *Should I pack a toothbrush?* I'd ask Mom teasingly. *It might be days 'til she lets me go.* My mom laughed and teased back, *I'll call the fire department if you're not back in a day or two. Now hurry along before the casserole gets cold.*

"Dakota, dear, can you get the door?" Mr. Trenton asked me since I was right by it. He and my Uncle Travis were on their second scotch and about to light up their Cubans.

"Sure, Mr. Trenton—I mean, Uncle Drew!" He preferred I addressed him as such. I opened the door to an incredibly good-looking guy. I'd guess he was in his mid-thirties. He was ravenously tall, dark, and handsome, and his muscular arms were practically bursting the seams of his camel-hair blazer. He reminded me of the shirtless guy you'd see holding a lady in distress on the cover of one of those supermarket romance novels. Up until my Nana's eyesight failed her, which was in her late eighties, I swore she read all the Harlequin brand love stories. It was hard to imagine an elder craving erotic fiction—or anything erotic, for that matter.

He tipped his cowboy hat and said, "Good evening, Dakota," in a very sexy way.

"Hi … how'd you know my name?" I was taken aback and mildly amused that this hottie knew me by name.

He smiled and said suavely, "I'm a private investigator, and the first investigating I do is of my client's own family."

"Yes, of course," I said. I invited him in and gestured for him to follow me to the study.

"Detective Michaels," Drew called. "To what do we owe the pleasure?"

I was beginning to leave the room when my uncle called, "Dakota, you can stay and hear what Detective Michaels has to say if you want."

Drew agreed. "Yes, Dakota, you can stay if you'd like." He went behind the bar. "Detective Michaels, how do you take your scotch—straight or on the rocks?"

Doesn't he know you have to be over fifty before you acquire a taste for scotch?

"No thank you, sir. I don't drink when I'm on duty," Detective Michaels answered.

"Dakota, dear, will you be a doll and check if there are any cold Heinekens in the kitchen fridge? There are none in here," he said, looking in the minibar fridge while ignoring Detective Michael's answer.

"I'll go check," I appeased him. I returned with a six-pack in one hand and an opened bottle in my other. I handed the bottle to the detective, who gently took it from me, saying, "Thank you." Then he gave me a wink! I tried to hide my smile—I don't know why.

I placed the remaining beers in the mini-fridge. "I'm actually going to head home. I'm tired. Good night."

Simultaneously, all three men said good night to me almost musically. I grabbed my purse and scooted out, laughing. I called Gloria, of course, to tell her about hottie detective. She made the drive home go by more quickly as we laughed and picked up from when we last spoke. She insisted, "Houston has way better-looking guys than Fort Worth ... even with the army base here!"

CHAPTER 43

Valentine's Day

Because Hubbell had been away for our first New Year's Eve, he promised our first Valentine's Day would be a memorable one—and the start to a very romantic weekend, since the holiday fell on a Friday. Luke and Savannah were going with Amber Lee to visit her parents in Georgia. I didn't have to go because I was going there in a couple of weeks for a bridal shower Amber Lee's godmother was throwing her. Therefore, I had the house all to myself!

Gloria was visiting but staying with Cooper at his apartment. Her parents didn't know Luke was out of town. And Luke didn't know her parents didn't know this! If Mrs. Gold had known, she wouldn't have allowed Gloria to visit. Gloria told me her dad was the cool one. *Our daughter's college bound—it's going to happen sooner or later!* But her mom always countered, *Let it happen later!* Let's just say Gloria was in the process of wearing down her parents' patience and was forced to fib in order to maintain some sanity for both parties!

It wasn't Luke's first time meeting Amber Lee's parents. The incredible guy my brother is, and the old-fashioned values he stands by, meant that he flew to Atlanta to ask Mr. Brickman for his daughter's hand in marriage. Thank goodness this was before Luke found out Amber Lee was pregnant; knowing him, he would have been nervous and fumbled.

Luke returned home with a one-carat solitaire diamond ring that had belonged to Mr. Brickman's mother, Amber Lee's deceased grandma. Luke decided to add half-carat emeralds—Amber Lee's birthstone—to each side. I told Luke how proud I was of him and how I really liked his personal touch to the engagement ring. And for Amber Lee's sake I asked, "So with the money you saved on the diamond, will you be going to Europe or Hawaii for your honeymoon?"

He beamed and quickly captured me, tickling my sides. "You think I'm going to tell you?"

"Why not?" I laughed, elbowing him and escaping his hold!

He smirked. "You'd tell my bride—it's still a surprise!"

"I don't know what you're talking about!"

He laughed. "Nice try, Dakota!"

Uncle Travis was back home and content to be on his own again. Pamela had been his Florence Nightingale since his release from the hospital, and I think she was a tad relieved he was back in Fort Worth. My uncle's a great guy, but he started acting ornery.

Pamela's ex, Carlos Sanchez, was out of jail and on parole. He wanted to work things out so he could see his daughter. Uncle Travis didn't believe he had any ties with the hit and run, and so far there wasn't any proof that he did—only suspicions, and the law didn't run on suspicions! My uncle was representing Pamela. Both parties were going to meet amicably and try to agree on an arrangement when Carlos could be reunited with his daughter. Even though he was an ex-con, he was still her dad. I couldn't imagine not knowing my dad. Besides, everyone deserved a second chance—well, maybe. It all depends on what they did in the first place, I suppose. Oh, I'd make a terrible public defender!

I picked Gloria up again at the bus depot, but this time I dropped her off at Cooper's instead of us heading to my house. He pulled in from work at the same time we did, and after their embrace he insisted I come up and see his place, even though I told him, "Hubbell's actually headed to my house right now."

Cooper said flatly, "He can wait." Then he audaciously added, "It'll make him want you more."

"Yeah!" Gloria agreed with raised eyebrows.

"Okay … but just a quick tour," I caved irritably.

Cooper's apartment wasn't typical of a twenty-three-year-old male. It looked professionally decorated with high-end furniture and was spotless. When he saw my surprised look, he confessed, "My grandma decorated it, and I have a maid. Lucky for us, she came this morning."

Gloria excused herself and ran to the bathroom after telling us she'd been holding it. "Bus toilets—ugh!"

"Is she an interior designer?" I asked.

"She was. She's retired now, but of course she still decorates for family."

"Amber Lee's an interior designer. Her place is incredible, too," I said, sounding enthusiastic.

"So you think this is incredible? Why thank you, Dakota. I appreciate the compliment. I'll let my grandma know."

"Gloria's the only one you should be boasting about to Grandma!" I replied rather sharply. I realized I might have been a little too harsh when I saw Cooper's brows furrow and a pout begin to form, like how he acted with Savannah when he told her he couldn't stay to read *Paddington Bear* with us.

But his puppy-dog act quickly turned to a grin when Gloria slipped her hands in his rear jean pockets from behind and nuzzled the back of his neck, moaning, "God, you smell so good." She didn't seem to care that I was just a foot away.

No, I wasn't harsh—he could take it! I said in a rushed voice, "Okay, great place. I've gotta go. You two lovebirds have fun. Happy Valentine's Day!" And I scooted outta Cooper's and headed to the elevator.

While I was waiting for it, Gloria bounced out to give me another hug and said, "Love you, girlfriend!"

The elevator door opened, and as I stepped in I spoke French. "Au revoir, mes amis." I waved good-bye as the door closed, calling back, "Love you, too!"

On the drive home my cell rang. I answered to a desperate Hubbell. "Where are you?" he asked, sounding terribly lonely.

"On my way. I'll be in your arms in less than fifteen minutes."

"Well, because you weren't here on my arrival, the first part of my surprise is shot," he said forlornly. I pictured him pouting.

"Really?" I asked with a pout.

"Really!" he answered in a childish voice.

I laughed. "I'll make up for it—don't you worry!"

I pulled into the driveway to a waiting Hubbell holding a large, fuzzy polar bear with a bouquet of fresh, red roses between its paws. "It's not shot," I exclaimed. "I love it!" And I acted as if I were about to kiss Hubbell but instead planted a loud kiss on the bear and told it, "Thank you for the flowers." Inhaling their scent, I sighed. "Divine." Then I took the bear from Hubbell's grasp and held it as if it were Savannah.

"Very funny! Now if you know what's good for you—you better give me one of those!"

"Is that a threat, doctor?"

"Yes! I can perform all sorts of operations on you!"

"You think? Save me!" I said to my new furry friend, sounding like a damsel in distress.

Hubbell grabbed us, and even with the bear in between, he managed to squeeze in a kiss. Naturally, I melted. We began walking to the house holding hands. "Your brother is very cool to let you have the house all to yourself. You and Gloria could really throw a crazy and wild party!"

"We could, but she wants to be with Cooper solo, and I ... well, I want to be with you. Besides, Luke trusts me, and I never want to break that trust." A twinge of guilt riddled me about Mr. and Mrs. Gold not knowing Luke was in Georgia.

Once inside I strode to the cabinet that held the vases.

"Dakota, sometimes I find it hard to believe you're only seventeen. You're so rational."

"Why? Why are you so surprised?"

"Because ... well, you don't want to know what I did when I was your age."

"I can only imagine! But I think I have a good idea. I bet you broke a lot of hearts."

"None. It was my heart—"With a fisted hand he knocked at his heart and pouted his lips. "It was my heart that was broken."

"Really? I find that hard to believe," I said as I was filling a vase with water. The bear was sitting up on the counter, leaning against the blender. I imagined it telling me not to believe him.

"Believe it, baby!" And he flipped the switch to the overhead speakers. Daryl Hall and John Oates played "Sara Smile." He turned off the lights. Only the under-cabinet lights were glowing. I was still by the sink, carefully placing each rose in the vase. Hubbell came from behind and massaged my shoulders, kissing the side of my neck, moving his hands to my ass, and telling me how great it was. I smiled, relishing in his touch. And then he softly spoke. "I love you, Mrs. Cavanaugh."

"Is this a proposal, Dr. Cavanaugh?" I asked coyly.

"Maybe ... and your answer?"

"Maybe," I answered seductively.

"You drive me crazy, Dakota." And he turned me around. We were face to face.

He clasped my face, looked directly into my eyes, and said, "You have no idea how much I love you, do you?"

"I do know. I'm also aware of the twenty-eight hundred miles that will separate us," I answered.

"That's not till August. Right now it's February—our first Valentine's Day—and you're my valentine." He kissed me passionately.

"You're my valentine," I whispered in between breaths.

And the next thing I knew, I was being carried upstairs.

CHAPTER 44

Bridal Shower

"Amber Lee, you're like a twenty-first century Annie Hall!" I declared as she shot at the shells Mr. Brickman was pulling. I felt like a genuine southern belle relaxing on a chaise lounge under a nine-foot ceiling porch with fans overhead and bluegrass music faintly playing in the background. All I needed now was a mint julep.

Their three Brittany spaniels were noisily panting by my side while an adorable little fluff-ball-type dog took to me right away and curled itself up on my stomach. Its fur was so soft, like angora. I couldn't remember its name, but its breed was a Shih Tzu.

I love dogs, but the panting was driving me crazy. "Don't you have a rabbit to hunt? Shoo," I told 'em, but they ignored me.

Mrs. Brickman returned with a tray of iced tea and a shiny silver bowl of mixed nuts. "Scat!" she cried. The three spaniels ran off, but the little fluff ball on my lap perked up. "April Showers, you come to mama," Mrs. Brickman cooed.

Ah yes, *April Showers*. She obeyed, and the heating pad feeling on my stomach quickly diminished. I sipped my lightly sweetened tea and examined the bowl of nuts. As I plucked a Brazilian into my mouth, Mrs. Brickman began, "So Dakota, dear, Amber Lee tells me you want to study in Paris."

"Yes, ma'am," I answered softly, chewing with my mouth closed.

"I studied at the Sorbonne and loved it. Paris is really, really, romantic," she said dreamily, as if she were inwardly reminiscing a love scene.

"Yes, so I've heard."

"Oh yes indeed. The entire semester was incredible. So romantic," she repeated with a heavenly sigh.

"So I've heard," I repeated, discreetly rolling my eyes. Mrs. Brickman reminded me of that crazy lady at my dad's funeral. "Anything else Paris has to offer other than being the city of romance?" I joked.

She shook a no and then guzzled more than half her iced tea as if she had just run a 5K. Then she took a silver flask from her pocket, twisted it open, and poured its contents into her glass, filling it to the rim. A-ha, now I see why she guzzled—she needed room for the booze, pronto! By the sweet smell of it I think it was bourbon—perhaps Southern Comfort. How apropos. Did Amber Lee know she had got a lush for a mother? Then she gestured it to me. "No thank you," I said politely. OMG! She then let April Showers lick at the top of the flask before she screwed the cap back on, praising the dog. "Good girl." *OMG, Whacko! Crazy lady!*

Within seconds I was saved. Amber Lee skipped up the three porch steps as if she were a girl scout selling cookies door to door. Mr. Brickman followed, but his gait had less oomph. I guessed he was in his mid-sixties and didn't exercise. "What are you three ladies up to?" Mr. Brickman asked in a jovial manner, a tad out of breath. Three? Oh, he was referring to April Showers as one of the girls. Mr. Wacko. Good lord, I really didn't expect this of Amber Lee's parents. How did she turn out so normal? Her sticky sweetness wasn't as weird … or did it come with age? Should I warn Luke?

"Mom, what's for dinner?" Amber Lee asked. She surveyed the bowl of nuts, picking out the almonds and putting a few in her mouth.

She chortled as if this was such an absurd question. "Well, I don't know, dear. Ask Miss Page."

Mr. Brickman gave a chuckle, too, and directed to me, "Since our daughter and son grew up and left home, my wife doesn't cook much."

Amber Lee remarked under her breath, "She never has."

Mrs. Brickman ignored her daughter's comment and defended herself. "We usually eat at the club, since it's just the two of us, or Miss Page prepares something for us before she leaves. We're really blessed when Amber Lee's brother, Wesley, phones and invites us over for supper. He married a great girl."

"They made a feisty boy!" Mr. Brickman boasted as he squeezed the lime into the cocktail he had just prepared. There was an old-fashioned cart on the veranda that held an ice bucket with an engraved B surrounded by matching tumblers. Bottles of spirits were housed in crystal carafes labeled with silver tags. Mr. Brickman's drink smelt of gin and was effervescent, so I presumed it was a gin and tonic. I was surprised he hadn't offered to make one for his daughter or asked if I needed a refill.

"Our grandson is a hellion!" Mrs. Brickman affirmed and then gestured her almost-empty glass toward her husband. "Honey, can you freshen mine?"

"Boys are different. Rambunctious!" Mr. Brickman defended as he took his wife's glass. "Sure thing, buttercup—one bourbon on the rocks coming up!"

"He has a name—Timmy!" Amber Lee reminded them, sounding annoyed at her parents.

"Yes, Tim-me," Mrs. Brickman slowly enunciated, trying not to slur.

"When am I going to meet them?" I asked, smiling, feeling sorry for Amber Lee.

"Tomorrow," Amber Lee answered. Then she suggested she and I head to the kitchen to give Miss Page a hand. Mr. and Mrs. Brickman remained on the porch. Both were on the loveseat with April Showers coiled up in between, their drinks in hand, looking very content—and *weird!*

"Dakota, I'm sorry about that," Amber Lee said quietly as we made our way inside.

"Sorry about what?" I asked, sounding as if everything were hunky dory.

"My drunk mom."

"It was the spaniels' panting that drove me crazy!" I declared, rolling my eyes. "Your mom's charming," I added to ease her worried mind.

She laughed. "Dakota, you're something else, kiddo! Has anyone ever told you that?"

"I thought I was your sweet cream?" I teased, elbowing her.

She put her arms around my shoulders. "You are my sweet cream," she declared with a chuckle. "I consider myself very lucky to become a part of your family, Dakota. Your brother is the love of my life, and Savannah—oh, she is a true gem. I don't understand her mother, though. How can this woman only see her baby once a month—if that?"

"I know. Don't get me started. I wonder if Savannah will start calling you Mom."

We entered the kitchen. Miss Page was fixing a big bowl of mixed greens—making a hearty salad. I could smell something delicious cooking in the oven. Amber Lee introduced me to her. She was African American, seventyish, heavyset, and had the straightest, whitest teeth I had ever seen on a person—seriously, she could have been an ad for toothpaste. And she wasn't shy about ordering me around in a fun and flattering way. "Now, Miss Dakota," she began, eyeing me from head to toe, "With those long gorgeous legs of yours, do you think you could reach up and grab me that big punch bowl?" She pointed to the tallest shelf.

"Be glad to, but I may need that stool," I answered, referring to the 1950s-era, nostalgic-looking chrome and faux leather stepstool in the corner by the phone.

"Well, go get it then—its legs don't walk, you know!" she instructed.

I chuckled while retrieving the stepstool and getting the large silver bowl down. As I handed it to her she brazenly asked, "You polish, Dakota?"

"Sure," I answered.

"Oh no you don't, Miss Page ... Dakota's our guest," Amber Lee reminded her, putting a halt to Miss Page's hints for help.

"Really, I don't mind. I can help," I said sincerely.

"See! The girl don't mind helping a poor old woman out. Besides, it's for *your* bridal shower, and ain't she the maid of honor?"

"Isn't she going to make a beautiful maid of honor?" Amber Lee boasted, ignoring Miss Page's rhetorical question.

"Yes. And I bet she can buff this tarnish straight to hell!" Miss Page declared, examining the bowl and then pushing it into my hands.

I laughed. This woman was a pistol.

"Miss Page, please. Please do your best tomorrow in abstaining from using such colorful language!" Amber Lee said with authority. She took the bowl from my hands and placed it back into Miss Page's. My mom also referred to profanity as *colorful language*—including the word *hell*. It was uncanny how many similarities Amber Lee and Mom shared.

Miss Page stood still and feigned an apology, "Sorry, Miss Amber Lee. Sorry, Miss Dakota." Then, eyeing Amber Lee's disappointed look, she quickly came to. "Oh, Amber Lee, I'm just teasin'. Dakota knows I don't mean no harm." Then she sweetly took a hand of mine and said, "Besides, I wouldn't want you to mess up those pretty nails of yours."

"Thank you. Amber Lee treated me to a French manicure yesterday."

"Oh how nice," she commented while walking over to the sink. "But I do have rubber gloves … in case you change your mind!" she attempted one last time before Amber Lee and I disappeared through the butler door and began setting the dining room table. I couldn't help but laugh. I thought she was funny. Amber Lee lightheartedly mumbled as she made the linen napkins look like fans, "Let's pray she behaves herself tomorrow!"

The floral arrangement arrived after dinner, but I overheard Amber Lee telling Luke, "It arrived just in time—before supper. I put it on the dining room table as the centerpiece, and we all remarked how beautiful it was and how thoughtful you are. I am just the luckiest woman in the world. And I can't wait to become Mrs. Lockwood!"

As Amber Lee turned the corner and rolled down a very long driveway with mature oaks beautifying both sides, we came to a grand home similar to the one in *Gone With The Wind*. Enormous pillars held up a two-story porch, and at any moment I was waiting for a Scarlet O'Hara–type woman to traipse out.

Instead, a very well-rounded, middle-aged black woman, modestly dressed with her hair pinned into a no-nonsense bun on the back of her head, bustled out from the large front door and waited.

We got out of Mrs. Brickman's classic 1990 silver Mercedes sedan. Amber Lee was almost running to this woman, who had her arms out and a smile as big as Louis Armstrong's. I initially thought this woman was the housekeeper, minus the apron, but was completely taken aback when Amber Lee happily shrieked, "Miss Ellie!"

And in a very boisterous and deep southern accent she replied, "Miss Amber Lee, you jump up these stairs as fast as a jackrabbit and give your ol' godmother a kiss!"

And Amber Lee did just that as I helped tipsy Mrs. Brickman out of the backseat. She must have snuck a few swigs during the short drive, and I immediately felt regret for not insisting that she take the front. Poor Amber Lee. Gloria would have given an *Oy* if she were here. I smiled just thinking about my crazy, fun friend, wishing she were with me to take hold of Mrs. Brickman's other arm. As it was, the woman was leaning all her weight on me.

I was very encouraged to learn that Amber Lee's parents were forward thinkers who weren't compelled to follow every white, Southern tradition of the past. In our drive I did notice a few homes still displaying the Confederate flag. It was such a pleasant surprise that a Southern black woman was godmother to a Southern white child and that not even the slightest mention was made of her race, because it made no difference. Mr. and Mrs. Brickman had just earned major brownie points in my book. My inner curiosity wanted to investigate, though, how Miss Ellie had become so rich!

Inside the grand foyer, a college-aged girl with her hair done up in a French braid, holding a tray of something delectable, approached me and offered, "Would you like an hors d'oeuvre?"

"Oh yes, please." I took the cocktail napkin the girl was handing me in one hand, and with my other I plucked a toothpicked scallop wrapped in bacon. "Thank you. My friend Gloria would love these!" She smiled and scooted to another guest. Before I wrapped the toothpick in the white cocktail napkin, I noticed it was personalized. In gold fancy lettering it read *Amber Lee's Bridal Shower* with the date. Very nice, I thought. My mom always noticed and admired little touches like that.

"Oh I do declare, Miss Amber Lee, that you are absolutely right. This here child is a movie star!" Miss Ellie then gestured her plump, wiggly arms out to me and ordered, "Get over here, child, and give Miss Ellie a hug. You're family now!"

I smiled and did as I was told. As Miss Ellie was squeezing me, almost suffocating me in her large bosoms, she observed, "Geez Louise, child, you are nothing but skin and bones. One week with me and I'll plump you right up!"

We all laughed. And even though Miss Ellie loosened her very loving embrace, she didn't let go of my hand. She remained holding it and told me, "You stick with me, child, and I'll introduce you to all my kin and Amber's. Now, many of these folks aren't blood-related, but down here in the South, your genuine friends are like family. Be around those who are sincere and have good souls and you'll lead a happy life, Dakota!"

I was going to tell her about Uncle Travis not being blood related but rather my dad's best friend since the third grade, but I decided to save it for another time. Besides, she would meet my uncle at the wedding. We walked out onto the veranda, still holding hands. As soon as she spotted someone she wanted me to meet, she put more bounce in her gait. "Dakota, I'd like you to meet the most incredible woman, Miss Betty Grounds." By the way she said it you could tell there was more to come. I noticed the rather large diamond on her finger and wedding band. It seemed that even married women were referred to as Miss in the South, regardless of their marital status. She turned around when she heard her name, and Miss Ellie continued, "Well, Miss Betty has a heart of gold."

"Oh Miss Ellie." Mrs. Grounds sighed. "Not again!"

I smiled, thinking about my dad and Uncle Travis reciting their Luanne story to newcomers, too.

"Dakota, this woman saved my son!" Miss Ellie declared.

"Miss Ellie, I did not! I only moved him along."

"Oh, quit being so modest!" Miss Ellie teasingly chided.

I finally asked after their loving banter, "Well, what'd you do—save him from drowning?"

"I taught her son to read—that's all."

"That's all? Miss Betty came along and flipped the switch! She changed his life—and mine. She's in special education and was the only teacher who connected with my son—understood his learning disability."

How frustrating for him. I love books and couldn't imagine not being able to decode them. Miss Ellie finally let go of my hand when she noticed the hors d'oeuvres weren't being passed on the veranda. "Where's that girl, Fiona, and her friend I hired to help serve today?" she said with both her hands on her hips, looking annoyed.

"The girl with her hair back in a French braid?" I inquired.

"Skinny girl?" she asked. "Is that who you mean?"

I nodded with a chuckle.

"She could stand behind a telephone pole and don't nobody see her! That'd be Fiona. She's a law student at Emory. Go figure—brains, beauty, and string-bean figure!" She gave a humph. "Well, where are they? Her roommate's the other girl helping out."

"They're probably replenishing the serving trays," I said, trying to ease Miss Ellie's mind. "I'll check for you, okay? I've got to head to the little girls' room, anyway."

I remembered one particular dinner party my parents hosted for a charitable league whose president was resigning from his post. Even with all the planning it was still stressful, so I could understand how

Miss Ellie felt with about fifty ladies to tend to. I smiled, remembering how funny it was when my dad sat my mom down before the guests arrived and sternly told her, *Loretta, you are not in any condition to take on another volunteer assignment. No matter how much the club pleads, telling you how invincible you are and how much your due diligence is needed, you cannot be the president of this one. Understand?* And as always, she was greatly appreciative and said in a very sincere manner, *Yes, dear. You're right. I understand.* Then with a tinge of nervousness she cooed, *just don't leave me alone with them—you know how weak I can be, and I may cave.* I laughed as if my dad were saving her from selling her soul to the devil. They were exceptional, and I wished I had told them that. It was inspiring to know that so many people felt in need of my parents and looked up to them. Their positive look on life and their mantra, *Service above self,* was definitely something for me to live up to.

"Okay," Miss Ellie confirmed. "And thank you, child. But hurry back. You're almost as important as the bride—I need to show you off!" She smiled and then set off to an elderly woman slouched over in a chair whose hand held a glass teetering on the verge of dropping. It looked like she had fallen asleep.

I heard Miss Page long before I saw her, asking a guest, "Could you help me, dear?" But I went instead and took the overly stacked, heavy tray that wobbled in her hands as I whispered to her, "Next time don't put so many glasses on it." She didn't like that. She gave me a beady-eyed glare and threatened under her breath, "You just wait till we get home, Miss Dakota."

I was a bit startled, but then a cloud of recognizable perfume swooped into the room, catching my attention. The woman bathed in Beautiful was attractive. She headed toward Amber Lee, bellowing in a deep Southern accent, "Amber Lee, is that you? I've been looking all over for you!" she exaggerated, as if there were hordes of people at this gathering. I quickly carried the tray into the kitchen, set it down, and hollered, "Miss Ellie's looking for you two." They were standing by the ovens.

"We're waiting on the stuffed mushrooms," they answered frantically.

"Well, they aren't going to cook any faster with you watching them!" I reprimanded. I eyed the shrimp cocktail on the counter all ready to go. "At least one of you should get out there and pass these around!" I pointed to the Mariposa shell-shaped platter.

The other one—not Fiona—hurried over to take the platter and scurried out.

On my return I overheard Amber Lee telling a small group of ladies, "Betty and my mama were best friends, which is why Sylvia and I got thrown together."

"Not a bad thing," Sylvia declared. She was the woman who wore my perfume!

"Really the best thing!" they both said in unison, as if they had rehearsed.

My first impression of Sylvia Grounds reminded me of the old but classic movie *Animal House,* based on National Lampoon's comic. Bear with me, because I have to set up the scene in order for you to understand *the effect of Sylvia!*

The late John Belushi played the grotesque frat boy. He stuffed as much mashed potatoes into his mouth as he possibly could, like a chipmunk would with corn and seeds. He knew he was sending this snobby, Southern belle sorority sister who was sitting across from him over the edge with his atrocious table manners. He decided to take his vulgarity one step further. He mumbled the best he could with stuffed cheeks, "What am I?" Sorority Snot was bewildered—she almost looked traumatized. And Frat Boy barbarically squeezed his cheeks and shouted, "Zit!" The mashed potatoes shot out onto her clean, pressed blouse, like pus from an overly ripe pimple, and she shrieked in a very aristocratic, southern accent, "You are a P-I-G, *pig!* That's what you are! A *pig!*"

I know it's too early to judge, but for some weird reason Sylvia reminded me of that character—the sorority snot!

"Hi," I said, putting out my hand to shake hers.

"Hello," she greeted back, giving my hand a limp shake. Oh no. My uncle warned me of people with limp handshakes.

"So, I hear my best friend decided on a small wedding party. She's only having *you* by her side—no Suzanne or Sylvia, *only you*, Da-coy-ya." She frowned. On top of not pronouncing my name correctly, her face even looked stupid.

"It's Dakota, like the state," I corrected.

"Are you North or South?" she asked, laughing at her own dumb joke.

"Huh?" No one has ever asked me that stupid question. She seemed like such a bitch.

Thank God Fiona approached with a tray of skewered somethings. Ah, curried chicken. "Dee-lish," I mimicked Gloria. She'd have a field day with Sylvia.

"So, Da-Ko-Ta." Sylvia enunciated each syllable obnoxiously, acting as if she were speech-impaired. Cooper would give her shit, too. "Amber Lee tells me you lost both your parents."

"Yeah, Sil-V-Ah," I shot right back and waited. Where was she going with her dumb-ass comment?

"How are you making out?" she asked, sounding as if it were my clunker of a car that had broken down.

"My brother, Luke, and his daughter are incredible and helped me cope." I eyeballed Amber Lee reappearing. I wrapped an arm around her so she couldn't sneak away again. "And then Amber Lee came along. She is going to be the beacon to our already happy home." And I gave her shoulders a squeeze.

"She is going to shine more light into our lives than I'll know what to do with!" I said in the most exaggerated, sticky-sweet Texan voice I could conjure up, as if I had taken a boot camp on phoniness. However, what I said about Amber Lee being a beacon was said with the utmost sincerity. She was really going to shine more light onto our already happy lives. Sylvia didn't exactly smile, but her thin lips were less grim.

Good timing—Miss Ellie announced while clapping her hands like Mrs. White, "All right, ladies, time to adjourn to the dining room and have us a feast!" I silently prayed, *Please don't have me sitting with Sylvia. Please.*

CHAPTER 45

Miss Ellie

After the bridal shower, I was so tired. Socializing was exhausting. I collapsed on Amber Lee's childhood canopy bed, my feet dangling so my pumps, dusty from the gravel driveway, wouldn't smudge her cream-colored, crocheted bedspread. I felt too lazy to slip 'em off. Amber Lee walked in, chuckling at my helpless state. She took my shoes off for me and placed them together on the floor. "Oh Dakota, you must be exhausted—cornered with people you don't even know and forced to make small talk. The food was excellent, though—wasn't it? I hope you had a nice time. Isn't Miss Ellie a hoot?"

"Thanks. I had a great time. Tell me about Miss Ellie."

"You mean, how come a black woman is my godmother?"

"Yes. I think it's great. I think she's wonderful. But it's not common—especially in the South."

"Well ..." She plopped down on the oversized chair in the corner. "Miss Ellie worked for two families, the Fields and us." She took off her own shoes and massaged her right toe, surveying the forming blister. "I knew I shouldn't have worn those shoes."

She sighed. "Where was I? Oh yes, the Fields. Unfortunately, the Lord did not bless the Fields with children. Oh, how they tried though—so my mama says. Mrs. Field was a pioneer patient for the newest fertility treatments. They even went as far as the Himalayas to some guru for some spiritual and herbal remedy. Since Mrs. Field couldn't conceive a child, she devoted her time to improving the city of Marietta and every charity you could imagine. Doctor Field was a prominent gynecologist and obstetrician, but by no means did he only help the wealthy people of Georgia. He paid visits to the less fortunate and delivered their babies for free. Then when Mrs. Field suddenly had a heart attack and died, Dr. Field became a recluse. He passed away in his sleep a few months later. Some say he missed his wife so much he died of a broken heart—couldn't go on living without her."

"Wow—that's what you'd call true love," I chimed.

"Hmm. I suppose, but it's awfully sad—to depend on your spouse for even the air you breathe. Anyway, Dr. Field bequeathed their home and its contents—all those gorgeous antiques you saw today, and fifty percent of their assets—to their long-time, loyal housekeeper, Miss Ellie May Washington."

That explained her wealth, and the plethora of nudes displayed throughout the house—most were modern artworks of the female anatomy. I think I rested my plate of finger food on a marble pelvis.

Amber Lee continued, "The other fifty percent was divided among the city's community college and local nonprofit organizations. The Fields were big advocates of the poor receiving a college education, so scholarships were set up. Anyway, when Miss Ellie became an heiress, she didn't let it get to her head. She still remained loyal to my mom, who was pregnant at the time with me. She adored my brother and missed her own son, who was in college. She needed to keep busy so she continued to help raise my brother, Wesley, who was five at the time. I also think she was afraid my mom was going to give into her temptation—the drink. She kept a watchful eye on my mother—supposedly frisked her throughout the day for the infamous silver flask. It was given to her as a wedding gift, engraved with her initials. Dad got one too—Mom uses his as backup."

"Geez, did your dad ever think about getting her some professional help?"

"He loves my mom, but at the time he thought it'd hurt her. I know, just the opposite is true, but it wasn't as easy as it sounds. You can't just send your spouse to the Betty Ford Clinic. It's not like sending an unwilling kid to summer camp. She would have had to agree on it, and she didn't think she had a problem—still doesn't. Seriously, because of Miss Ellie May, Wesley and I don't have Fetal Alcohol Syndrome."

"I'm so sorry, Amber Lee," I said solemnly. I couldn't fathom drinking while pregnant.

"But the real reason why Miss Ellie remains loyal to us is that she truly loves us, and we truly love her. Miss Ellie was an everyday fixture in our lives. She will always remain family regardless of skin color ... And Miss Ellie delivered me!"

"What?" I guffawed.

"Miss Ellie was spending the night to help out with my brother's party. He was only having a few friends sleep over, but with my mama so far along, it was best an extra adult was on hand. My dad was at his poker night with the boys. My mama's water broke while she and Miss Ellie were quilting. They were finishing the last touches of my quilt." Amber Lee pointed to a pretty, crib-sized quilt hanging on the wall next to her bureau. It was of pastel fabrics, and each letter of her name was represented with an animal. I liked the pink and blue elephants in *Lee* the best because their trunks were entwined. "Her contractions came on so quickly and close together, and she was fully dilated. I was born at home—slithered right into Miss Ellie's strong and loving hands."

"You're kidding!"

"Nope. My parents asked her if she would like to be my godmother."

I knew Miss Ellie was the staple that held the Brickmans together, but I didn't know she literally delivered Amber Lee. It reminded me of Mammy from *Gone With the Wind*— Hattie McDaniel—the first African American to win an Oscar. "Amber Lee, your mom may be a lush and your dad a—I don't know, a guy's guy? But it is pretty cool they recognized that Miss Ellie deserved to have the honor of being asked to be your godmother."

"I know. Thanks. Hey, let's say we slip into our pajamas early and head downstairs to watch a movie. My parents have quite a collection, and my father always likes company."

"Music to my ears—I'm always interested to see what movies people collect," I said, springing from the bed and practically skipping to my sweats, which were hanging on the back of the bathroom door. Amber Lee followed, chuckling.

CHAPTER 46

Triumph Way

"Luke, I have decided I am ready."

"You're ready for what?"

"I am ready to visit my old home."

"Really? Why? I mean, I'm glad but any particular reason you're ready now rather than later?"

"Yes."

He stood waiting. "Well, are you going to tell me?"

"I want to find something."

He looked at me with puzzled concern. "You want to find something. Are you going to tell me what this something is?"

"No! But it's a good thing." I made sure not to say *Don't worry,* although I could see how that'd work for the moment. "You'll be very pleased and happy with me."

"Okay, so I oughtn't worry?"

"No, you'll like what I bring back."

"Okay. When do you want to go? Do you want me to take you?"

"No, I'm gonna drive myself."

"All right, but be careful. Are you going to sleep there or at Gloria's—or at your uncle's?"

"I haven't decided yet. I'm going to wait to see how I feel. They already know I'll be in Fort Worth for the weekend. I told 'em I'd call them if I felt too shaken to spend the night in my old home."

"Oh, so I'm the last to know of this weekend road trip you're taking? Hmm …"

"Oh, wipe that puppy look off! I'm doing it for you. The reason they know before you is because I asked them for their opinion—of the brilliant surprise I have planned for you!"

"All right, you're forgiven. Now let's go eat. We've got to swing by Drew's to retrieve Savannah."

"What restaurant?" I asked. "I'm starvin'."

"I was thinkin' Rhonda's Road House."

"Great, I could go for barbecue." I also was really happy Luke didn't have any ill feeling toward that place, since it was where we ate the night Janet asked for a divorce.

When we turned down Drew's very long driveway—it was almost the length of a neighborhood block—another car was slowly headed out. When it saw us, it decelerated even more. I could have walked faster than it. The driver put down his window to survey who we were. I immediately recognized it was that good-looking PI. Luke slowed too. Both cars came to a complete stop, and Luke was first to give a friendly, "Hello."

"Hi, I'm Detective Michaels." Then he jutted his head out to me and said, "Hi, Dakota. How are you?"

Luke asked suspiciously, "You know each other?"

"Kind of," I answered with a shrug.

"I just met your sister here the other night. Mr. Trenton hired me to help investigate the accident."

"Oh," Luke said. "Good."

"Your daughter's awfully cute—she's waitin' for you."

Luke nodded, saying nothing.

"Well, I've got to head to another job. Good night Luke, Dakota." He rolled away.

"How'd he know my name?" Luke asked, puzzled.

"Duh. He's a detective, remember?" I said freshly.

"Oh, yeah," he said hesitantly. "It's nice Drew is taking such an interest in finding the mystery driver, but why? Unless he knows somethin' we don't."

CHAPTER 47

Driving with Cooper

"I'm headed out," I hollered at the foot of the stairs.

Luke called down, "Wait. Savannah wants to give you something."

As Luke came down carrying Savannah, who was carrying Paddington, I knew what she wanted me to have. Only on rare occasions did Paddington ever leave the second floor.

"Aunt Dakota, I want you to sleep with Paddington tonight—in case you're sad or scared."

"Are you sure?"

"Positive!"

"Okay." I took the bear from her willing hands and held it like a baby. "Thank you. I already feel safer."

She smiled.

Luke began his litany of questions. "Did you fill your tank?"

"Yes," I answered.

"Did you check your tires?"

"Yes."

"All four?"

"Check!" I answered, sounding like a private—he was the commanding officer, of course.

He smirked. "No unusual noises?"

"Nope. No funny noises. Purring like a kitten."

"No unusual lights coming on? You know the one that looks like a little genie lamp means you need an oil change?"

"Really? I thought it meant I had to stop for ice cream!" I teased.

"Don't be fresh!"

I laughed, "And you—don't be paranoid."

"I can't help it. This is your first long road trip by yourself. Are you sure you don't want us to come?"

Savannah looked excited, hoping I'd say yes.

I assured him, "I'll be fine. Quit worrying." I looked at Savannah. "Cutie, it's not that I don't want you to come—it's just something I need to do by myself. Besides, it's a surprise for you, too!"

Luke didn't let go of his worried look. "Oh stop! You're getting me nervous!" I relented.

"Okay, but it is your first road trip by yourself," Luke annoyingly repeated.

"Yes it is, and it won't be my last. Now, let me go without making me feel guilty!"

"Okay. I'm sorry. It's just that I love you so darn much," he said like the adoring brother he is. Then opened his arms for me to come in. Savannah had hers open too, and I was cradled in the middle holding Paddington—the four of us literally bear hugged!

I was only thirty minutes in when a light came on on my dashboard. Oh shit! I had just gotten onto the interstate. so I was going to have to wait till there was a rest stop. I tapped on the dashboard, calling, "Come on, Betty—don't let me down now." That was what Dad did with his ol' Ford pickup when it started making rattling noises. But I had Mom's loyal Honda Civic, which never gave her problems—at least not that I could remember. Ten minutes later smoke started billowing from the hood. Oh shit! The smoke became denser—it was getting harder for me to see. I cautiously veered to the breakdown lane just when my car decided to die. My head fell down on the steering wheel in a helpless state. "Oh Betty, how could you?" I cried. I couldn't believe this. Then, within seconds, a black Toyota 4-Runner pulled in behind me, and out walked Cooper. This was even more unbelievable!

"Oh my God, is this purely a coincidence, or are you following me?" I teased, practically jumping out of my car. I was grinning from ear to ear, feeling overly ecstatic and greatly relieved that a familiar face had come to my rescue. I wanted to jump into his arms, or at least bow down to him like an Egyptian slave. God knows he looked worthy. He too was surprised to see me. The Good Samaritan he was, he had just stopped to help out a bystander.

"I'm headed to Dallas. My grandpa isn't feeling well. My grandma seems worried—more so than usual," he answered, looking sorrowful.

"I'm sorry. It's probably nothing serious," I said to ease Cooper's mind. "Does Gloria know?"

"No. And neither do my grandparents. Where are you headed?"

"My old home," I answered.

"Does Gloria know?" he asked

"Yes. I may stay with her, depending how I feel," I answered.

"She didn't mention it to me. What do you mean, how you feel?"

"I haven't stayed alone at my house since my dad passed." Then curtly I asked, "And why do you think Gloria needs to let *you* know?"

"Don't get defensive, Dakota. Do you want a ride or not?"

"Let me call Luke. I'll let him know and see what he thinks I should do," I explained.

Without even a hello, Luke answered in a panic. "Dakota, is everything all right? You shouldn't be on the phone while driving!"

"Yeah, I know. I'm not driving. My car broke down."

"Where are you?"

"Just got onto Interstate 610. I'm not alone ..."

Before I could finish, Luke interrupted. "What do you mean? Someone pulled over? Dakota, don't get in their car. I'm on my way." He sounded worse now, and I feared for when Savannah learned to drive—she'd only be allowed up and down the driveway!

"Luke, will you calm down? First of all, I'd never do something that stupid, and secondly—it's Cooper."

"What, Gloria's Cooper?"

"Yeah, he's headed to Dallas—to his grandparents."

"Thank God it's Cooper! There are crazy people, Dakota, and a beautiful young girl with a broken-down car on the highway—it's downright dangerous! I asked you if your car was …"

"Luke, I know—I know," I said, sounding rash. I hated being wrong. "Tell me, what do I do about the car? Cooper said I can hitch a ride with him."

"I'll call Triple-A and have the car towed to a garage. I'll call you back to let you know their ETA."

"English, please," I snapped.

"Estimated time of arrival. You have to stay with the car until they get there," he said impatiently. "Bye." And he hung up.

I let Cooper know, and we waited in his car listening to the radio without speaking. Luke phoned me back to tell me a tow truck would be coming within the hour.

Luckily, it arrived about twenty minutes into our wait. A pot-bellied, grungy-looking guy in his midfifties got out. He reeked of cigarettes, his hands were filthy, and his dirty fingernails needed trimming. When he removed his cap to scratch at his balding head, I noticed the American flag with initials *RIP* tattooed at the nape of his neck. He eyed my glancing and told me what it stood for. "Rest in peace—for all the servicemen who died saving our country."

"Nice," I responded.

"Yeah … nice," he said smugly, giving me the once-over. He repeated, "Nice."

I shuddered.

He finished hitching the car and pushed the button to start the crane. Over the noise he loudly asked, "So you two married?"

Cooper gave a big-ass smile, amused at the thought. And I wanted to shout to the moron, *What? Don't I look my age? Why in the world would I be married!* Instead I answered defiantly, "No!" And then like an idiot I threw in, "He's my friend's boyfriend."

"Your friend's boyfriend, eh? Sounds scandalous," he said, giving a suggestive sneer to Cooper and a wink to me. Cooper, who was chuckling, nodded with an I-wish look. Should I just head back home to Luke and forgo this road trip with Cooper? But I could not fathom sitting in the tow truck with the slimeball. He gave me the heebie-jeebies.

Cooper and I carefully weaved out as my car was being hauled away. "Why'd you laugh when that scumbag implied you were cheating on Gloria with me?"

"I didn't," he said evenly, not the least bit phased at my accusation.

"Yes you did," I tried again.

Cooper turned the volume higher. The tail end of "Call Me Maybe" was playing. "Oh, I hate this song." He was about to change the channel when I stopped him. Our hands touched for a miniscule second. "Okay, if you like it, I'll persevere."

"It's Gloria's favorite song, too," I said somewhat defensively. "Or don't you know that?"

"I think it's every teenage girl's favorite song," he rebuked.

It ended, and a commercial started. Cooper lowered the volume. "So why do you want to visit your old home all of a sudden?"

"I want to get some photos together of my dad. I had already rummaged through Luke's boxes. His mom wasn't a scrapbooker like mine, but she took plenty of pictures showing Luke's progression all the way up to Savannah's third birthday."

"Then what ... she grew tired of taking pictures?" Cooper asked in a joking manner.

"No, she died."

"Oh, sorry," Cooper apologized.

"She had stage four liver cancer and died within a short few months of being diagnosed."

"I hate cancer," he said soberly.

I wanted to be a wise-ass and ask him if he knew anyone who *liked* cancer. I abstained. After all, I was the damsel in distress. "I thought it'd be neat to make an album combining both—Luke and our dad—depicting them from their babyhood all the way up to adulthood. It's amazing how much they look alike."

"That'll be really something special ... it's just like you, Dakota. Does Luke know?"

"No. It's my wedding gift to him. I also want to find my mom's veil for Amber Lee to wear—her mom's perished," I answered, ignoring his snuck-in compliment. *Why does he keep making innuendoes—can't he just concentrate on Gloria?*

"That's really nice of you, Dakota."

"Thanks. Do you think you're going to go?"

"Go? Go where? Their wedding?"

"Yeah. I know Amber Lee's planning on inviting Gloria—naturally, she'll want to bring you along. Amber Lee will give the thumbs-up—she thinks you're adorable!"

He blushed, and I regretted telling him that. Like his head needed to get any more inflated! Why did he get me so ... so anxious? I wasn't sure if that was the right word. It was hard to explain. It was as if I were trying hard to dislike him, but deep down ...

"Really?" Cooper said excitedly, like a kid scoring an A. "I never gave it any thought, but I don't see why I wouldn't go to the wedding as Gloria's guest. Are you in it?"

"Yes. I'm the maid of honor."

"Who's the best man?"

"My Uncle Travis."

"That's great! Where's it going to take place?"

"Her parents' home in Georgia—a mansion. It's absolutely beautiful, too."

"When is it?"

"April 13."

"Well, that's a long way off. Who knows if Gloria and I will still be together?"

"No, *this April*—next month!"

"Huh? Why so quick? Is she pregnant?"

"I don't know," I lied. "Why do you think that—about you and Gloria not being together?

"Dakota, I'm being realistic. She's starting college, in Connecticut no less. That's a *long* way from here." There was an awkward silence. "How weird is it that Hubbell's going to med school at Yale?"

"Weird that your girlfriend and my boyfriend will be at Yale or weird that Hubbell wants to become a doctor?"

"Both. I never figured him for the doctor type."

"Well, I never figured you for the Harvard type."

"Touché!" He snickered.

"How'd you like Boston?" I asked, changing the subject.

"Loved it—it's a great city with a lot of history, culture, and diversity. Even as a kid I loved visiting Boston. My grandparents have a summer house on the North Shore in a little town called Rockport—an artist colony. You'd love it."

"Sounds quaint. My mom would have loved it—she was more artsy. Are your grandparents from Boston?"

"Just outside. Have you heard of Boston College?"

"Yup."

"They didn't live far from it. My mom moved to Texas when she met my dad. They got married—had TJ and me. My grandparents soon followed—said they missed her too much and wanted to be hands-on grandparents. So they sold their home in Chestnut Hill—a mansion as well—and bought a home in Dallas, just down the street from us. They kept their Rockport home, and we'd all go there every summer. Sure beat staying in Texas for the summer."

"Sounds nice."

"My dad would always stay for the week of Fourth of July but then had to get back to Dallas for work. My mom signed us up at various day camps to give her a break. We were rambunctious boys."

"That doesn't surprise me." I smiled. I enjoyed hearing about his family. Somehow he had burrowed into my heart. Was it because he helped save my uncle? Or was it before that, when Savannah threw back her head giggling at what he had just whispered in her ear?

"I caught my first Blue out of Gloucester—sixteen feet!" For a split second he took both hands off the steering wheel to show me just how big a-fish he hooked. We took art classes. I did a watercolor of some famous red house and gave it to my grandma. She framed it. I even made a toy dory at the Shipbuilding Museum in Essex that actually floats." He chuckled. "TJ and I loved racing our boats to see which one was fastest."

It was nice to hear someone else reminisce for a change.

"She still has that, too!" he proclaimed proudly. "Essex is another quaint town in Massachusetts. You'll see how charming New England is when you visit Hubbell. Not so much where Yale is, but there's a ton of other sweet spots. Hopefully he won't be too busy to whisk you off to New York for a weekend—Manhattan's another great city."

"I plan to," I said evenly. *I plan to see it all with Hubbell—not you,* I thought nervously. I was enjoying listening to Cooper's childhood stories. But for some strange reason I was beginning to feel that this was wrong, as if I were cheating.

He asked, "Did you ever see the movie *The Proposal*?"

"Heard of it. Who'd it star?"

"Sandra Bullock. Anyway, the set was really downtown Rockport, not Alaska."

"Cool. I'll rent it. How'd you and TJ end up in Houston?"

"Jobs ... and the herbal sisters."

"The herbal sisters?"

"Twins. Rosemary and Sage." His reminiscing brought a smile to his face.

"That good, huh? Wasn't TJ with Linda?"

"He was. The twins were mine!"

"Yours? You went out with both sisters?"

His smirk was worse now, like a teenage boy at Hooters. "That is so wacked! Did they know?"

Cooper chuckled. "It was their idea."

"All right, I don't need to know any more. You're a perv!" And I blared the radio to the Rolling Stones. "Sympathy for the Devil" was playing—how apropos.

Cooper's smug look was still plastered on his face. Geez, he drove me crazy!

CHAPTER 48
The Kiss

W e pulled in. "Are you sure you don't want me to come in with you?"

"No, I'll be all right. Unless you need to use the bathroom?"

"Yeah, I could drain the vein."

"Oh my God, why do guys say that?" I grimaced.

He had no answer. He just shrugged his shoulders.

I unbuckled Paddington. Cooper had, adorably, put a seatbelt on him. I unlocked the back door—an awkward feeling because we rarely used to lock it. When we entered, a musty smell overpowered us. I placed my purse and Paddington on the kitchen counter.

"Nice place," he commented while dropping my duffle bag.

"Thanks. Of course, it was a lot nicer when my mom was alive. She always had a scented candle lit, and nothing was out of place. My mom would preach, *Everything has a home, and if you don't put things back where they belong, you won't be able to find them when you need them!*

He chuckled and remarked, "All moms say that. They're right, of course." He surveyed the wall in the hallway between the guest bathroom and the living room on his way to use the john. Every inch was covered with framed photographs, now layered with dust. He stopped and stared at the only black-and-white one. I was about four years old and licking around a dripping ice cream. I was concentrating and looking very content, not caring that half of my face was covered in it. He smiled and asked, "Do you remember what flavor?"

"Strawberry," I answered.

He stepped toward me. I felt his breath upon my face, "You were adorable."

"Thanks." I stepped back. "But all little kids with ice cream look adorable."

"Yeah, but you still are."

I ignored his flattery and told him, pointing to a closed door, "There's the bathroom." *Now use it and get out.*

I returned to the casual living room. It was dusty, cool, dim, and quiet. I closed my eyes to remember the smells, the sounds, and the coziness it had once contained. I imagined Mom and Dad, laughing and dancing and telling me to join in. I missed them so much and wished they'd appear—ghost form would be all right. I slowly began to feel cold and tired. A chill had crept upon me, weighing me down like wet clothes. I was feeling woozy, as if I had been drugged. I found myself shivering. I wanted to curl up in my bed, but I knew I couldn't yet. Cooper was still here. That was a mistake. I shouldn't have had him come in. But it was only polite of me to offer the use of the bathroom, right?

"Dakota, are you okay?" Cooper reappeared.

I nodded and blinked back my tears. "I'm sorry," I mumbled. My nose began to drip. *Do not cry, Dakota.* From behind I felt Cooper's hands on both my shoulders. He began rubbing them. The shoulder massage felt incredible … and wrong. He then whispered, his warm breath near my ear, "Dakota, I know how you're feeling; you're not alone." Suddenly I just let it out. I was bawling like Niagara Falls. *Oh my God,* I thought. Cooper was now facing me. He pulled me to his sturdy chest. *Did he just kiss the top of my head? Oh my God, what's happening?* I found myself pushing him away, creating space between us. But I didn't let go of him—why? I was looking up into his sexy, smoldering eyes—also teary. And after what felt like an eternity, we kissed. *Stop kissing him, Dakota.* This was wrong. My conscience struggled. Finally it won. I pushed myself out of his firm hold and stumbled back. The floor felt as if it were rising and falling, like the deck of a ship. I fainted.

When I woke up, it was dark outside. A lamp dimmed in the far corner of the room. My Mom's afghan was laid over me as I lay on the gingham blue sofa. And sitting in Dad's chair across from me was Cooper, asleep. Shit, what had I done? Why was he still here? What would I tell Gloria? Wait, she didn't know. Why hadn't he gone to his grandparents'? Why was he still here with me? He could have left and written me a note. He started to stir. His eyes opened ... to me staring at him. *Look away, Dakota.*

"Oh good—you're up. You fainted. I carried you," he said. "How's your head? Luckily it missed the table by a hair's breadth."

"Fine," I answered, feeling for a bump. "I fainted at my dad's funeral too, when Uncle Travis revealed Luke. I should see a doctor about it." And I rested my head back down on Mom's pillow and covered my face with both my hands. I took a deep breath and prayed our kiss had been only a figment of my imagination. I mumbled, "You can go now. Thank you. I'll be all right."

He stood up. Just when I thought he was headed for the door, I felt him kneel beside me. He removed my hands from my face, looked deep into my eyes, and said softly, "Dakota, you're so beautiful ... inside and out. You're so young to have gone through all this. It's understandable. We have a lot in common."

"Cooper, I'm sorry."

"I'm not."

"You're my best friend's boyfriend."

He bent over to kiss me, and I reciprocated. He was an incredible kisser—better than Hubbell. *Geez, what am I doing? Stop!* I pushed him away and jumped up off the sofa as if something had just bit me. In a firm, loud voice I said, "Cooper, this isn't right! You know it and I know it! Let's stop, okay? Can you please just leave?"

I was beginning to feel pissed off—at myself and at Cooper for taking advantage of my vulnerability. He shook his head but got up anyway and headed to the door. He hesitated, his hand on the doorknob. "I'm going to end it with Gloria," he said while keeping his back to me.

"Don't—please don't, Cooper."

"I love. I love you, Dakota." And with that, Cooper walked out the door, leaving me with only my houseful of memories for company, feeling more bewildered than when I had entered it two hours ago, with the taste of his kiss lingering on my lips.

CHAPTER 49

Alone

The house was cold. I turned up the thermostat and turned a light on in every room and drew its shades. I didn't need anyone seeing in, especially old Mrs. Turner. I've had enough excitement for one day. My cell rang. It was Hubbell. I let it go to voicemail. I couldn't talk to him right then. I felt guilty and was afraid of sounding nervous. But then, he was probably worried. He'd call Luke to see if I had checked in. Luke would tell him my car broke down and Cooper came to my rescue—and that I hitched a ride with him! Then he'd call Gloria to see if I was with her because of Cooper. Then she'd find out about Cooper being here with me—the snowball effect. *Ugh.*

I decided to call Luke. "I'm safe and sound in my old home," I said, sounding all cheery so he needn't worry anymore. "It feels great!" I lied.

"Yes, the doors are locked. No, we didn't stop for food." I didn't even think of that. Suddenly I was feeling hungry. "I'll order takeout and have it delivered. Yes, the heat is working. So is the electricity and water. Uncle Travis told me he left it on because of my uncertainty. I'll let you know when you can pick me up at the bus depot. No, I don't want to depend on Cooper—he may need to stay longer. His grandpa's ill." *But really, it's because we kissed and I feel terrible and I can't look at him.* "All right, I've got to start my project—your surprise wedding gift. Good night, and give Savannah a kiss for me." Click.

I had promised Gloria I'd call her when I got here, but what would I say about Cooper driving me? She'd become upset at him for not letting her know he was in Dallas, so close to her. She'd want to see him, but would he want to see her? I sketched the synopsis in mind as if it were a trailer for some love story. He held me, whispered in my ear, kissed me. I surrendered. We passionately kissed. And he told me he loved *me!* Usually those three little words makes people feel good, but I felt terrible.

Instead I decided to call Uncle Travis. It was brief. He was still at the office. He asked if everything in the house was working and reminded me the one utility he did shut off was the phone—and cable, of course. I told him I'd be too busy looking in boxes and wouldn't have time for television anyway. He said he'd pick me up in the morning to take me out for breakfast. I already was looking forward to it.

Okay. Now I knew I needed to call Hubbell, but before I did I listened to his message. *Hi Babe—my dad's not feeling well, so Mom's making me take his place and take her to some play. I have to turn off my cell—don't want you to worry. I'll call you in the morn. Bye. Love you.*

Awesome! I decided to wait until Gloria called me. I rummaged the junk drawer for Pizza Hut's menu. I ordered a small pepperoni, a garden salad, and a liter of Pepsi. I noticed my cell was running low. I searched my duffle for the charger. Shoot, I had absentmindedly left it at home. Luke's checklist didn't sound so dumb after all—although he didn't ask me if I had my charger! I put the kitchen radio on. It was old and spotted with splattered food—a far cry from Luke's Bose, but it worked. It was still tuned into Dad's station, the Oldies but Goodies channel. I jiggled it a bit to erase the static, and Aretha's voice came in clearer. "Respect" was playing.

I knew where Mom kept Dad's childhood photos—in the attic—but I wouldn't be able to hear the doorbell from there when the pizza arrived, so I decided to start with the albums in the family room. Both shelves housed them from bottom to top. Dad built them custom for that purpose. I got out the sticky notes from the junk drawer so I could mark which pages I needed to scan. In addition to putting together an album for Luke, I was going to make a slideshow with music. He loved a lot of the songs my dad did, so it'd be easy and add a sentimental touch.

My pizza arrived. After eating, I pulled down the stairs to the attic. My mom was a collector, but not of anything worth auctioning off at Sotheby's! It wasn't the monetary value my mom cherished—it was the sentiment behind the many trinkets in her possession that held great meaning for her. Whether they were her own purchases or gifted to her, she kept them. I was with her when she found a small sculpture of two dolphins leaping out of a wave. It was made of cheap resin with "Made in China" stamped on the bottom, but she bought it because it reminded her of the time she and Dad swam with the dolphins during their honeymoon.

She also kept everything I made in school and at home on those rainy or scorching-hot summer days where all you could do was stay in with the air conditioner as your best companion. I patiently opened the long-buried treasures and soon was lost in a sea of memories. Although my life hadn't stopped spinning since my dad's death, I felt the past was more alive in my heart right at that moment than my present aloneness was. Object after object stirred a sentimental hunger in my heart, like the longing a gardener felt in the winter for the fragrance of jasmine, lilac, and heather. I chose lilacs to be placed on my mom's casket because they smelt the prettiest, like her. I unearthed a wind chime my mom wrapped so carefully that its strings easily became untangled as I held it up. We had cleverly made it from a wire hanger and seashells Mom and I collected when Dad surprised us with a trip to Sanibel Island. Then I unwrapped a decoupage box that had once been a milk carton. I made it for Dad for Father's Day. It used to be on his dresser and housed his loose pocket change—my money for when the ice cream truck drove down our street, playing its come-hither tune.

Mom was very organized, so finding what I came here for was effortless. In black marker the box was labeled "JETHRO'S CHILDHOOD PHOTOS" in Mom's neat penmanship. Gosh, it was heavy. How'd she get it up these stairs unless she filled it up here? I decided to sit on my purple childhood stool and go through the box there. I carefully ripped the clear packing tape away and opened the filled-to-the-brim box.

It was uncanny. Even though Savannah was a girl, there were a few photos of Jethro between four and five years old that resembled her. I put those in the take-pile. Dad would have loved being a grandpa. He would have devoured Savannah, doting over her and spoilin' her rotten! I missed him terribly—more so now than ever before. I started getting teary-eyed. The take-pile grew and toppled. I decided I had enough. It was time to pack up and get to bed. Out of the many empty bags my mom had hanging, I chose the sturdy LL Bean canvas beach bag monogrammed with a big, capital B in navy blue. We never used it for the beach but for our arts and crafts projects that required lots of supplies. Now I was filling it with mementos. I hauled the heavy bag down and placed it near the back door. I made one more trip up to find my mom's wedding dress bag. I knew the veil was inside, too. I found it hanging up and labeled—easy peazy! I carried it down and placed it on my parents' bed. I pushed back the hideaway stairs and flipped the light switch. I was so tired. The oven clock read 11:35. I washed up and afterward headed to each room, turning off the lights I had foolishly turned on because I felt scared. Before I climbed into my bed, I thought it'd be a good idea to shake my bedspread free of dust. But I was childishly scared to go outside in the dark, so I decided to shake it in the garage. And that's when I became most terrified.

CHAPTER 50
The Intruder

Oh my God. A million questions came to mind. My body was quickly covered in goose bumps like a bad rash. With shaking hands and a racing heart, I cautiously walked around it as if a dead body might be inside—inside the phantom-black Cadillac Escalade with tinted windows. What was Mr. Jennings' car doing here? The front grill was smashed in. Oh my God, it was the hit-and-run vehicle. Why did he want my uncle and Pamela killed? I had to call Uncle Travis.

Suddenly the garage door was opening. I ran back in, quickly flipping the light off and closing the door. I tried to lock it but remembered Dad had never fixed the lock. I ran to my room, turned off the light, and scurried under my bed. My cell was on the dresser. Did I have time to get it? Did I even have enough juice to call 911? It was too late. The intruder was in—in *my* house. A disturbingly familiar voice called my name. "Dakota."

I lay absolutely still, paralyzed like an animal surprised by a hunter, uncertain whether to stay or flee. I was so scared—more scared then when I had lost my parents at the mall. I was eight, and supposedly it was maybe three minutes, but those were the longest and most frightening minutes of my life until now.

"Dakota, I know you're in here," the intruder said firmly. Then he added creepily, as if this were a game, "Come out, come out, wherever you are."

The freaky dad from *The Shining* popped into my mind. I didn't move. "I won't hurt you … let me explain." If I hadn't shaken my bedspread, I wouldn't have seen the car. I would have been in bed when he broke in. "I just spoke with your uncle. He mentioned you were here—came to get pictures of your dad. Dakota, I'm gonna find you, and when I do …"

He was in my room. His polished, chestnut-colored cowboy boots were staring at me. They moved away, but within seconds I was quickly and painfully pulled out by my legs. I screamed and flailed desperately. I grabbed onto the bed sheet that hung over—of course, it didn't help me in any way. I was fully out from under my bed, and I squirmed ferociously, trying to break free of his tight grip. In his hands I struggled like a dying fish, praying a neighbor would hear my screams. My nightgown was pulled up to my shoulders, and my breasts were showing. I was thankful I had underpants on. He slapped me so hard across my face that his big-ass college ring cut me, and blood started to form. He pushed me down onto my bed, and his two-hundred-pound body smothered me. His hand pushed down on my mouth to muffle my screams. "Shut up!" he shouted. "Shut up!"

My face was throbbing. I stopped screaming. I was terrified he was going to hit me again. And that's when I realized who it was—I could put a face to the voice. I stopped screaming and heaved, "Mr. Jennings."

"Shh, that a girl. Shh," he said breathlessly with his piercing eyes on mine like I was his prey. I was trying to calm down and reclaim some composure, but I couldn't get past what was happening to me. "You've blossomed. Sweet, sweet Dakota," he whispered in heavy breaths with a sinister Jack Nicholson smile. After my unsuccessful struggle to break free, our bodies were covered with perspiration. His heavy body weighed down on my scantily dressed body—I was wearing a silk nightgown of Mom's. I stared at him as perverse thoughts spun through my mind. Oh my God, was he going to rape me? I nervously sniveled, "What do you want?"

"Okay. I'm going to get off of you, but promise me you won't run. I have a gun, Dakota. Please don't make me use it on you tonight."

Tonight as opposed to another night? I could not believe the owner of Jennings Petroleum, my dad's boss, was a killer. And I could not fathom that I might be his next victim. My cell rang. I had the urge to run for it and shout for help. Mr. Jennings threatened, "Don't you dare." It stopped ringing on the second ring—either the person hung up or my phone died.

He sat across from me on my worn-down, comfy chair as I stayed on my bed. My back was propped up against the wall. I felt almost naked and wanted to cover myself. "Can you throw me my robe? You're sitting on it." Surprisingly, he did. And it was then that I saw his gun, tucked in its holster. He wasn't lying. Funny, I hadn't felt it when he was on top of me.

"I didn't kill your dad, despite what your uncle is trying to prove. What he told you is a lie."

What is he talking about? My uncle hadn't mentioned a word of this. I pretended like he had. "Lies ... they were lies? Why should I believe you?"

A contemptuous smile formed on what I used to think was a handsome face. Now he was a monster. "I had a lucrative business until your dad's accident messed it all up."

I knew my uncle didn't strip the company in my lawsuit. But I remained quiet.

"Yup, my other source of income was assisting one of the largest drug cartels in South America," he said nonchalantly. He went on to explain, as if he were a teacher about to pull up a PowerPoint, "I was the middleman—point B. I made sure it got to point C—the distributers. I was making millions until the accident. His death attracted all kinds of people, drawing in unnecessary publicity from journalists, investigators, stockholders, even environmentalists—the worst. The cartel was afraid our operation would be blown. They went elsewhere and found another middleman, but it's only a matter of time before they kill me. I know too much. Your dad's carelessness sabotaged my business."

I was slowly nodding, like a bobble head on a car's dashboard, trying to process all this info. I was puzzled—more like shocked, really.

"Petroleum disguises its scent—the dogs walk right by it." He chuckled mischievously, feeling very pleased at this.

"Dogs?" I asked.

"Yup. The dogs the drug traffickers use to sniff out the drugs. You see, Dakota, I supply the fuel for Dallas/Fort Worth International and George Bush Intercontinental airports. My fuel gets pumped into the planes. Then my barrels are emptied, but that sweet scent of gasoline permeates them. The empty barrels discreetly get filled with bags of coke and ride right out of the airport scot free—brilliant, isn't it?"

"Sounds incredible," I said sarcastically. "So what—my dad found out, and you made his death look like an accident on the job?"

He didn't answer me but decided to divulge further about his drug business. "It was all so good. Carlos Mendez made sure everything ran smoothly at the airports ... until his stupid wife halted our operation."

"So you wanted to kill Pamela, not my uncle?"

He ignored my question again. His face was suddenly stony. "She only set us back. She didn't stop it—another narc was involved in the operation, Carlos's partner. No fingerprints led to him. He was a lot smarter than Carlos. He didn't have a bitch that'd rat him out!"

"Pamela's not a bitch!" I defended. "She's an incredible mom." A fleeing thought of Alexis becoming motherless made my heart ache.

"Your uncle became suspicious when he fought for your settlement. You're a poor little rich girl, Dakota—worth millions. My millions!" His face twisted with anger, and for a moment I could see the madness alive in his eyes, "What I made in a year with the cartel took Jennings Petroleum five years to acquire. Fuel's a lucrative business, don't get me wrong, but the money was faster and easier with the drug cartel."

"Yeah, and also illegal!" I reminded him. I thought of Mathew from my old school, who died of a drug overdose. He was the richest kid in school. He drove a red Corvette. He was a real showoff and party boy, but he was too stupid to realize his limits. He thought he was invincible. In a way, Mr. Jennings played a part in his death.

"Your uncle just couldn't stay away after we settled. The check was astronomical, too. Don't think for a minute he was doing it all for you,

Dakota. His take was thirty percent. His fee was close to a million dollars. You won three million dollars, Dakota!" He said matter-of-factly.

"I won? I don't consider my dad's death a contest, Mr. Jennings," I said sternly. I didn't care about the money. I'll probably end up giving most of it away. I could never spend that in my lifetime—I'm just not an extravagant person.

"Please call me Jake," he said calmly, as if he wanted to make peace.

"So the machine really did go berserk, Jake? You didn't make it look like an accident?"

"Dakota, why would I want to attract attention to my company if I was running drugs for the most prestigious drug cartel in South America?"

"Oh, so drug cartels are prestigious now?" I said facetiously, feeling relieved he hadn't killed my father.

He laughed. "Dakota, you're very wise for your age." He smoothed down his hair with both his hands, reminding me of Cooper. What if Cooper had spent the night with me? Would we have been in my bedroom making love, or would he have slept on the sofa and cut Jake off at the pass?

"And you're very stupid for yours. You should have kept your machines running smoothly like your drugs," I said evenly, reminding myself of the cop shows Dad and I watched together.

"I was planning on having your dad killed," he rebutted. I could feel my blood boil. I wanted to lunge at him and beat him to a pulp. Instead I remained fixed on his sinister face. "Just not at my company. I didn't want to jeopardize the family's business," he finished with an evil sneer, like a villain.

I cried, "My dad murdered? Why?" I dried the sweat off my palms, rubbing them back and forth on the knees of my terry robe. Then I began twisting its tie around my fingers like I had with the handkerchief at Dad's funeral.

"I heard him talking on the phone late one night, still at the refinery. Why'd he stay so late when he's got you, his sweet daughter Dakota, waiting for him at home? When your mom was alive, he punched out on the nose. At 5:01 he was out the door, headed home. I bet you started rebelling, didn't you, Dakota? You got interested in boys and stayed out past your curfew. Your father couldn't handle you no more."

"Shut up! You don't know what you're talking about," I yelled, having the urge to punch him.

He smiled as if my anger amused him. "Jethro said he thought he saw what looked like the remnants of cocaine in one of the barrels. There must have been a busted bag—probably happened in transit," he explained.

"You make it sound as if it were groceries you were transporting," I said angrily.

"Your uncle told me your dad called him that morning, but he didn't get the message until after the accident. Travis became suspicious. He even threatened me. I assumed he was going to let it go after he cashed his million-dollar commission check.

"You can't put a price on someone's life," I reminded.

"Who says? I bet you didn't know your uncle lowers his fee for female clients—sometimes he even waives it for the pretty ones, if they perform. Did you perform, Dakota?" He sneered, reminding me of the slimeball tow truck driver.

"You're disgusting!" I charged.

"I know he wasn't blood-related, Dakota. He was friends with your daddy since the third grade, right? Every time they told that story it sounded more stupid."

"Shut up!" I shouted, hugging my arms to my chest. I felt fire surging through my body. I knew my uncle was a big flirt, but I didn't know he was disreputable.

Jake didn't shut up. He was sounding more worked up, getting angrier with each hateful word he spewed. "Travis raised the red flags, sending all types of environmentalists to the refinery checking for gas leaks. Those stupid green thumbs, tree huggers, are worse than the police—they're fanatics!"

"You killed the taxi driver. He was a dad. He was innocent—like my dad, you son of- a bitch," I said, feeling overheated and full of rage. The doorbell suddenly startled us. Within seconds we heard knocking, followed with a voice—a familiar voice.

CHAPTER 51

Because of Angela

An elderly female voice rang out. "Dakota, Dakota, are you in there? Are you okay, dear? I thought I heard screaming." *Yeah, but that was like, twenty minutes ago. What took you so long Mrs. Turner?*

Jake asked, agitated, "Who is she?"

"Angela Turner—a neighbor. She's persistent. If you won't let me answer, she'll call the fire department. Honest. I wouldn't put it past her." *Shit, why did I tell him that? That would've been good. I was so dumb during times of crisis.*

"Okay … but one false move, Dakota—" He opened his jacket to show me his gun. He concealed himself in the hallway behind the opened bathroom door. I then opened the front door. Even though it had been less than a year since I saw Mrs. Turner at my dad's funeral, she looked as if she had aged ten. She was frailer, and her slouch was more prominent.

"Dakota, what in the world happened to you? Your face—it's cut. Let me help you." She pushed her way in past me.

I had forgotten about my face. "No, no, please. I'm fine," I lied. "I fell looking for my mom's wedding dress." But it was too late—she was standing in the pint-sized foyer, and she slowly made her way to the kitchen. I followed her wobbly gait.

She tore off a paper towel, wet it, and then turned to me. "Sit," she said sternly, gesturing me over to the stool by the vintage-looking wall phone that Mom ordered from Pottery Barn. I obeyed and allowed Mrs. Turner to gently dab my left cheek. She said as she cleared away the already-crusted blood, "Dakota, are you getting married? You're too young, dear. How old are you, twenty-one?"

I could see that dementia had set in, too. "Mrs. Turner, you were at my dad's funeral less than a year ago—I was sixteen then. I turned seventeen in October."

"Honey, your dad died seven years ago."

"No. My mom did, Mrs. Turner," I corrected, hoping it would refresh her memory.

She became flustered. "Oh heavens. That's terrible. Put the kettle on, dear. Let's have some tea and talk about it." And then just as quickly as a person with short-term memory would, she asked, "Are your parents asleep? I don't want to wake them."

Oh my God, it was worse than I thought. I eyeballed Jake spying on us, and I shrugged my shoulders at him behind Mrs. Turner's back. Well, I thought it was behind her back. What my mother always said about the woman was true. *Nothing gets past her—she's like a hawk.*

"Dakota, do you have someone here?"

"What?"

"Dakota, I may have been born at night but not last night! Are you hiding a boy? Does your father know?" she asked angrily.

Just a minute ago she thought my parents were asleep. Now she thought I was a slut? "Mrs. Turner, what are you talking about?" I asked, trying to sound surprised. Inwardly I was thrilled Mrs. Turner was still sharp as a blade … at some things.

"I saw you looking over there," she said, heading in the direction where Jake was. Oh my God, was he going to hurt her? She looked behind the door. "Nothing here." Where'd he go? She peeked her head into my bedroom. "No one here." She eyed my parents' open bedroom door and asked, "Where's your parents?" More importantly, where was Jake Jennings? Suddenly the teakettle howled. I ran to it and quickly turned off the burner. She stopped her sleuthing and said excitedly, "Our tea—I almost forgot!" Making her way back into the kitchen she lightheartedly ordered, "I take one teaspoon of sugar and a squirt of lemon."

Poor Mrs. Turner—forgetful was too light of a word for what she had. I opened the fridge in hopes there'd be a lemon. There happened to be a lonely one. Its skin was as pruned as Mrs. Turner's skin. I sliced into it in hopes it would have some zest for her tea. Thankfully it had, and she commented, "Dakota, you make a lovely cup of tea, like your mother."

"My mother had you over for tea?" I asked, surprised.

"Oh yes, all the time. The minute you got on that bus to school, she told me to come over."

I really didn't believe my mother did that. I think Mrs. Turner was mistaking Mom with someone else. I knew my mom had a heart of gold, but her patience grew thin with Mrs. Angela Turner. I once over-heard Mom telling Dad, *That woman doesn't fit her name. She's the far-thest thing from an angel—closer to the devil!* My dad chuckled and asked, *Loretta, what did she do now?*

"Mrs. Turner, I don't mean to be rude, but I am really tired. I need to go to bed—okay? You need to leave."

She glanced at the oven clock, which read 12:34. "All right, dear. It is very late. But let me use the little girls' room first."

I suppose, with her one-mile-an-hour gait, she probably wouldn't make it home before peeing her pants. "Certainly," I said as she toddled to the toilet.

I heard a faint creak—the loose floorboard Dad never had fixed. Jake crept up, closing the distance, quiet as a cat. He slowly touched my shoulder with his hand, startling the shit out of me, as he demanded in a hushed voice, "Get rid of her."

A surge of energy shot up through my body as if I had nothing to lose. I brazenly asked, "What then, Jake? When she leaves, what are you going to do? You can't get away with it … unless you kill me! Are you going to kill me and make it look like an accident?" I spoke loudly, ignoring the fact Mrs. Turner was only a few steps away and could hear.

"Lower your voice, Dakota!"

"She's hard of hearing, too!" I declared matter-of-factly, even though

I really didn't know if this were true or not. Instantaneously from behind I spied Mrs. Turner with a can of Lysol, ready to shoot! Jake turned, and Mrs. Turner sprayed into his eyes like there was no tomorrow. He screamed bloody murder. I grabbed my mom's heaviest casserole dish and smashed it on his head. He fell. Jake Jennings was down! Angela stared at him and then up at me with a look of utter amazement. Her eyes bulged like a cartoon character's, ready to pop from her head. "Call the police!" she shouted. I returned the astounded look. "Call the police," she repeated with iron in her voice. The urgency sunk in. I instinctively ran to the wall phone. Shit—nothing. I ran for my cell in the bedroom. Shit—that was dead, too. "Mrs. Turner, we need to run to your house and call the police!" I yelled, returning to her out of breath.

She gripped my forearm and stared into my eyes. "You run, dear—the door's unlocked." She was squeezing my arm hard, using it to help hold herself up. "I'd slow you down, dear." I walked her to a stool. "Go, Dakota." She saw my worried look. "I'll be okay—Go!"

I fled my home for hers but not fast enough—I was shot. Shot in the leg. The pain wasn't anything you could imagine unless you've been shot. At first it was the sound—the gun going off—that scared me the most. Then the sight of blood—my blood spewing from my leg as I collapsed on Mrs. Turner's lawn—put me into a state of delirium. This couldn't be happening to me. I felt as if I had been drugged. My dentist, Dr. Samuels, appeared, giving me laughing gas. I was hallucinating. All the people I loved flashed in front of me as if a soundless movie starring my family was playing right before my eyes. I felt helpless and hopeless. Looking up into the deep sky, I examined the heavens. The stars marked the dark sky like diamonds in a mine. Then I heard my dad's voice shouting *Run!* as he had at my Little League games. *Run, Dakota!* I suddenly felt powerful. My endorphins kicked in, and I said to myself, *I'm not ready to die!* I gathered my stamina, put all my life into my legs, and scrambled up like a cat and ran with my heart full of fire to live. I furiously limped into Mrs. Turner's home. It was a matter of life or death. I grabbed the phone and pushed 911 like I was giving it CPR. "Help! I've been shot. Come to Triumph Way—10—"

CHAPTER 52

Nurse Penny

The police traced the call and sped to the Turner home, where I had passed out from loss of blood. They found Mrs. Turner and Jake Jennings at my house—one dead and the other unconscious.

I cried, "No!" when I had heard it was Mrs. Turner who had died. A female officer rode in the ambulance with me. As she sat next to me, holding my shaking hand, she gently spoke. "The old woman put up a strong fight. She knocked the guy unconscious with an iron skillet and had herself a heart attack seconds later." Tears streamed down my face. She must have put all her strength into hoisting Mom's heavy pan to save *my* life. I repeated aloud to the nice officer, letting her know the old woman had a name, "Angela. Angela Turner ... saved my life."

"She certainly did. She was your superhero!" The officer confirmed with a smile and a squeeze of my hand.

I don't know why. Maybe delirium was the cause, but I imagined Mrs. Turner saying, *Hasta la vista, baby!* Although I doubt she ever watched those Arnold Schwarzenegger movies, in my mind, at that death-threatening moment, she *was* the Terminator! "I'll never forget her as long as I live," I said with a hint of a smile.

"I surely hope not. This one's going in the book—*My Years on the Police Force*. Wait till the precinct hears about Old Lady Turner saving Dakota Buchannan from Jake Jennings—gone mad!" she said, sounding heroic. She gave my hand a light squeeze. "Unbelievable! Was it the money?"

She didn't wait for an answer; "Money does funny things to people. But you deserved every bit of it!" Then as quick as lightening she
realized she had been rambling on—and about a not-so-comforting
topic, considering my current circumstances. She stopped talking after
saying, "Sorry about your dad" with genuine sincerity as she rubbed
my hand with both of hers as if to warm it.

I looked up to the hospital ceiling—the direction of heaven—and
spoke aloud, not afraid of anyone overhearing and thinking I'd gone
crazy. "Mom," I called. "Angela Turner's name suits her. She really was
angel material!" I imagined all three—Mom, Dad, and Mrs. Turner—
smiling down upon me. I chuckled at the image of them giving me the
gung-ho arm thingamajig and saying, *You did it, girl!*

As I fell asleep, it came to me. People come into your life and go
out again in their own way, in their own time, in concert with everything else. Things happen for a reason—they may seem unexplainable
or unbelievable, but nonetheless, there's a purpose behind them. And
maybe Mom or Dad would explain this to me, in my dreams or through
someone else. Those we love never leave us; they are only transformed.

Mrs. Turner's funeral was well attended. Although her personality
was overbearing, she meant well, and people who knew her realized
that. I thanked her endlessly in my prayers as she was laid to rest. If
it weren't for her, I might have been the one being lowered into the
ground. I chose a blanket of tea roses to be placed on her casket in
remembrance of our last time together, with her complimenting the
tea I had made and supposedly the teas she had treasured with Mom. I
hoped those tête-à-têtes really had existed and weren't a figment of Mrs.
Turner's senility or imagination.

Two weeks after I came home from the hospital, Amber Lee and
Luke threw a party. It seemed like everyone Amber Lee and Luke
knew were at my house, Dr. and Mrs. Cavanaugh included—I had
never told Luke and Amber Lee what a jerk Dr. Cavanaugh was. If
Luke knew what Dr. Cavanaugh had implied, I didn't think he would
have invited them to this party. And now that he had, that meant they
were getting an invite to the wedding. Great! I was being facetious,

of course—I wanted Hubbell all to myself. Luke had hired my friend Zach to be DJ. My welcome-home party was also a prenuptial party for Luke and Amber Lee. I was thrilled; honestly, I hated being the center of attention.

I was on crutches, and Hubbell was right by my side as we made our way through the crowds onto the pool patio. For a brief moment I felt like Moses parting the Red Sea. All the guests looked at me like I had survived so much, which I had. Unlike the strangers and acquaintances at my dad's funeral, these party guests didn't ask me what they could do for me. Instead they congratulated me for my bravery, and this time I wasn't annoyed at being called brave.

Cooper and Gloria were slow dancing. Mr. and Mrs. Brickman were sitting at the bar, knocking back what seemed like their third, perhaps fourth cocktails. Luke and Drew looked intent, listening to my uncle. He was probably projecting Jake Jennings's case. Jake Jennings was out on bail. He was on trial for assault and battery and the murder of Chris Regal, the taxi driver.

I presented Amber Lee with my mother's veil. Naturally, she cried and was touched with my sentimental generosity and thoughtfulness. Her tears were contagious, and Hubbell pushed tissues into my hands. Amber Lee and I blew our wet noses and giggled at our outward emotions, feeling slightly embarrassed—people were staring! I wasn't too worried, though. I knew more tears of joy were going to flow among many party guests, especially Luke—he needed his own box of tissues handy as the pièce de resistance was revealed. The slide show began as Louis Armstrong's What a Wonderful World played and the black-and-white photos began flashing onto the enormous movie screen Mr. Trenton had rented. Thanks to Nurse Penny, I was able to pull my movie off.

When I was transferred to Memorial Hospital from the hospital in Fort Worth, Nurse Penny recognized my name. She remembered who I was and took a special interest in me, giving me extra TLC. Cooper and Gloria had brought the beach bag full of old photographs, the one I had worked on filling before Jake showed up. I was relieved Cooper decided not to break up with Gloria—at least for now. Penny stayed late one night, looking at them with me and listening to me reminisce. I had her full attention, and she acted like a member of the family would. At a few moments it felt as if she wanted to say, *Oh, I remember that time!* She insisted on helping me with my project. She took on the arduous task of scanning each photograph onto a disc—there were well over one hundred photos. She didn't complain, but it must have taken her at least four hours.

Pamela brought me my laptop, and I was able to make the slide-show I wanted to for Luke. Penny was amazed at how suave I was with technology and all the different applications I knew how to use to make a home movie look like a Hollywood one! I added some special effects, plus of course the Motown music he and my Dad had in common.

It was a huge success, and everyone loved it. The applause seemed endless, and I felt accomplished. It was as if I completed an arts and crafts project with my mom rather than abandoning it and tucking it under my bed. Mom really would have enjoyed this project. Even though Luke wasn't her son, she would have loved him as if he were. I knew she would have been proud of me and happy Luke and I had each other.

"Penny," I called as I eyed her arrival at the party. I hobbled over to her, and we embraced. Hubbell stood by.

"Hi, cutie," she said to Hubbell, who blushed.

"I'm so glad you came, Penny. I want to introduce you to everyone, especially my sweet Savannah," I said excitedly. Just then, Savannah ran to us, pleading, "Auntie Dakota, our song is playing—let's dance!" I could hear "Call Me Maybe" was playing.

"Hi, Savannah. I'm Penny, your auntie's nurse. It's really not a good idea she go dancing in her condition. But seeing what song's playing, we'll make an exception!"

Savannah giggled, and Hubbell swung her up into his arms as the four of us shimmied to the dance floor.

That night I gave in willingly to my exhaustion and drifted off like a lazy bump on a log. Savannah was by my side. She was set on sleeping with me since my release from the hospital. Something deep in my heart, unmeasured by my own consciousness, soared unburdened for the first time since my mother's passing. My father and I coped after losing her and grew into our relationship as the best father-daughter team possible. When he died, I felt hopeless and questioned God's wisdom. But then when Luke entered my life unexpectedly with his daughter, Savannah, my hopeless state gradually disappeared. And I realized it has to be impossible for God to save everyone, but somehow he turns a tragedy around. God had a mission—to supersede my dad's love with Luke's. And at this moment beside Savannah, snuggled like bunnies under the duvet, it was her embrace that warmed me. Because of Savannah, I felt safe and full of hope.

Thank you for reading my debut novel.
Stay tuned for its sequel.
Feel free to e-mail me at becauseofsavannah@gmail.com
I'd love to hear from you and I'm committed to e-mail you back.
Sarah Patt ☺
www.sarahpatt.com

Dakota gives into the temptation of Cooper—the young, handsome man who helped save the life of her Uncle Travis, a high-profile attorney. As her new romance blossoms, Dakota discovers evidence, which may have been tampered with over a vendetta—another family secret she wasn't privy to. Since the media paints Dakota as a messed-up, orphaned teenager with an over-the-top imagination, the validity of Dakota's testimony is on the table. Just when circumstances are getting heated, the key suspect is conveniently found dead— an apparent suicide. Dakota is half relieved and half suspicious, especially when there's no note to be found. Just how does Dakota survive another surreal blow? Through the eyes of a child, *Savannah* reminds us all to never give up hope—everything happens for a reason!

About the Author

Sarah Patt earned a master's degree in Special Education from Simmons College. She currently teaches at Landmark School in Massachusetts, where she never takes for granted the short commute, brisk salt air, and the devoted faculty, staff, and students who help make her work inspirational and rewarding.